CW00550950

# The Ultimate Londoner

## James Ward

COOL MILLENNIUM BOOKS

2

Published in the United Kingdom. All rights reserved. No part of this publication may be reproduced, distributed or transmitted in any form or means, without written permission.

Copyright © James Ward 2018

James Ward has asserted his right to be identified as the author of this Work in accordance with the Copyright, Designs and Patents Act 1988.

This is a work of fiction. All names, characters, and events are the product of the author's imagination, or used fictitiously. All resemblance to actual events, places, events or persons, living or dead, is entirely coincidental.

First published in KDP 2018.
This edition published 2021.

A CIP catalogue record for this book is available from the British Library.

ISBN: 978-1-913851-12-5

*Cover picture shows 30 St Mary Axe ('The Gherkin') from beneath St Helen's Church, Bishopsgate.*

This book is sold subject to the condition that it shall not, by way of trade or otherwise, be lent, re-sold, hired out or otherwise circulated without the publisher's prior consent in any form of trading or cover other than that in which it is published and without a similar condition including the condition being imposed on the subsequent purchaser.

This novel was produced in the UK and uses British-English language conventions ('authorise' instead of 'authorize', 'The government are' instead of 'the government is', etc.)

To my wife

## Chapter 1: So Where Exactly Have You Been?

As he entered Thames House, he caught sight of himself in the glass of the interior door: a blond, curly-haired, stocky guy in his early thirties. Not everyone's idea of the ultimate Londoner, but hey.

He brushed his lapels and walked into the lobby. Colin Bale, the chief receptionist, stood in his regular position behind the far desk. He seemed momentarily wrong-footed, then regarded the new arrival with his chin drawn back. "My God," he said. "You've returned."

"A bit late for you to be on duty, isn't it?"

But Colin had turned away. He was on the phone, speaking energetically. He swivelled back. "Stay there," he commanded. Then he faced the other way and continued talking.

Soundproofing-wise, it was a failure. He'd make a terrible spy. To make matters worse, he'd raised his voice, like he was agitated.

"Yes, *John Mordred*," he was saying. "*Him*. He's *here*, ma'am, *in reception*. Just arrived, just *now*, this very moment. No, he looks *fine*, ma'am! He actually told me it was *a bit late for me to be on duty*, as if he'd simply strolled in casually with a view to doing a bit of overtime!" He giggled slightly. "No, ma'am, as I've just said: he looks well. He does, er – how can I put it? - *smell* a little? Yes, of course I'll keep him here, ma'am. No problem. Absolutely."

He hung up and gave the security guards a non-verbal signal whose meaning was all too obvious. *Don't let him leave.*

"I'll just stand here then, shall I?" Mordred said.

Colin swallowed. "Yes, please, John. Sorry. Ruby Parker's, er, she's coming up from the basement."

"I gathered that. Am I in trouble?"

"I don't know."

Mordred chuckled. "Nor do I, actually. I've no idea about anything that's happened to me in the last hour."

Suddenly, the lift in the recess behind the desk pinged. Its doors swished open revealing a small black woman in a skirt-suit, flanked by a tall, long-haired white woman of about Mordred's age, plus a man perhaps ten years his senior with a widow's peak and a frown. Ruby Parker, Phyllis Robinson and Alec Cunningham. They considered Mordred with roughly the same expression Colin had, earlier. Then Phyllis ran over and wrapped her arms round him.

"Oh my *God*," she said. "John, we were so *worried!* Where the hell have you *been?*"

"I don't know," he replied hoarsely, as she squeezed the air from his lungs. "I vaguely remember leaving here at five - "

"*Five?*" She held him at arm's length, wiped her eyes and laughed manically. "*Five o'clock?*"

"It's been *three days*, John," Ruby Parker said gently. "I need you to take a moment and think very hard. Where exactly were you?"

Three *days?* The floor lurched unpleasantly. He suddenly felt as dislocated as everyone else looked.

"I – I've no idea," he said.

## Chapter 2: Unlegendary

*Four days earlier.*

3.20pm. Mordred logged off, rose from his desk and strode across the open-plan office to meet Alec, already standing by the exit. A handful of others were slipping jackets on, taking last mouthfuls of coffee, standing impatiently by monitors to make sure they'd properly shut down. The eighteen or twenty who'd chosen to stay in the office carried on as if nothing was happening.

Thames House lectures always began like this. Some people were required to attend because their job descriptions entailed it. They always looked self-important and disgruntled as they got up, like they had better things to do.

Others had arrived at work the day before to find formal invites in their inboxes. These tended to look more enthusiastic as they stood up to leave because they were the accepters. The decliners had already bowed out. A variety of things might be behind an invitation, including – so some cynics said - the fact that you were deemed capable of sitting up straight for two hours, making a few notes, and asking at least one coherent question at the end. Still, an invitation was an invitation. Not everyone got one.

The third category of attendees was the most interesting. These were people who'd opted in after the first two categories were confirmed. Because the remaining places were offered on a first-come-first-served basis.

You might opt in for several reasons. Most trivially, that sitting in a lecture theatre with a notepad was vastly preferable to poring through files relating to phone taps. Equally inconsequentially, that you stood a chance of leaving work early, if, say, questions from the floor dried up before 5.30.

But these were the opt-in motivations of a small minority. They were dwarfed by another, much stronger. That your muse had flown and you didn't anticipate finding her in encrypted reports about comings and goings at provincial mosques, or the ruminations of extremist right-wing bloggers. In short, that you planned to publish an espionage novel when you left the service.

The novelists also looked self-important and disgruntled as they got up to attend. They too had better things to be getting on with. But in their case, it was the next chapter of *Forces of Destruction* or *The Spy who Grew Orchids*.

As for the quality of the lectures themselves, it varied. Sometimes they were as engaging as TED talks. But at worst, the speaker read from his or her notes in a monotone, sometimes stopping mid-sentence to take a long sip of water. Today's was entitled, 'Quantum Computing and Other Fabulous Beasts'. Which boded well. If you could be bothered to devise a quirky heading, you probably cared about entertaining the troops.

Mordred and Cunningham entered the lecture theatre without talking and sat down at the far end of the middle row. The speaker, a slim middle-aged woman with black hair in a ponytail and an expensive suit, sat on a chair on the podium. She was trying to make eye contact with every new arrival in order to cast them a little smile. Perhaps they did that sort of thing in Nottingham, where she'd come from. Mordred smiled back at her, and upped the stakes with a small wave.

"Do you two know each other?" Cunningham asked as they sat down. The room was half-full and people chatted quietly. Still six minutes to kick-off.

"I don't think so," Mordred said.

"The way you gave her that wave."

"People do that sort of thing sometimes. It's called 'being friendly'."

"Were you invited, by the way, or did you opt in?"

"The latter. You?"

"Same. Apparently, this is the most popular lecture this year. They're thinking of asking her back in a few weeks' time, to do the same talk. Assuming she at least half-crushes it, of course. Do you actually know anything about quantum computing?"

"I've read about it," Mordred replied. "A quantum computer would be good at optimisation, among other things."

"Is your wife here?"

"Phyllis? Somewhere, I believe. I don't recall actually marrying her."

"Maybe you should ask her."

"Thanks for the highly random advice. I have. She said no, remember?"

Cunningham shrugged. "I mean, *again*."

"We've had this conversation."

"Everyone knows she regrets turning you down. And it was yonks ago. Surely you can ask her again. Look, there she is. Two rows back from the front, with Suki. Wow. On the other hand, why bother? As I see it, you've already got a perfect relationship. Separate flats but somehow still living together. Both worlds. Marriage is just a word nowadays."

"Remind me how we got onto this subject. Valentine's Day's been and gone."

"I'm just trying to make conversation. It's called 'being friendly', John. More specifically than that, though, I asked if Phyllis was here. I'm just trying to give you the benefit of my worldly wisdom, that's all. What do *you* want to talk about?"

"Hang on. When you said 'everyone' knows she regrets turning me down - "

"It was just a turn of phrase," Cunningham replied. "What I meant is, *I* know that."

"Er, how?"

"From Annabel."

"I see. Where is Annabel today, by the way?"

"Cyprus, apparently. Phyllis told Annabel, Annabel told me, now I'm telling you."

"This is what I'd call a teenage conversation," Mordred said.

"Granted. Just one more thing. If I were you, I wouldn't ask her. You're better off as you are. Let sleeping dogs lie, that's my advice."

"Thanks for nothing. Oh-oh, here we go."

Another middle-aged woman had appeared at the front of the room, someone Mordred recognised from the canteen, although they'd never spoken: a mid-level section officer in another department. She introduced the speaker – Professor Camilla Burkewitz from Nottingham University – and said how important it was to know something about quantum computing in today's world. Then she went to sit on the end of the front row. The novelists shifted tetchily along to make room for her.

Camilla Burkewitz spoke for fifty-five minutes about cryptanalysis, quantum supremacy, decoherence, complexity theory and the Church-Turing hypothesis. She didn't pause once to sip her water. After twenty minutes, Mordred lost the thread and couldn't get it back. Afterwards, he felt increasingly stupid. He guessed he wasn't alone. When Burkewitz finished her talk, the chairwoman returned to the podium to supervise a Q&A. The novelists all put their hands up. Alec sighed miserably.

After four questions, it was obvious the novelists were much more interested in artificial intelligence than they were in quantum computing. As a sneaky way of signalling the fact, they began by asking about the connection. *Where were the other 'fabulous beasts' of the lecture title?* one guy, an MI7 probationer with a goatee, demanded. So far she'd only talked about quantum computers.

Camilla Burkewitz did her best to respond, but, fatally, she lapsed into opacity again, and the novelists spotted an easy kill. One of their number, a twentysomething woman in a pinafore frock, declared confidently that quantum computing would eventually lead to super-human consciousness, because consciousness was merely lots of deep, quick, interconnected calculations constrained by a programmable feedback loop. Some of her fellow authors murmured their agreement; others groaned. Then they argued heatedly amongst themselves. It wasn't clear what Camilla Burkewitz thought, or even whether she'd ever want to come back. The chairwoman raised both arms in a vain plea for calm.

"Bloody hippies," Alec grumbled. "What the hell's artificial intelligence got to do with anything?"

"Didn't *you* once write a novel?" Mordred asked.

"No, John, I didn't. It was a screenplay. And I didn't finish it. I grew up instead."

The noise gradually abated. The chairwoman thanked Camilla Burkewitz while she still had the chance, and there were twenty seconds of applause. The novelists continued to argue vehemently as they left.

"Maybe we should follow them," Mordred said. "They'll probably be going round the corner. The Marquis of Granby or the Regency Café."

"What for? *You're* not writing a novel, are you?"

"Absolutely not, no, but - "

Alec shook his head. "If you think they'll be having an interesting discussion, forget it. There's no reason to believe any of them actually know anything."

"What about that woman who said artificial intelligence was just millions of calculations feeding back on themselves?"

"I'd say she's mastered the art of turning tripe into soundbites. Let's take the stairs. Did you see the look Camilla Burkewitz gave her? Like, who let the loonies in?"

"She probably knew exactly what she was talking about. The whole of MI7's full of computer experts. It's mainly what we do nowadays."

"Knowing how to troubleshoot Microsoft Word and zap the Melissa Virus is a far cry from building Hal 9000."

"Which sounds more than a bit patronising."

Alec scoffed.

They'd stopped between two flights of stairs to continue the discussion. As far as Mordred could tell, they were alone. Whatever happened now, they'd probably lost the novelists. Still, the principle was worth fighting for.

"All right, put it another way then," Alec said. "You're right. Seriously, you are. All sarcasm aside for a moment, I'm being far too negative. Probably a fair number of the novelists down in the front row *were* computer experts."

"Bit of an about turn. So should we follow them? Or try to?"

"Nope."

"Okay. Not a complete about turn then."

"What sort of a conversation do you think I'm likely to have with a bunch of IT boffins? I quite liked Professor Burkewitz. She had a passion for her subject and obviously didn't realise she was incomprehensible to mortals. But an hour of feeling like the class dunce is more than I'm used to. I don't want to add to it by feeling like the pub or the café dunce too. Some of those guys actually look up to me. And they look up to you a hell of a lot more - "

"Me?"

"'There goes the legendary John Mordred.' That's what they say."

"Right."

"If you go to a pub with them, it'll take a mere thirty minutes for the Mordie Magic to dissipate. You'll become permanently unlegendary."

Mordred laughed. "Not sure that's a word."

"It will be."

"So effectively, we're not going to follow them because we're scared."

Alec drew his chin back and flicked his eyebrows. He emitted a little 'whoa'. "I see what you mean," he said. "Well spotted."

"If we're so legendary, surely we can exert our combined charisma to change the subject if the going gets tough."

Alec nodded sceptically. "We can, but they'll probably twig. Look, John, you've got to choose your battles. 'Never allow the enemy to meet you on his own territory': Sun Tzu, *The Art of War*."

"We're overthinking this. They *know* we're not computer experts. When we show our ignorance, that's not going to influence their opinion of us. Anyway, why do we have to engage them in discussion? Why can't we just sit and listen?"

"A bit like sitting and listening to Camilla Burkewitz, you mean? But with beer? Not even that if we go to the Regency? No thanks."

"We might learn something."

"That's what I love about you, John. You're a child of the light; I'm a wizened old man of the darkness. Your Dartington crystal wine glass is forever half full; my Poundshop ale tankard's always completely empty."

"So shall we follow them, or not?"

Alec sighed. "Okay, you win. Even I'm beginning to despise my curmudgeonly attitude now. I half wish we'd met twenty years ago, and you'd been a woman, and we'd struck up a relationship. I might have turned out completely differently."

"I'd have been a twelve-year-old girl."

"Let's not go there. Forget I ever spoke."

They went to reception to sign out. As expected, the novelists were nowhere in sight. Mordred's assumption that they were headed either for the Marquis or the Regency wasn't underpinned by any evidence, and actually, there were a large number of places they could have repaired to. They might even have gone for a meal together. Novelists sometimes did that. 'Having a literary supper', they called it.

Luckily, Colin was on duty.

"Did you see where the novelists went?" Alec asked him.

"Er, who are 'the novelists'?" Colin replied, nervously. He was oddly afraid of Alec in a way he didn't appear to be of anyone else, certainly not John Mordred.

"Don't give me that," Alec said. "You know exactly who I mean."

"A group of men and women from the lecture, arguing about artificial intelligence," Mordred put in gently. "Four women and about seven or eight men. Mostly young. Probably IT personnel."

"I, er – they left by the front door," Colin said.

"Did you hear them say where they were going?" Alec demanded.

"I, um, heard someone mention the … Barley Mow? I, er - "

"Thanks," Alec said. He was already on his way to the exit. Mordred skipped to catch up.

Outside, they turned left, and did another left turn at Horseferry Road. It rained and a cold wind blew from the river. The traffic was dense, buses and taxis and vans packed together like they were sheltering from the sky in each other's company.

The Barley Mow was just before the turn on the corner with Arneway Street, a three minute walk. The décor was one variety of olde-traditional: dark wood with a narrow tiled area round the bar, rustic chairs, plain circular tables. When they entered, the novelists had already taken up residence on the other side of the room; they'd already bought drinks and snacks. They were still arguing. A few of them looked up. One waved at Mordred. For the first time, he noticed what Alec had intimated: they regarded him as *a person of interest*.

"So now what?" Alec whispered.

A rhetorical question. Answer: so now nothing at all. They could hardly stride over and say, 'Mind if we join your discussion?' They were experienced intelligence officers; the novelists, by the look of them, were all relatively new recruits. The way MI7 worked, it would look like a clumsy attempt to put a pair of spies among fledgling pigeons. It would give entirely the wrong impression, in other words, and might even lead to a few people resigning. Not everyone enjoyed working at Thames House, and sometimes a straw inadvertently broke a camel's back.

"Let's just get a pint each," Mordred said. "We'll drink it quickly, and get out of here."

"Look at the way they're staring at you. I knew you were legendary, but I didn't realise how much."

"I don't call those admiring stares."

"What's your interpretation? Two pints of Satan's Pelvis, please," he told the barman.

"I'd say they're willing us not to approach. They're having an enjoyable discussion and they don't want it ruined by a pair of arses."

"Check. They're snobs, in a word."

"Anti-arse snobs."

Their craft beers arrived. Alec paid. They drank up without saying anything more and left.

"Makes you realise you're getting old," Mordred said, when they were outside again. "When young people spurn your company."

The rain suddenly switched to a deluge. Both men realised their coats were completely ineffective. They silently resigned themselves to the prospect of a swift and thorough soaking.

"I'm ten years older than you," Alec said, raising his voice slightly so he could be heard above the mingled noise of traffic and hard rain on the pavement. "If this was a BBC drama, I'd be your stereotypical male bemoaning my diminished ability to 'pull'. But the truth is, I don't care, and neither do you. Youth's rubbish. It took at least twelve of them to get anywhere near making their contempt known to us, whereas we effectively despised them without even trying."

"You say 'effectively'."

"They knew exactly what we thought of them and their literary pretensions."

"I think they were probably just shy."

"Look, John, you're a great guy and everything, but sometimes your tendency to see the best in everyone, no matter how repellent, really does grate. And it's not good for you either.

15

Spies are supposed to be cynical. We're not meant to err on the side of generosity. They weren't 'shy'. They were up themselves. There's a big difference."

The door behind them creaked open and they knew to stop speaking. "Excuse me," a timid voice said.

They turned round to find a young bearded man in a pale blue crew-neck jumper and chinos, standing under a huge black umbrella. He smiled awkwardly.

"We, er, saw you at the lecture," he said. "We wondered if you'd like to come and join us. We're just having a few drinks and a bit of a discussion. We think the next big thing in espionage won't be spy versus spy, it'll be spy versus computer. It's already happening. The drinks are on us, by the way."

How to reply to that sort of invitation when your face was covered in rain; when you were blinking rapidly from the effort of keeping your eyes open; when your clothes were soaked through, and all of those things must be obvious to anyone within twenty paces?

"Thanks for the invite," Mordred said. "We've just been called back to base."

"Really kind," Alec assented miserably.

"Would you like to borrow my umbrella?" the young man asked. "The rain seems to have come out of nowhere. It wasn't like this an hour ago. And the forecast didn't say anything."

"No, thanks," they replied together.

"But thanks," Mordred added. "Really kind."

"If it's a false alarm, feel free to come back and find us," the man said. "Well done on your nomination, by the way," he told Mordred. "I hope it goes well." He went back inside.

"I wonder what Sun Tzu would say," Mordred said when he was sure they were alone again.

They turned east in the pretence of heading back to Thames House.

"We should call it a night," Alec said levelly. "How are you getting home?"

"Tube."

"Westminster okay? We could walk there together, get another drink on the way. I could do with one. Or three."

"What do you think he meant, *Well done on my nomination?*"

"'Congratulations on the fact that you've been summoned by your boss to deal with a national emergency'," Alec said. "God, how embarrassing. We looked stupid. We might as well have joined them in their discussion. It couldn't have ended any more badly than that."

"Un-legended."

"The gods must love you, John. You never lose any arguments with me, you make me feel bad about myself, and worst of all, something mortifying always happens when I slate you. On the other hand, I *was* right."

"Comforting. For you."

"If we'd gone home like I suggested, instead of coming here, we'd have been spared everything. And we wouldn't be walking along now like two sodden man-sponges."

"The reason it all went wrong is because we made allowances for your hyper-caution. If we'd simply followed them to begin with, we'd be in the Barley Mow now with free drinks and good company."

"So what's the moral of the story? Have a bit more faith in human nature?"

"What's wrong with that?"

"Nothing," Alec said sulkily. He suddenly looked completely defeated. "Nothing at all."

Mordred's phone rang. *Phyllis.*

"Hi, Phyll," he said.

"Where are you?" she asked.

"Horseferry Road. With Alec. We're on our way to get the tube at Westminster. We might call in at St Stephen's for a drink in a moment. Assuming it's not jam-packed. Fancy meeting us there?"

"I have to go home. I mean *home* home. My parents', in Donnington."

"Bloody hell, that's a bit sudden. Is everything okay?"

"As far as I know, fine. I can be back by tomorrow morning, of course. They're being very mysterious about it, but apparently it's 'something good' and it requires my presence in person. I've been trying to think what it could be."

"Something that might involve a solicitor. Or a large gift of some sort. Or both."

"Roughly what I thought. Which leaves me very 'hmm'. I'll keep you posted."

"Enjoy the lecture, by the way?"

"It was outstanding. Afterwards, I went up to the canteen with Suki for a coffee. We've just been talking about it."

"About quantum computing or artificial intelligence?"

"Both. Hey, look, no one knows whether they're connected. Scientists can't even build a decent quantum machine yet, but Suki says Roger Penrose's view about quantum gravity effects in microtubules… "

"Hello? Are you still there?"

"Apparently, my taxi's arrived. I love you, John. I'll call you later tonight."

"Have a good journey."

She hung up.

"That was Phyllis right?" Alec said. "Is she okay? I mean, I heard you ask."

"She's fine. Her parents have called her back to the ancestral home for reasons unknown. But they're fine too."

Alec nodded. "St Stephen's Tavern, then?"

"If we can get in. Mind you, it should be okay, this time of night."

"Quick pint, then home. I apologise for what I said earlier. It wasn't your fault. It was mine."

"To be fair, the way it panned out was a lot funnier than if we'd just done the common sense thing. Therefore, a better evening, in a strange sort of way."

"On the surface," Alec said, "that doesn't make any sense whatsoever, but strangely, I know what you mean. Agreed."

Ten minutes later, they called into St Stephen's. Mordred ordered two pints of Dung Beetle. They stood in silence, drank, slowly deposited two pools of rainwater on the floor, then used the toilets.

"Did you see the way everyone looked at us?" Alec said indignantly, as they came out. "Like they'd never seen two wet people before."

"See you tomorrow."

They'd reached the tube station now. And they were feeling the cold. They descended the steps together and parted without further dialogue. Mordred picked up an *Evening Standard* from the metal dispenser, and made for the Circle line. He looked at his phone. *6.20.*

When he reached the platform, he became conscious for the first time that some people were looking at him.

He was wet. So what? A lot of people down here were. It was raining.

Strangely, though, these were roughly the same looks the novelists had turned on him in The Barley Mow. They were the same glares he'd stood through in St Stephen's Tavern. For some reason, he'd become *generally* worthy of note.

It couldn't just be that he was wet. There were all sorts of peculiar-looking people in London – in every big city, for that matter – and, on the spectrum of interestingness, wet clothes must surely be fairly near the bottom.

Maybe they thought he was getting a cold.

Possibly, yes. They were looking at him because they thought he might be infectious.

Yet their body language wasn't consistent with that. There wasn't much room to give any one person wide-berth down here, but still, under the right circumstances, it'd be natural to at least try.

Yet no one was.

19

On the contrary, some of them seemed infinitesimally *drawn* to him.

He should probably try to ignore it. He'd be home soon. He could shower and warm up. He'd eat dinner - some kind of mushroom thing with cheese and tagliatelle he'd bought from Tesco - then wait for Phyllis to call.

On the other hand, it wasn't always wise for a spy to try and ignore things.

But it couldn't possibly be prearranged, all this staring. It would have to involve the novelists, the punters in St Stephen's and a clutch of would-be passengers in Westminster tube station. People who couldn't conceivably be related. Much less in any plot against him.

Maybe he was cold, and coming down with something like the flu, and feeling subtly paranoid. That would explain it.

Not very *well*, though, because they really *were* staring at him.

But it *would* explain it. And it was probably the best explanation on offer.

Unless some prankster had attached something to his back. He took his jacket off.

Nope.

The train arrived. He sat down on one of the middle seats, leaving his jacket off, since the seat of his trousers was relatively dry and he didn't want to wet the upholstery for the next passenger.

Again, though, the odd way the seat seemed to be *left* for him, like he was silently being invited to take it, so people could have a better gawp at him.

He leaned forward. His jumper was wet and he didn't want to flatten it against the chair. He looked at the floor. Ten or twelve pairs of feet beside his.

He unfolded his *Standard*. Time to find out what Rihanna had been doing lately.

He suddenly became aware of an intensification of the interest in him. People leaned forward a little more, a little less unguardedly.

My God, it was something *in here*, in the paper! They were looking to see his reaction to something in the *Standard*.

How could that be? Could he be dreaming? Could he have fallen asleep somewhere between Thames House and Westminster?

No, because he hadn't sat down anywhere else. And you knew when you were awake. You just did. This wasn't a dream.

He turned each page as fast as was consistent with scanning it for clues. A couple of whales had swum into the Thames – pretty amazing, but it couldn't be that - the Mayor had attended a charity ball in Regent Street, an MP had been knocked off his bike in Hounslow.

It wasn't until he came to the centre that he saw.

He was looking at a picture of himself.

Himself. John Mordred. With his name written beneath it. And a paragraph about him.

It was him. It was *his name*. My God, he was floating, like it had filled him with helium.

He looked up and around the carriage apologetically. All the stares turned quickly, ashamedly away.

*I can see why you've all been looking at me now,* his helium self announced from the ceiling, *and you've no idea how sorry I am, but I promise you I didn't put it there. I've no idea how it got there. Hey, I'm really sorry, everyone.*

He closed the paper. He needed to get off the train. He had to get back to Thames House. Apart from anything else, this was a major breach of security.

Who'd put it there? Why?

Actually, what *was* it?

He opened the paper again, flicked through to the centre. He was shaking. Not much – as much as was consistent with being a legendary spy – but enough to augment his self-consciousness. If that were possible.

The heading: *The Ultimate Londoner!* And right at the bottom of the page, beneath ten photographs in two rows of five: *Shortlist!*

Shortlist? When had the longlist gone up? And where? It couldn't have been in *The Evening Standard*. Even if he hadn't noticed, someone connected to him would have.

His phone was ringing. *Ruby Parker*.

He picked up. "Hello?"

"John," she said, "have you by any chance seen tonight's *Evening Standard?*"

"I'm looking at it right now."

"And?"

"I've no idea how it got there. Or what it is."

"Where are you?"

"On the tube. About to double back and return to base."

"Good." She hung up.

The train was coming in to Embankment now. He needed to get off and find a taxi, pronto.

Before he closed his newspaper, he noticed the sentence immediately beneath the heading. *First prize: FIVE MILLION POUNDS!*

For a hallucinogenic-type moment, he knew exactly who was behind it.

Five *MILLION* pounds was exactly the sort of sum Dr Evil might have come up with.

## Chapter 3: In a Nutshell, No One Knows

Mordred stepped off the train at Embankment, and climbed the escalator two steps at a time. He swiped his Oyster card on the exit barrier. His phone rang. *Phyllis.*

"I know what you're about to say," he told her, "and I've no idea."

"The ... 'competition'?"

"In *The Evening Standard.*"

"We're both on the same wavelength then," she said. "I'm on the train to Newbury now. Would you like me to come back? You're going to be in big trouble when Ruby Parker finds out."

"She already has. I'm not sure what use your returning would be. Don't take that the wrong way. If you're as much in the dark as me. You - "

"Moral support?"

"You're giving me that now. No, your parents have something important to say. That's your priority."

"Have you any theories? I mean, about who's responsible?"

"I've only just seen it. Hang on." He was on the street now. He flagged down a crawling taxi, and got awkwardly onto the back seat. "Lambeth Bridge, please," he told the driver. "Millbank end."

The car pulled enthusiastically out into the traffic.

"Everyone's been looking at me since I left the lecture," he continued, "like I'm some kind of – Good God."

"What is it? Are you okay?"

"Alec and I followed some of the junior staff to the Barley Mow, hoping to join their discussion about artificial intelligence - "

Phyllis chuckled. "The novelists?"

"That's right. And we shied off at the last minute. But one of them followed us outside, and he congratulated me on my 'nomination'. I had no idea what he was talking about."

"But it makes sense now."

"I haven't even read the details. I'm in shock. Have you read it?"

"It says you're from the North East, you're a Magpies supporter and you live in Islington. You're a civil servant in the Foreign and Commonwealth Office and you're known for your vegetarianism and incredible support for good causes."

"Bloody hell. That's a lot of information. Even the FCO bit's not that far off. And it definitely says 'vegetarian', not 'vegan'? Because that's quite rare nowadays."

"I'm looking at it now. And yep, that's what it says. Haven't you got a copy?"

"I can't read and talk to you at the same time. And I'd much prefer to talk to you."

"That's sweet. Still, five million pounds, eh? Quite a nest egg, if you're sacked."

"Let's not joke, eh?"

"Words I never thought I'd hear John Mordred utter. And you say you've no idea who might be behind it? Because I have."

"Really? Go on."

"Hannah Lexingwood, née Mordred. Your sister. An internationally famous rock impresario who feels deeply sorry for her runt of a brother, and would probably do anything to give him kudos and a bit of a leg up the social ladder. Only, he's so damned independent he won't accept help by any normal channels - "

His stomach plunged, like it recognised the description. "Bloody hell, that sounds disturbingly plausible."

"And it hadn't occurred to you? Who else knows that much about you?"

"You think she could be behind the entire competition?"

"Or she merely nominated you," Phyllis said. "But I'd imagine it's the former. It would be a very good way of slipping you a cool five million – a drop in the ocean to her – without the messy complication of you feeling indebted. Don't tell her I said any of this, by the way."

"Obviously not. Who are the other shortlisted candidates?"

"I see your reasoning. If they're all duds, we've got her bang to rights. A Russian oligarch, a pub landlord, a female retiree, a female DJ, a parliamentary intern, a community worker, a comedian, a former conservative councillor, a novelist."

"Difficult to see how I might be the clear front-runner in that sort of field. And there'll be rioting in the streets of London if a Magpies supporter wins its ultimate citizen award."

"True, it would have been in her interests to play down your North Eastern connections. And you're not *much* of a football fan, are you? I've never heard you drone on about it. And you don't go to matches. Only when your dad's around. I don't even think you've got a replica shirt, have you?"

"One. About two sizes too small, with 'Shearer' written on the back."

"Means nothing to me. I'm a Donnington supporter. But you're right. Maybe your sister isn't behind it. If it was six fabulously wealthy rogues versus you, or if there was less about your connection to the so-called beautiful game, I'd be convinced. But a female DJ, a community worker, a pub landlord? Where's the glory in raising *their* hopes only to dash them? It certainly doesn't sound like her."

"There's no second prize?"

"Nothing. Only the five million, 'to be awarded in a special ceremony on the top floor of 30 St Mary Axe' – the Gherkin – 'in exactly twenty-eight days from now.' Which means, aha! all we have to do is find out who booked it! I genuinely don't think it is her, now we've talked. I might ring Ruby Parker and ask if I can spearhead the investigation."

"Good luck with that. She's not keen on people working cases they've a personal involvement in."

"You and me, you mean? Oh, I think that would work in my favour. Me investigating you, when you're a suspect in something: no. Me trying to help you when you're in trouble: obviously, yes. I'd be doubly effective. Who else could be relied on to give a hundred per cent round the clock?"

"How do I win? If people have to vote for me, I've no chance."

"They don't. It's - "

"Whereabouts would you like dropping?" the taxi driver asked as they crossed Lambeth Bridge.

"I'd better go," Mordred told Phyllis. "We've arrived. I'll talk to you later. Horseferry Road," he told the driver. "Corner of Thorney Street."

"Best of luck," Phyllis said.

She hung up. She was obviously overflowing with ideas about how to ride to his rescue, and talking to him in person had served all the use it was going to.

He looked at his phone as the car pulled to a halt. *43 missed calls*. Bloody hell.

He paid the driver, got out and scanned the list as he walked. Six from his sisters – including two from Hannah - four from Alec, two from his parents. Good God, there were people he hadn't spoken to in years here. And sixty-two texts, all, by the looks of them, variations on 'Congratulations!'

Alec had left a voicemail. "John, if you haven't yet seen tonight's *Evening Standard*, I strongly advise you to get hold of a copy – even if you have to pick one out of a bin – and turn to the centre pages. You've been shortlisted for some sort of competition. If you're not responsible – and I hardly think you'd put a hole in your own head – perhaps think about who might be. My guess is, your big sister. Failing that, Soraya Snow. If you need help fending off Ruby Parker, give me a call. Remember that guy outside the Barley Mow who said - "

Mordred hung up and climbed the steps to the front door of Thames House. Colin Bale stood in his usual place, his face completely unreadable. "Er, are congratulations in order, John?" he asked, as Mordred signed the register.

"Commiserations more like."

"Ruby Parker's expecting you. I imagine you already know that. She's in her office."

"Thanks."

He took the lift to Basement One, walked the short distance to her door and knocked. Her 'Enter' was usually a good indicator of how your meeting was likely to go. This one didn't sound half as apoplectic as he expected.

He obeyed to find her sitting behind her desk. She had a copy of *The Evening Standard* open at the centre pages. "Sit down, John," she said neutrally. "I've just been speaking to Phyllis. She's just about managed to persuade me that your sister's not behind this. You do realise that, professionally, it could be bad for you? Not as bad as retirement, but at the very least it would mean you having to take lessons on how to spy in plain sight."

"I'm already a tiny bit famous," he replied. "We've always recognised that."

"You exhausted Andy Warhol's five minutes a few years ago," she said. "I don't think many people today would recognise your face on the strength of your family connections, impressive though they are. No, before this came up, you were making a very satisfactory return to obscurity."

"I've no idea where it came from," he said.

"I've been on the phone to *The Evening Standard*, and interestingly, they don't know either. You'll notice it's a sponsored pull-out. A glorified advert, in other words, and not actually the *Standard* itself. Evgeny Lebedev's a big supporter of press freedom. Providing advertisers don't breach his paper's policies prohibiting promotion of inequality, racism, illegal activity, etcetera, they'll usually find ready acceptance. Don't forget, this is a free newspaper: advertising's how it makes its revenue."

"You mention 'illegal activity'. What about breaching the data protection act?"

"You mean, the *Standard*? From their point of view, 'shortlist' implies prior rounds, at which the candidates' consent would already have been procured. And, of course, there's supposedly five million pounds on offer. Who wouldn't want a one in ten chance of that? On this occasion, a certain incautiousness on its part was probably to be expected. It's certainly understandable."

"*Were* there any prior rounds?"

"Not that we've so far been able to discover. You've got to remember, MI7 found out about this at roughly the same time you did, about an hour ago. We've had very little time to dig, but we've a lot of people working on it."

"Someone at the *Standard* must have taken a *name* when they accepted the advert? And what about bank account details? Whoever placed the ad must have paid up front."

"As I say, John, we're working on it. But we need you to do something as a matter of urgency."

"Call Hannah."

"The fact is, all Phyllis's arguments to the effect that your sister's not behind this only merely add up to a convincing case that she didn't micro-manage it. But Hannah may be responsible for the overall idea. She might have hired others to flesh out the details."

"We're running a big risk of making this all about me. There are nine other candidates."

"From our point of view, and until we discover otherwise, it *is* all about you. Granted, we've no idea who might benefit from exposing you to public scrutiny in this way, or why they've chosen such a roundabout way of going about it, but we can't afford to be complacent. Now, stop prevaricating. I need you to ring your sister. I want you to record your conversation, and then I want you to send the MP3 to Tariq for analysis. I need you to ask her directly whether she's responsible for the Ultimate Londoner competition, and, if not, whether she nominated you. And if the answer to both those questions is no, whether she *knows who did*. If at all possible, ask to speak to Soraya Snow, and ask her the same questions. And put it on speakerphone. I need to hear what she has to say. Afterwards, I may have to ask you your opinion: whether you think your sister was lying at any point in your conversation. You're good at detecting telling voice modulations. But I won't take your verdict as final. Are you happy with all that?"

Mordred sighed. "Probably not in the Pharrell Williams sense, but I can live with it."

"In your own time then."

He went to Contacts and pressed Call. It rang four times, then Hannah's voice. *"John!* Oh my God! Did you get my text? *Congratulations!"*

"Thank you. I - "

"You'll have to keep the paper. I haven't got a copy. I'm in Berlin now, with the band. Tim sent me a photo. Bloody hell, you're a dark horse! I don't even know what it is. What *is* it? 'Ultimate Londoner': what do you have to do? How did you get nominated? It says 'shortlist'!"

"I know. I - "

"Mum and Dad are over the moon. Mind you, you shouldn't have told them you're a bloody Newcastle fan. Couldn't you have said Arsenal or Tottenham, or West Ham? Even bloody Leyton Orient would have been better than Newcastle! You do realise you've thrown it away, don't you? Anyway, well done. It's still a fantastic achievement. And at least you've been true to your roots. Even though you're not what I'd call a proper football fan. You're an idiot, really."

"Thanks."

"Still, good for your CV. And a swanky dinner at the Gherkin, eh?"

"Listen, Hannah, I - "

"Are you okay? You don't sound as over the moon as you should be. Sorry, I probably shouldn't have said all that stuff about Newcastle. Look, it won't necessarily scupper you. What the hell do I know? I should just keep my big trap shut. Anyway, it must be working for you. You wouldn't have got this far otherwise."

"I'm not bothered about winning. I'm just disturbed, that's all."

"What do you mean, 'disturbed'?"

"I'd never heard of the 'Ultimate Londoner' competition before tonight. I've no idea who organised it, or who nominated me. I spoke to a friend. He said he thought you might have organised it."

*"Me?"*

"As a way of helping me get on in life."

*"What?"*

"An act of kindness - "

"Bloody hell, John, you *really do* need to get yourself a new set of friends! If they think you can only get anywhere with the help of your sister, who *of course* would set up a big competition with a five million pound prize pot, then fix it so you'd win, they're not worth hanging on to! Good God, what must your *enemies* be like?"

"You didn't even nominate me?"

"I'd never even *heard* of it before Tim sent me that photo. I'd have rung and congratulated you on being *long*listed if I'd known."

"Do you think Soraya could have nominated me?"

*"What?* Because you're my brother and she wants to curry favour with me? John, I don't want to sound tactless, but Soraya and I are together all the time, she's one of the world's biggest rock stars, and she really doesn't need to go poring through *The Evening Standard* on the off chance that there might be some kind of competition she can nominate John Mordred for, as a kind of oblique favour to her manager. Apart from anything else, she'd have said something. For God's sake, John, has it not actually

occurred to you yet that you might *actually be worth it?* that someone might have nominated you because they honestly think you deserve it? And that they might be right? Listen carefully: *it's got nothing to do with me.* Skype me and watch my lips. *It's got nothing to do with me, or Soraya, or Lady Luck, or Father Christmas.* Now go and get a celebratory drink and have a bit more faith in yourself. I love you. Over and out."

She hung up. The room filled with a huge silence.

"I'm pretty sure she wasn't putting that on," Mordred said at last.

Ruby Parker sighed. "Agreed. Send it to Tariq anyway."

He flicked through the list till he found Tariq, and pressed Send.

Ruby Parker read the newspaper again for a few seconds then looked up. "This is a long shot, but has your sister any fabulously wealthy enemies of the kind that might try something like this? I mean, whose names spring to mind."

"She organised a global rally against tax avoidance a few years ago, and she's known for her anti-capitalism. I'm pretty sure she's got oodles of enemies. Names: I'm not sure, off hand. I can find out. But I don't follow. Why are you asking?"

"You're likely to get a lot of flak from this. Ultimate Londoner, and yet it emphatically underscores your Northumbrian connections. Reading this, one might be forgiven for thinking you're an outsider, an immigrant with a perverse loyalty to an area hundreds of miles from London, and why do you deserve such an accolade? Its author seems to have gone to extraordinary lengths to make you look anything but the ultimate Londoner. At the very least, you come across as the odd one out. All the others were born or grew up here. Where it mentions their support of sports teams, they're all local."

"You mean, it could be designed to provoke an anti-Mordred backlash."

"With her as the main target. You know how suspicious the British are nowadays. They see conspiracies everywhere. With this as your manifesto, it might not be long before some people start claiming she pulled strings to get you nominated. And if you win, it'll be even worse for her."

"It does sound plausible…"

"Although speculative. I'll keep it in mind, although we do need to consider the simpler hypotheses first. Chief amongst which is that this is all a mix-up. Do you remember where you were when that photo was taken, by the way? I mean, it's not one of yours: stolen, in other words?"

"Apart from ID for passports and the like, I don't keep any photos of myself. Even on my phone." He looked. "I'm sitting on a chair somewhere. That's a jacket I wear a lot. And it looks like a zoom-in. Sorry, but anyone could have taken it."

"When we find out who's behind it, we'll insist you're withdrawn. You may need to confirm that in person, so keep your phone switched on. I want you to leave the capital at the first opportunity, lie low somewhere and await further instructions. Don't answer any calls unless you're absolutely certain of the caller. It won't be long before people start inviting you onto radio talk shows and trying to take your picture in the street. If we can staunch the whole thing at source, it should blow over in a few days."

"I'll catch a train out of London first thing tomorrow morning."

"Speak to Amber before you leave the building. Hopefully, no one knows exactly where you live yet, but you probably need to go home incognito, just to be on the safe side. She'll arrange that. If it turns out your address isn't secure, then turn round, come back here, and you can spend the night in one of the pods. As for getting out of London tomorrow, let us know your travel and accommodation details as soon as you've worked them out.

"I'll probably go back to Hexham for a few days, see my parents. They're due a visit, and I can't see anyone caring about The Ultimate Londoner up there. I'll tell them I'm unhappy about the competition anyway." He stood up. "They'll shelter me."

"I have an uncanny feeling this may not be something to quip about, John. Let me know when you've arrived, and check in by phone daily at eight am."

"Will do." He left the room.

## Chapter 4: A Kind of Touchie Basie Thing

Phyllis got off the train at Newbury. The taxi her parents had sent was waiting outside the station. She got onto the back seat, confirmed her identity for the driver, and closed the glass partition separating them. She needed to think.

She'd have to get back to London tonight, ready to start probing tomorrow. Ruby Parker hadn't sounded entirely convinced by the idea that Hannah Lexingwood wasn't behind all this, but it was obvious she didn't discount the possibility either. If there was to be an investigation, and Phyllis was going to head it, she needed to be there. Get this over and done with, whatever it was.

But so difficult to think straight. Why had they insisted on knowing her *precise time of arrival*? What could be so important that it was worth summoning her all this way for? What could require her presence in person?

Something to which her parents needed to gauge her reaction with precision, presumably. Phones didn't allow that.

Maybe they were getting divorced.

She didn't know how bad she'd feel about that: just bad-bad or horrendously bad? She couldn't picture them apart. Somehow, it was inconceivable, like their sudden disappearance into a sinkhole.

Or maybe her brother, Francis, was getting divorced – which, technically, would be more serious: he had a young family. Maybe he'd broken up with Melanie and he badly needed to see his older sister for advice or comfort.

But no, Francis wasn't the sort of person to go crying to Mum and Dad when things went wrong. And he certainly wouldn't involve Phyllis.

My God, parental divorce. It had to be. They'd had some gigantic row, decided they had to get away from each other *right this minute*, as people in those circumstances often did, and they'd called her in as a way of tying up loose ends. If you were angry enough with each other, and sufficiently frantic to make a new start, you wouldn't care about inconveniencing your daughter with a nearly two hour train journey. You'd just want it over with.

Okay, okay. Get a grip. Hear them out, don't try to change their minds – it was probably useless anyway, and what right did you have? – and get back to London. Be level-headed. Think about the future: the investigation, John and… Well, in the long term, life after spying.

She'd always told herself MI7 wasn't a forever option; or rather, to the extent that it was, it'd become increasingly dull. In the end, she needed to rediscover the other strings to her bow.

John complicated that. He didn't seem to have any career goals. If she was honest, she thought he saw life in some kind of whacky religious way, like most of its highest values were in some sort of different dimension. Career-wise, he was governed by the law of inertia. He'd continue on whatever path fate had chosen for him. Since he was already a spy, he'd carry on being a spy. It was as good a job as any, and money wasn't important. Overall, it wasn't an outlook calculated to make him a comfortable pension, or get him a villa in Tuscany. Ultimate Londoner, good God.

The taxi pulled onto her parents' drive and she got out. The evening was clear and breezy with a thin moon. The driver waved away her attempt to tip him: it had all been taken care of already. She looked at her phone. *8.30.* Exactly when she'd said she'd arrive. Whatever happened now, they couldn't complain she'd kept them waiting.

The house was detached Georgian, with a big garden surrounded by gloomy firs, and room at the front for six cars - useful when you were entertaining.

She had her own front door key, but it seemed more prudent, and more polite, to knock. Keep it formal. If they were going to break bad news, you were best to start as you meant to go on.

Her mother and father answered the door together. A tall, thin woman with lots of jewellery, voluminous dark hair and a well-preserved face, and a bald, double-chinned, apple-shaped giant. Both were dressed for a formal occasion. Her mother wore a brown skirt and matching blouse. Her father wore a brass-buttoned blazer and tie. They had their shoes on. Their good shoes.

Yet their delighted simultaneous exclamation of "Phyllie!" was instantaneously clinching. There was no divorce on the cards here. They gave her a warm hug.

"Are we going out somewhere?" Phyllis said.

"Going out?" her mother said, looking quizzically at herself. "Oh, you mean, these clothes? No, no, absolutely not. Come into the front room. I've made you sandwiches. I take it you haven't eaten?"

"I grabbed some sushi at M&S," she replied.

"I don't call sushi eating," her father said good-naturedly.

"It's only a kind of snack, really," her mother said.

"Too trendy for my liking," her father said. "It'll die a commercial death when people realise it's unsatisfactory in every significant way. No disrespect to the Japanese."

Her parents were nervous. Something wasn't right.

Why the front room, for example? Why not the living room? And why sandwiches? If her mother thought she was hungry, she unfailingly served a hot meal. She didn't do sandwiches. Not at this time of night. And why were they dressed up?

"Is Francis here?" Phyllis asked.

Her parents looked perplexedly at each other.

"Why would he be?" her mother asked.

"That depends on why you've asked me to come home," Phyllis replied. "Until I know that - "

Her mother put her finger to her lips. "Ssh!"

"Come into the front room, Phyllie," her father said. "Consume some sandwiches, have a nice cup of tea, and we'll explain everything. Well done again for getting here on the dot. I mean, on the *absolute* dot. It's a great achievement."

"Be quiet," her mother said. "You're just confusing her even more."

They went into the front room. Phyllis's father made a point of closing the door gently but firmly behind him, unintentionally emphasising the mystery.

The room contained two sofas, two floor-to-ceiling bookshelves filled with antique books that weren't really meant for reading, a coffee table laid with sandwiches and a tea set, and a Victorian fireplace with a disused grate. There was the usual variety of polished wooden surfaces topped with ornaments and plants. A huge window on the left would have looked out onto the forecourt, but the curtains were closed. The central heating was on.

Buster, a two-year old Labradoodle, got laboriously to his feet when he saw Phyllis, and came over for a stroke. Then he retired to the corner and sat down, as if even he didn't know what was going on, but he really hoped they'd get it over with.

Her mother pointed to the sandwiches. "Egg mayonnaise, salmon and cucumber, cheese and pickle, ham. Sit down, darling. How's, er, 'John' by the way?"

She always said John's name as if the inverted commas were tweezers that would make contact with it more palatable.

"Fine," Phyllis said. "And we're still together." She sat down, picked up a random sandwich and put it in her mouth. She was annoyed now. A full day at work, two hours on the train, and now *guess the event?* "What's going on?"

Her mother lowered her voice, although - unless someone was hiding under one of the sofas - there was no chance of her being overheard. "Cynthia Cartwright's in the living room," she said, "with Innes Mount and Sir Anthony Hartley. They're here to see *you*."

For a moment, Phyllis had no idea who the three were, but then her memory powered up like someone had just pulled a start cord. Cynthia Cartwright: the chairwoman of the local Conservative party association; Innes Mount, the local MP; Sir Anthony Hartley, the Conservative MP for somewhere in Hertfordshire.

"Me?" she said.

Her mother was suddenly on the verge of tears. She faced Phyllis, took her hands, and looked her in the eyes. "Innes is going to retire at the next election. They want *you* to take the helm."

Her father stood behind the sofa, suitably distant. "They've talked about you at the *highest levels*, apparently, Phyllie. You've done a lot of work for the party in the past, canvassing on doorsteps, fundraising, all that sort of thing, and managed to combine it with a high-powered job in London. You've served your country with distinction in Afghanistan; at the other end of the sublime-ridiculous scale, you've been in *Vogue* and *Harper's*. You've travelled and you're an idealist. You're a Tory PR dream of a thirty-two-year-old, in other words. And you're a local girl."

Buster groaned and sank to the floor.

"'Future Prime Minister material'," her mother said emotionally. "Sir Anthony actually used those words!" She rose to her feet to manage her tears, and went to stand at the window. Had the curtains not been closed, she'd have been looking outside. As it was, she faced three metres of fabric.

"You could do a lot of good," her father said. "The country's really been through the mill since Brexit."

"Tonight's just an informal chat," her mother said. "A kind of touchie basie thing."

"*Touch base*," her father corrected her. "You don't have to decide anything. Think of it like the first round of any high-powered job interview. You're evaluating them as much as they are you. But don't undersell yourself. You *are* big on their radar. They're looking to attract the next generation's vote, and to do that, they need fresh, attractive young faces. The Blue Rinse Brigade's had its day."

"Eat up, Phyllie," her mother said. "We're going in there in a few minutes for sherries." She and her father exchanged solemn looks. "We've, er, told them about 'John'," she said. "But not much. They seem to have taken it for granted that, since you have impeccable taste, anyone lucky enough to call himself your boyfriend must be the most suitable of eligible bachelors."

The silence that followed this sentence conveyed much more information than its constituent words. It said: *don't ruin everything with the truth.*

Phyllis felt light-headed. Her face filled with blood, and suddenly the central heating was overpowering.

My God, this was what her life had been building towards!

She'd never considered the possibility of a political career before, not seriously. Apart from anything else, she had at least another decade's in-the-field spycraft in her. But this was a once-in-a-lifetime opportunity. It wouldn't come back. And it felt right. It felt strongly like what she really, really wanted.

"You are *okay* with all this, aren't you, Phyllie?" her mother asked.

"It's your life," her father said. "We only want what's best for you. If this isn't your bag, we'll go in there together, and break it gently to them. Together."

Phyllis put her hands on her temples. "Wow."

Her mother sat down next to her and put her shaking fingertips on her shoulder. "Good wow… or bad?" she asked huskily, as if a million pounds rode on the answer.

"The former," Phyllis said. She beamed. "The former, of course! Let's go into the living room."

## Chapter 5: Checking Out the Competition

After his interview with Ruby Parker, Mordred went to see Amber Goodings, a stout fifty-year-old with frizzy yellow hair and red-framed glasses. Amber ran MI7's wardrobe department. She claimed that good concealment employed the magician's art of misdirection, so she preferred to avoid greasepaint and latex prosthetic facial features except in emergencies. Or as she herself put it, "I'm not a costumier." Often, the best disguise was a hair-covering hat, spectacles with tinted lenses, and something singular worn at chest level - a blazer badge, say, or a loud T-shirt slogan – all in a style the wearer wouldn't normally choose.

She gave Mordred a trilby, sunglasses, a smart mid-length coat and a *Financial Times* to hold at chest-level whilst walking and to 'read' on the tube. "Although why anyone would read a newspaper about money is beyond me," she added, as she trimmed his hair slightly to fit his hat.

He arrived home at 8.40pm after a pleasingly uneventful journey, plus one stop to get a falafel pitta. His flat contained a living room, a bedroom in which the bed took up three-quarters of the space, a tiny bathroom, and a kitchen miniscule enough to make every cupboard, utility and implement reachable from a single spot. It was owned by the British government, and sat within a secure block accessible only by keying a six-digit code-number into a pad. He flopped down on the sofa and switched the TV on. *Last of the Summer Wine*.

After ten minutes, he imagined Phyllis coming in and saying, "Why are you watching that?" He could almost feel her presence.

Imaginary-her had asked a good question. He didn't know, except that virtually the characters were northern. And there were northern houses and northern streets and northern moors.

Northern. Like him.

*Too* northern, in fact. A weird cross between the *Wigan Pier* era of boots and braces and the present day.

But Phyllis wouldn't be in tonight. She might not even call. If she thought it was too late, she'd wait till tomorrow.

Anyway, he wasn't northern. Not any more. He was the ultimate Londoner, for God's sake, or one of them.

What a joke.

Time for a look at his competitors. He took his laptop from the drawer beneath the TV and switched it on. While its cogs ground, applying group registry policies, applying his user settings and preparing his desktop, he went into the kitchen and poured a glass of orange.

The prize's official website was easy enough to find. A clean white background with navy blue text, large photos of the ten candidates, accompanying information, and a link to the Gherkin. *John Mordred is a vegetarian and massive supporter of good causes. Known to his friends as a stylish man-about-town, he has lived in Islington for nearly ten years, and works in the civil service at the Foreign and Commonwealth Office. Originally from the north of England, John still supports Newcastle United Football Club, and confesses to an enduring loyalty to the place of his birth. "But I also love London," he says, "and winning the Ultimate Londoner Award 2018 would be a dream come true. With so much social mobility nowadays, probably most Londoners have a strong sense of belonging in two places. In that sense, paradoxically, I'm probably one of its most representative citizens."*

Bloody hell, he hadn't said any of that!

But then, he knew that. Calm down. Have a look at the others.

First up, Russian oligarch, Igor Lazarev. A grey-haired, moustachioed man in a suit who looked to be in his mid-sixties. *A big player in the capital, Igor owns February Rose Park in Mayfair and the Golden Gazelle Hotel in Chelsea. A Russian by birth, a Londoner by adoption, he made his fortune during the privatisation of Russia's gas industry following the Soviet Union's collapse 1991. He supports Arsenal Football Club, and rarely misses a game. "Arsenal first,"* he says, *"but every other London club second. I love London. It is a great city. New York is good also, but is overhyped. Paris is nice, but its dog-lovers have yet to discover the virtues of the 'poop scoop'. Moscow I love, of course – and I will not hear a word said against it - but not as much as I love my beautiful London."*

Next up, the pub landlord, Martin Coombes. Another middle-aged man. Open-neck shirt, pint of beer in one hand, big grin, big nose, big face, big sideburns. *A Londoner born and bred, Martin loves to spend his free time in Brighton, and travels there by scooter. He runs The Mermaid in Hammersmith with Judy, his wife of seventeen years. Not quite an original Mod, his love of everything Parka and Lambretta related was sparked by Paul Weller and The Jam in 1978. "My favourite beer," he says, "is London Pride. And that tells you everything about me. Brighton, yes, but only because it's London by the Sea. London. London, London. I AM the ultimate Londoner. Bring it on the rest of you. And you're always welcome in The Mermaid. For you nine, the drinks are on me. And everyone else when I win!"*

Gloria Shipton looked about seventy with cropped grey hair and a pashmina. She looked fed up. *Retired and not quite loving it, Gloria's had a difficult two years since being diagnosed with cancer in 2016. Chemotherapy has apparently worked its magic however, and Gloria's now well on the road to recovery. A good thing too, because she'd be sorely missed by Great Ormond Street Hospital, for which she's raised thousands of pounds by participating in the London Marathon each year - even just after she'd been given the all-clear last February. "It was a hell of a difficult run," she said. "But I'm just an old woman now, and I've had my life. Little children who get ill, well, what kind of God is there in heaven? As long as I've lungs to breathe with, I'll keep fundraising."*

The next candidate was a young Asian woman in a vest, standing behind a set of turntables and giving a peace salute with both hands. *Mehreen Shah is a twenty one-year-old DJ and human rights activist, and loves London's cosmopolitanism. Her YouGov petition calling on MP's to take stronger action against women trafficking last year was signed by over a quarter of a million people, and led to a debate in Parliament. She lives in Lambeth. A member of the*

*Hillsong evangelical community, she is also an ardent Londoner. "I was born within the sound of Bow Bells, so I'm a genuine Cockney. Nuff said, as Stan Lee put it."*

A young, uncertain-looking black woman in a suit, holding a pen. *Specioza Byanyima is a parliamentary intern looking to pursue a career in the civil service. She has appeared in every Notting Hill Carnival since 1996, and her grandfather, Delroy Shearer, was a pivotal member of the committee that inaugurated it thirty years earlier. "The carnival belongs to the whole of London nowadays," she says. "It's as much contemporary Britain's signature as Rio's is Brazil's. It represents inclusion and diversity and a bright future. It has helped make London what it is today: something both post-imperial and globally exemplary. I am proud to be in contention for The Ultimate Londoner Award."*

A thin white man in a T-shirt, jeans and baseball shoes, holding a microphone and grinning. *Marcus Jobs is an up-and-coming comedian with a string of successes behind him. The Amused Moose Comedy Award, which he won at last year's Edinburgh Festival, put him firmly on the national media radar. He has since appeared on* Have I Got News for You, The Now Show *and* The News Quiz. *Marcus was born in Croydon and grew up in Haringey. A fervent Tottenham supporter, he hasn't missed a home match since 2004. "I love-stroke-hate London," he says. "Depending on whether an unhealthy degree of arse-licking or a healthy dose of cynicism will help me win. Delete as applicable."*

A stout middle-aged woman in a hijab and an unkempt brown trouser-suit who looked surprised and delighted, as if she'd already won the five million. *Aisha Mirzakhani, 32, used to work in the City as a financial analyst, but after three years she decided she'd prefer a job working directly with society's most vulnerable people. She is now a full-time community officer in Newham. In her spare time, she enjoys tennis and fencing and helps coach the Walter Hancock Community School U14 netball team. "I don't really see myself as the ultimate Londoner," she says, "because there are so many more deserving people out there. But I'm flattered to have been shortlisted, and I'll do everything in my power to live up to the honour."*

An elderly white man with thin hair at the sides, and wispy dark eyebrows, was the next candidate. Expensive suit, expensive shirt, expensive tie. *Francis Shaylor is a former army major, company director and retired councillor from Richmond upon Thames. During his thirty years of service to the community, he helped extend home ownership across the borough and restore community pride at grass roots level. He chairs his local Rotary Club and has helped raise thousands for local charities. He is a member of The Worshipful Company of Merchant Taylors, one of the 110 livery companies of the City of London. "I've always considered myself the ultimate Londoner," he says, "but only insofar as that implies a fundamental, exceptionally rigorous duty of service to my fellow citizens. Life is about helping others."*

Last up, the novelist. A slim bearded man of about forty, standing on the Thames Embankment with grey skies and the Shard in the background. Like all good novelists, he looked utterly miserable. *Euan Frederick is a prize-winning author whose capital-based series* My Okey-Dokey Life *was adapted for BBC television in 2012. Euan is passionate about LGBT issues and the politics of inclusion. His latest novel,* Arrowed Circle Quest, *is about a young man seeking to fix his male identity ("an undertaking both logocentric and deeply nostalgic") in a future world in which everyone's gender changes frequently and predictably, according to precise divisions of the day. Described by one critic as ground breaking, it has been nominated for the Costa Book Award (novel section). "It's lovely to be considered an ultimate Londoner," Euan says. "My favourite writers are Dickens and Iain Sinclair. If my own name could be included, even on a humble level, alongside theirs, as a significant London writer, I'd be absolutely thrilled."*

Bloody hell. *John Mordred. Known to his friends as a stylish man-about-town …*

His head was caving in.

The great thing was, he stood no chance of winning against this lot.

On the other hand, something definitely didn't look real. None of the photos looked posed, for example: they all looked as if they'd been taken by a third party without the subject's knowledge.

Then there were the candidates themselves. All very worthy, no doubt – himself excluded – but more like someone's idea of a community cross-section than like a group of people who might actually head the field in a genuine Ultimate Londoner competition. Because most people's idea of the Ultimate Londoner would probably be the Queen, or failing that, Vera Lynn. Michael Caine, at a pinch. It wouldn't be Specioza Byanyima or Francis Shaylor. Where were Davina McCall, Alan Sugar, Zadie Smith, Ray Davies, Kate Moss, Will Self, Lily Allen, Prince Charles, Helen Mirren?

And then there was the voting. No indication of where the votes had come from, how many had been cast, who'd been in the previous round, or even whether there had been a previous round.

On the right, at the bottom, a live twitter feed. Most of it, if the first thirty entries were anything to go by, pretty anti-. The latest - *Pointless competition, pointless people #UltimateLondoner* – was broadly representative. *Waste of time, waste of cash. Why not give £5M to charity? #UltimateLondoner.* And there were a number of comments explicitly directed against him and the other candidates.

But mainly him. *What's skanky #JohnMordred doing in our competition? Go home, Loser! #UltimateLondoner.*

Fair point, but surely against Twitter's terms of service. In any case, it wasn't the only remark in that mould. The whole site was overflowing with them. As far as he could tell, the race to the bottom of the pile – Least Popular Contender – was pretty much tied between himself and Igor Lazarev.

Aha: here was something. *Visit our Facebook page to have your say and register to vote!*

Another site, a similar story. Lashings of troll vitriol directed against him and Igor.

The other candidates weren't faring much better. If ever a competition looked set to be a PR disaster for the capital, this was it. Right now, London looked like the Global Home of the Hopelessly Embittered.

He hoped his parents weren't looking at it. They'd worry themselves sick. They didn't think London was safe at the best of times, and, in their world, Islington was supposed to be a war-zone.

Time to ring them.

His mum picked up. "John!" she exclaimed. "Oh, you must be psychic! I was just about to ring you. I've just been saying to your dad: 'Do you think John's all right? We should probably ring him.'"

"Why wouldn't I be all right?"

"Well, we've just been looking at this 'Ultimate Londoner' competition you're in. Well done for being shortlisted, Love, but it doesn't look like it's very nice. It certainly seems to be bringing out the worst in everyone. We didn't know you worked for the Foreign Office, by the way. That's really great. Why didn't you tell us before?"

Mordred laughed. "Because I don't, really. I have *done* a bit of work for them, once or twice, in the past. But you know how these competitions are. They always fix on things they've got garbled."

"Are you at home?"

"Yep."

"Make sure your front door's locked. There are some very funny people in London."

"There are funny people everywhere, Mum."

"No, London's different. It's just too big, and people don't really belong there. They think they do, but they don't. No one does. Like your sister Charlotte says, it's just an expensive stage-set for people's fantasies."

"Okay, don't worry. I'll be careful. In fact, I'll be more than that. I've been given a bit of leave. I thought I might come back and see you for a short while."

"Oh, that'd be *lovely!*"

"I don't want to impose on you. I can stay in the town. Hexham, I mean."

She sighed. "We've been through this before, John, and I know you feel you've got to say it, but the answer's no. You're coming here, you're going to eat home-cooked food and you're going to sleep in your own bed. When are you coming?"

"When would be best?"

"The sooner the better – tonight, if you like - especially with all that going on in London. Your dad thinks you should ring up and ask for your name to be taken off the list. The whole thing sounds like ten times more trouble than it's worth. Oh, I know what you're going to say: it's five million pounds. But money isn't everything, and an awful lot of it dropping from the sky usually brings unhappiness. You're better off earning it."

"I'll get a train tomorrow morning. I should be there by three at the latest."

"Oh, that's *wonderful*. Ring us before you set off from King's Cross and when you get to Newcastle."

He said goodbye, hung up, and texted Phyllis to tell her what he was doing. Too late to ring her. Maybe they could see each other at the weekend, anywhere but London.

As he showered, brushed his teeth and got ready for bed, his mum's words began to play on him. *Certainly seems to be bringing out the worst in everyone… Some very funny people in London…*

Once or twice, in the silence between events and actions, he half-imagined he could hear the goblins scratching at his front door, trying to get in. He didn't belong here. They didn't want him around. They'd show him exactly what they did with strangers.

## Chapter 6: And You're an Idealist

Phyllis sat alone by the window at a Great Western Railway laminated table. She was exhausted and depressed. Three other passengers occupied her carriage, all alone, looking as frazzled as she probably did. *The 23.39 from Newbury to Paddington, estimated time of arrival, 01.21.* The ticket inspector had passed five minutes ago. Technically, she could now go to sleep. Realistically, she wouldn't until she got home, probably just after two.

She was too stimulated. Too many new experiences, too much excitement, too much having to keep her wits about her. This was the last train back tonight. Not catching it hadn't been an option. She was expected into work as usual tomorrow morning.

It had taken her exactly seventeen minutes to realise she didn't want to be the next MP for Newbury. Good God, the interview. Like talking to the living dead.

But she hadn't said anything, because even now, madly, a small part of her was still in two minds.

A small part growing bigger? She honestly didn't know.

Odd, how before she'd gone into the living room, she'd wondered how she could make John compatible with what she was about to commit to, or whether, and how, to endure the agony of leaving him. Alternatively, whether she'd be unable do either. *Ultimately, she chose the man she loved,* like some soppy romantic potboiler, completely out of synch with nowadays.

In the end, though, the living room conference had been a dispiritingly starchy, distant affair. Nothing to indicate anyone 'interviewing' her might ever become a friend. All as if they were doing her a massive favour. Which they probably were, only…

My God, if that's how they did *in*formal, what the hell must formal be like?

And that's when she'd remembered. It had been years since she'd had much to do with these sorts of people, but she'd cut them out of her life for a *reason*.

Political officials of all kinds were the same. They lacked something it was difficult to put your finger on; some very specific variety of the *spark of life*. Perhaps because they'd allowed civil society to refashion them in its own image; perhaps because they'd deliberately cauterised a large slice of their private selves. Yes, they knew they were more powerful than most people – and oh, how they relished it! - but they couldn't conceal their deeper insubstantiality. Presumably, it was a trade-off. Your God-given *joie de vivre* for the conviction that you were someone to be reckoned with. Hardly everyone was offered that exchange, and because it was so rare, you were supposed to grab it with both hands. Her good fortune – if that's what it was – lay in seeing through it.

On the other hand, insanely, it *was* tempting. *Phyllis Robinson, MP for Newbury.*

Because maybe the resulting you wasn't a cauterised version of your present self, after all. Maybe it was a completely different being, only similar to you, like a *Body Snatcher*.

That would explain its appeal. There was another Phyllis, a humourless, grey thing with limitless aspirations, who wanted to hijack her body. Its goals were all public: pleasing her parents, inspiring envy and awe, accumulating praise, honours, high ranking offices, titles. It wasn't really interested in this life at all. It lived for posterity, calculating that people in a hundred, two hundred, even a thousand years would speak of it like they nowadays spoke of Cincinnatus or Pitt the Younger. *Rose through the ranks to distinction, imperious, dominated its age,* etcetera. It would only be sated when she was dead.

By contrast, the Phyllis now occupying her body was geared entirely to this life. It didn't want recognition. It wanted happiness and a good night's sleep. It believed that when she was dead she wouldn't be here any longer so what was the point of worrying?

It was sane.

But it wasn't a question of which Phyllis was sane and which wasn't. It was about which was stronger. Why hadn't she told anyone she didn't want to be Newbury's next MP? Well, because the real her wasn't decisive enough. Other-Phyllis would marshal countless inducements and arguments over the coming days and weeks, because it knew it had an opening. And also what it was up against. And truth be told, its vigour came from the fact that it wasn't actually another Phyllis at all. Not behind the mask. It just looked and felt like a second her from her present perspective.

In reality, it was everyone of its type who had ever lived and was now dead. It was Themistocles and Pericles, Cincinnatus, Cicero, Julius Caesar, Pitt the Younger, Peel, Disraeli, and so on, and so on, for ever, all presently impotent in Hades, all rolled up into one and pathetically clamouring to relive through her.

Why her? Well, it had to take every chance it got, however unpromising, because it didn't get that many.

And she *was* unpromising, really. When she thought about it. Her father's *And you're an idealist* kept coming back to her.

What sort of idealist was she? The sort who wanted people to be fair, and innocent people not to suffer, that's all. She had some specific ideas, but how to make them into a distinctive political programme? She couldn't.

The country didn't need her. The constituency didn't need her.

On the other hand, maybe she was just tired. She looked at her phone. *00.14.* Your blood pressure usually went down during the night. You often thought you were a dud.

Thank God she hadn't rejected it on the spot, really. She needed to re-think with a bit of sunlight around her. They might not have shown it, but they probably did want her. As far as she recalled, she hadn't come across as too eager, which was good. *Phyllis Robinson, MP for Newbury.*

She had no idea how John would take it.

Or had she? They'd been together for a while now, and they were best friends as well as lovers. She ought to have *some* notion of how he'd react.

Bloody hell, she hoped he wouldn't say something wishy-washy. "I want what you want" or "I only want what's right for you." She needed some sort of guide to action. She needed him to embrace or reject it for its own sake.

But he wouldn't. His family were largely Corbynistas, as far as she could tell, and he didn't even vote. The best she could expect was that he wouldn't object.

Which wasn't enough. If she did want this – which she might or might not – she had to contemplate leaving him. Because in the longer term, they couldn't work, not if he was lukewarm. And she had to realise that now. No use being sentimental.

How to broach *I'm thinking of running for Parliament?*

It wasn't the sort of thing you could drop into a casual conversation. She needed to tell him she had something important to say, then choose a neutral venue, and ring-fence sufficient time for them to explore all the ramifications, or as many as possible at this stage. This was serious. It was their future.

Or absence of it. Her phone dinged. A text. *John.*

Her heart sank slightly when she saw it had been sent two hours ago. *I've been ordered to leave London. I'm going back to Hexham for a few days, just to avoid the hatred. I'll call you first thing. Hope everything's okay with your parents. I love you. J.*

'Hatred'? What was he talking about?

The competition: Ultimate bloody Londoner. She'd forgotten all about it. She went to the official website, then to Facebook. She scrolled down the posts. Her mouth popped open.

My God.

Poor John.

## Chapter 7: Bad Train Journey

Mordred didn't sleep well. At 2am, he got up and watched two episodes of *Shetland* on iPlayer. He could sleep on the train tomorrow – well, today, now. At 4am, he went back to bed for another try. He fell into a doze and his alarm went off at eight.

No real need to get up, except that he'd promised to ring Phyllis. He might as well combine that with packing a suitcase and getting ready to leave for Hexham. It'd probably be sensible to wear Amber's disguise to the station too. He didn't like to overestimate his own importance to strangers, but better safe than sorry.

He called Phyllis at 8.30 when he was certain she'd be on the bus.

"I was just about to ring you," she said. "Are you okay?"

"So far. Just in the middle of organising my escape from the capital."

"There are some pretty nasty people out there. I read the Facebook stuff. If it helps, I'm more than ever determined to get to the bottom of it."

"I haven't looked at it this morning. For all I know, Ruby Parker may have succeeded in getting me withdrawn."

"Sorry to be the bearer of bad news, but you're still very much in contention. I've just looked at the website."

"Was everything okay last night?"

"I guess so."

He sat down on the sofa. "You don't sound very certain."

"I need to talk to you."

"We're talking now. Is something wrong?"

He heard her sigh. "In one way, yes," she said. "In another, no: anything but. We need to have a long conversation, John. There isn't time now. I'll be at work pretty shortly."

"Longer than thirty minutes then?"

"Yep."

"We can see each other at the weekend, hopefully. Would that be okay?"

"It'd be ideal. But not at Hexham. Somewhere in between." She laughed. "Listen, I've suddenly realised how I must sound. Like *Dear John, there's someone else. It's not you, it's me.* That's not what this is."

His normal metabolism began to reassert itself, then the truth dawned. "In that case, someone's offered you another job."

A beat. "Maybe."

"And you can't tell me what it is over the phone? Presumably, it must be top secret. Another department. Grey or Blue?"

Another pause, longer this time. When she spoke there was a tremble in her voice. "Okay, I was going to save it, but it's nothing like that, although it is pretty hush-hush right now. In another way. Not a national security, for-your-eyes-only way."

"I take it I'm involved somehow."

"Only if you want to be."

"If being involved means we stay together, then yes I do. Does it entail moving abroad? By the way, this is beginning to sound a bit like *What's My Line*."

"They're considering offering me a safe parliamentary seat."

He had to replay her words in his head. 'They'?

"Are you still there?" she asked.

"A safe parliamentary seat?" he said, the only words he could think of. He should sound pleased. Maybe he *was* pleased. "Wow, that's amazing!"

"And I really don't … don't know what to do about it. And…"

"Hang on, are you upset?"

Another long pause. *"Yes, I am upset, you idiot! I hadn't banked on telling you today, and I'm completely conflicted. I wanted your honest advice, which is why I wanted a proper face-to-face conversation. The last thing I bloody wanted was, 'Wow, that's amazing!'"*

"But it is amazing. And in any case - "

"Look, John," she said, "stop talking." There was a sudden coldness in her voice. "I'm putting the phone down. Don't call me back. I'll text you on Friday and we'll book a hotel somewhere and talk. Like we should have done all along. In the meantime, I want you to consider what you think I should do, and whether you're prepared to stand by me if I accept."

She hung up.

He let out a deep breath and looked at the ceiling.

Bloody hell, they'd reached a major fork in the road, and it had just come out of nowhere. Depending on what happened in the next week or so, they might not even be together this time next year. Or they might be, but in different jobs, being slightly different people. He felt giddy. No wonder she was furious with him. Something like this, you needed tight control of all the variables for the sake of your mental health. You could do without your boyfriend chucking *What's My Line* into the discussion.

She hadn't said don't text her. He rattled off an *I love you,* pressed 'send' and switched on the TV as a way of clearing his mind.

Another episode of *Last of the Summer Wine.*

Five minutes later, his phone beeped. A text.

*I love you too. Enjoy your break. See you at the weekend. x.*

An hour later, he got on the train at King's Cross. Perhaps he was coming down with something, or maybe Phyllis's confession had kick-started something, but he felt distinctly queasy when the train departed. He called Ruby Parker to let her know his plans, then his mother to inform her that he'd set off. When the train pulled in to Harringay, he removed his disguise. He'd lost interest in whether anyone recognised him. What were they going to do, anyway, punch him? In broad daylight?

When the train reached Potters Bar, he had to put his head between his knees to ward off the urge to vomit. The passenger sitting next to him – an elderly woman in a T-shirt and trousers - leaned over solicitously and put her hand on his back. She didn't say anything. If you were reasonably young, alone, and on your way back from a morning in the capital, you might well be drunk.

Everyone in the carriage was against him, even the ticket inspector.

Hang on, that was insane. Suddenly, everything sped up. Brookmans Park, Welham Green, Hatfield all went by in a flash. Then everything slowed down. They seemed to be in one station for an age. He couldn't even see its name, and it looked deserted.

When they set off again, he was alone in the carriage.

Where had everyone else gone? Had there been some sort of emergency? If so, why had no one thought to tell him?

What was going on?

He'd been drugged, that's what. The paranoia, the nausea, the delusions, there was no other explanation. He needed to phone Ruby Parker. Or even the police.

Suddenly the door at the far end of the carriage swished open and a middle-aged man walked in. Smartly dressed: grey woollen coat, matching trilby, black polished brogues, striped tie. He sat down next to Mordred and turned to look at him.

Mordred couldn't find his phone in his pocket. It was too late now anyway. From the edges of his vision, blackness raced in.

## Chapter 8: What the Virtual Personal Assistant Knew

Phyllis received Mordred's text message twenty minutes after it had been sent, when she was almost at Thames House. She texted him back something conciliatory.

But she was still annoyed. *Wow, that's amazing*, bloody hell. Talk about glib.

Her fault, though – partly. She shouldn't have told him. Have let him pressure her. It'd have been far better to leave it hanging.

On the other hand, at least he'd have time to think about it now. When they next spoke, she might get some sense out of him.

And actually, to be fair, what had she really expected? She was thirty-two, like him. Not the sort of age people normally got offered seats in government. Not his fault his mind got blown. It really *was* mind blowing. How would she have reacted, had the boot been on the other foot? Suddenly, he didn't look so ridiculous.

The wind blew hard from the river and shook the trees on the embankment. She climbed the steps to Thames House, signed in at reception and went straight to her desk. Edna, a tall black woman in a casual maxi dress, was waiting for her with a cup of tea in her hand. She obviously had something to say.

"Is everything okay?" Phyllis asked.

"Have you seen all the shit about John?" Edna replied.

Phyllis chuckled. "The Ultimate Londoner? Some of it."

"Where do people get off, writing that kind of drivel? I hear he's been given leave. Is that a kind of 'for his own safety' thing?"

"Partly. Also, to keep him out of the public eye. We don't want people prying any more. Out of sight out of mind, as they say."

"Who nominated him? Do we know?"

"No, and neither does he. I'm just about to go and see Ruby Parker, ask if I can investigate. Assuming she hasn't already solved all the outstanding puzzles."

"Mind if I join you?"

"On the investigation, or just in her office?"

Edna shrugged. "Both. I'm only working carousels at the moment. Just ticking boxes to show they've had fresh eyes on them before the mandatory six months expires."

"Ditto. Clerical stuff and boring as hell. I'll just log on, see if my programme for the day's been tweaked. If not, I'll request a meeting."

She switched her computer on and went straight to her personalised *Today to Do* space. "Bingo," she said. "I've been summoned."

"Ruby Parker? When?"

"Right now."

"If you can possibly ask for a partner, you know where I am."

"I'll do my best."

Phyllis locked her screen and took the lift to Ruby Parker's office. She knocked twice, heard 'Enter' and went in.

Ruby Parker sat behind her desk with a tabloid newspaper open in front of her. She gestured for Phyllis to sit down.

"Have you seen this morning's *Metro?*" she asked.

Phyllis's heart sank. Talk about an inauspicious start. "I, er, didn't pick one up on the way in," she replied. "Sorry, I was talking to John on the phone."

"It's not a veiled accusation. It's hardly required reading. Only, had you done so, you'd be aware there's another Ultimate Londoner supplement. Slightly different information, completely different photo. Someone knows an awful lot about John, and they're lying so low, we can't seem to locate them."

"When you put it like that, it sounds quite sinister."

"We've no reason to think John's being targeted for anything, but we can't afford to be complacent. And we need to get to the bottom of it. If it happens once, perhaps it can happen again. Next time, you or I could be the target."

"You've ruled out his sisters, I take it."

"He called his oldest in my presence. She denied it. The analysis of the voice recording was pretty conclusive: she's telling the truth. The others aren't really suspects. Apart from anything else, given how badly it's gone, I think if any of them started it, she'd have owned up with an apology by now."

Phyllis nodded. She needed to take charge of the discussion now. "You said we need to get to the bottom of it. I'd like to investigate."

"I thought you might say that. I confess, asking you had occurred to me."

"I'd like to take Edna, if possible."

"Your reasoning?"

"She's expressed an interest, and, since she's famous in her own right, and a Londoner, she's well placed to raise informal questions about why she herself wasn't nominated. She's got a huge network of contacts, some of whom might be very helpful. At the moment, she's only working on carousels. She can easily be spared."

"Excellent reasoning. Remind me again why *you* need to be involved."

Phyllis felt the pause in the conversation like a shove out of nowhere. She'd fallen into a trap of her own making. "Because I can work extra hard on this and I'm – I know enough about John to – make a good job of it."

"That's too vague, I'm afraid. We only need one person on this at the moment, and, from what you've just told me, Edna sounds much more suitable."

Another pause. But it was checkmate. "Granted," she said quietly.

"On the other hand, I do understand that you have personal reasons for wishing to be involved, and although that would normally count against you, in this particular instance it doesn't.

I'm prepared to put you both to work, but, because I know you'll probably work around the clock, with a tight deadline. You've got three days. If you haven't come up with any leads by then, we'll let the competition run its course. The award ceremony's on 21st May. We'll probably get our answers there."

"Do we know who's booked the Gherkin?"

"A shell company called Colander. We're in the process of following the usual smoke and mirrors trail. I'll let you know."

"Obviously, that makes it even more sinister."

"It also makes it less likely that you and Edna will find anything. Anyone who's taken the trouble to cover his or her tracks to that extent is unlikely to have left clues lying around on the ground."

"Well, if we've got three days, maybe we should get started."

Ruby Parker folded her hands in front of her. "There is something else."

Phyllis sat down.

"I understand the Conservative Party in Newbury's made you an offer."

That shove again. Wow. She pulled an involuntary face then realised. "That's right," she said.

"We haven't been spying on you," Ruby Parker went on. "Sir Anthony Hartley Brown inquired about your background. For the record, he now knows what you do for a living. He won't tell, but I understand the Tories are very keen on stealing you from us. It's only fair to warn you I intend to stand in their way. You're one of our most talented officers, and certainly our best all-rounder. John and Annabel, and to a lesser extent Alec, are all brilliant officers whose overdevelopment in certain areas compensates for skill-sets they lack. But I don't have to weigh pros against cons with you. You're all pros."

She was suddenly aware of everything in the room. She instinctively recognised what was happening: another of those *remember for the rest of your life* things. Two in twenty-four hours. She cleared her throat. "Thank you."

"Before you express too much gratitude, you may be interested to know I don't think you're cut out to be a politician. In that regard, you're much more like John than you probably realise. Compromising to increase your public standing isn't in your nature. You can change, of course. Everyone can. But it'll be a change for the worse."

Brutal. From one extreme to the other. She felt like she was absorbing blows from all sides. "I haven't decided anything yet. The thought of being MP for Newbury's a very attractive one and it's once in a lifetime."

"And obviously, you stand very little chance of being killed in action."

"There's that too. I don't know if that's a plus. For all I know, I may be an adrenaline junkie. In any case, we may both be jumping the gun. I've had no formal offer yet. Last night was just exploratory. Sir Anthony Hartley Brown may want me, and he may be a very senior figure within the party, but he's not local. His enthusiasm might even be counter-productive if Newbury's finest perceive him to be exerting unwanted pressure."

"On the other hand, there aren't many candidates of your calibre anywhere in the country, let alone, I would imagine, in a single constituency. Realistically, if you want it, it's probably yours for the taking. That's the assumption I'm working with at the moment. It's one of the reasons I'm allowing you and Edna to work the investigation you've just proposed together. Pretty soon, you're going to have to make your mind up. And I don't want you doing that against a background of feeling even slightly frustrated with your job here."

"I never have. There are dull parts to all jobs, and no career gives you a hundred per cent satisfaction all the time."

"You're talking yourself out of the investigation again."

Phyllis chuckled and got up. As she went back to her desk and Edna, a thought struck her: what if all that spiel about her being MI7's most rounded officer had simply been flimflam? Supposing Ruby Parker believed – as well she might – that if Phyllis left, John would inevitably follow? What if her real concern was to hold on to him?

But that was stupid. Ruby Parker was easily intelligent enough, but she was never less than completely honest with her subordinates.

More disturbingly, what did it say about her, Phyllis? How self-confident was she, if she could think something like that?

Enough to be an effective politician?

Enough to be a really effective anything? She stopped on the stairs, leaned against the handrail and put her fingertips to her temples. First *Future Prime Minister material*, now *You're certainly our best all-rounder*.

A crisis of confidence? She could feel it, like a coming thunderstorm. A kind of malign electricity in the air. Of all the times in her life, why *now*?

But then, just as suddenly as it arrived, it passed.

In its place, a great sense of peace. It was going to be okay, all of it, whatever happened next. She went to find Edna.

Two hours later, she sat at a small circular table in The Greyhound, Kensington Square with Timothy Grendell, the sub-editor of *The Evening Standard*, a slight forty-two-year-old with a well-trimmed beard, hairless scalp, pink V-necked jumper and chinos. Both had half-pints of ale of them.

Grendell believed he was talking to a police officer called DI Susan Nicholson. The trick was to introduce yourself vaguely, show a card, allow the interviewee to draw the inferential conclusion, and not to disrupt it. It helped if you then relocated somewhere congenial, bought drinks and took notes.

"It's not actually our competition, or anything to do with us," Grendell said. "We agreed to run the supplement, and happily – I mean, 'Ultimate Londoner': it's right up our street. We had no idea the whole thing was going to blow up in our faces. When you're presented with something that says 'shortlist', you tend to think there must have been prior stages. You assume the participants must have given their consent already. Of course you do. You don't question it."

"You're saying you now know they haven't?" Phyllis asked.

"You wouldn't be here otherwise, would you? The police don't come round asking questions when you haven't done anything wrong."

Phyllis shrugged. "So you're simply inferring?"

"Not quite," Grendell went on. He deflated. "We've had complaints from four of the contestants. They say they didn't know anything about it before yesterday evening, and they're thinking of suing. We let the *Metro* know. We assumed they might be running the same thing. But it was too late. So now they're in trouble too."

"Which four contestants?"

"I don't know their names. But you might recognise them from their descriptions. The Russian guy's most worrying."

"Igor Lazarev."

"Sounds right. He definitely has the financial capacity to sue, and he probably wouldn't settle out of court. He might even get brownie points from Putin. The only question is whether he'll be able to show enough of his privacy was breached. He probably can't. There's an awful lot of information about him in the public domain. He could assert that he didn't say the exact words the supplement attributed to him, try and build grounds to sue out of that. But it's pretty slender. There's nothing defamatory in what we published."

"Who are the other three?"

"Well, the old woman was the first. The chemotherapy patient. You know: London marathons…"

"Gloria Shipton."

"She was the first to call. Absolutely bloody apoplectic. Sue, who took the call, said she didn't know someone that old could be that potty-mouthed. In some ways, she's our biggest worry. It looks very bad indeed, the *Standard* making a community-spirited cancer victim's life miserable. And she might get legal aid. In that case, we might be able to fob her off with a donation to charity. I mean, I'm going with what the supplement said about her now, which could all be cobblers. If it is true, and she sues us, she'll probably give the proceeds away anyway, but it'll be minus the lawyer's fees. That gives us leverage. On the other hand, she might be the kind of woman who rings up to give you a bloody good shouting at, then calms down and leaves it at that. Who knows?"

"The other two complainants?"

"The DJ and the comedian. Marcus Jobs. I saw him on *Have I Got News for You*. I can't remember the DJ's name. Something Khan, I think."

"Mehreen Shah."

"That's the one. They were both quite nice about it, apparently, but pretty firm: they didn't want to be associated with the Ultimate Londoner Award."

"Why not?"

"They're not worthy, apparently. I don't mean in comparison with the other candidates. I mean, they don't want to get to gigs and punters are like, *There goes the Ultimate Londoner*. Snarky. When you've got people like Stormzy and Josh Widdicombe on the scene, it could easily work against you. The proverbial poisoned chalice, if you see what I mean. Would you like another beer? I'm buying."

"It's very kind of you, but I should probably be getting back to work in a minute."

"Me too," he said sadly.

"I appreciate the offer."

"Are you … Okay, I know this is going to be… Well, I'll just come out and say it. Would you like to go for a drink sometime? I mean, not like this. Socially."

She smiled. "Thank you, but I'm in a relationship."

"Well, if you ever, say … *leave* that relationship - "

"I'll bear you in mind. I'm flattered."

"You're very attractive. Sorry, I'm coming across a bit stalker-y now. It's just, you remind me a little of that supermodel, a few years ago. Phyllis something."

"I've had that before, believe it or not."

He laughed and put his hands up. *"Really?* Oh my God, I'm surprised anyone else remembers her! Robinson, that's the one. She was only on the scene for a short while. I used to do fashion at *The Mail on Sunday*, that's how I recall. Long memory for useless details."

She smiled and finished her beer. She'd been here once or twice before. It didn't faze her.

"Well," he said awkwardly, "now that's out of the way, let's get back to the Q&A!"

"I've only one more question. Can you tell me anything at all about the company that placed the ad? Colander, I believe it's called."

"Nothing. Posted us the copy, paid the fee, disappeared from sight."

She put her notepad in her bag and got to her feet. "Thank you ever so much for your time. You've been very helpful. May I get back to you, if we need anything else?"

He drank what remained of his beer, got to his feet, looked her in the eye and accepted her handshake. "I'd be more than pleased Susan. *More* than pleased."

Five minutes later, just as she was about to enter High Street Kensington tube station, her phone rang. *Edna.*

"I'm just on my way round to your place now," Phyllis told her. "Is everything okay?"

"I haven't got anywhere with my contacts," Edna replied. "It worries me that I'm beginning to sound a bit desperate. *Do you know anything about the Ultimate Londoner Award, and if so, maybe you could tell me why I wasn't nominated?* I'm not saying I actually put it like that, obviously, but I'm beginning to get the sense people are reading between the non-existent lines, so to speak.

But I'm calling you because I've discovered something really weird."

"Go on."

"Well, first off, I rang my agent. I'm a gold-medal athlete, why wasn't I, blah, blah. Anyway, she didn't know anything about it, so she put me on hold and asked her Siri. Have you come across Siri?"

"Apple's virtual personal assistant?"

"It sits on your kitchen table and you give it instructions. Like an Echo. *Alexa, could you play Road Rage by Dizzee Rascal,* that sort of thing."

"And?"

"Moira's Siri knew all about the Ultimate Londoner competition. It actually knew how many votes each of the candidates had."

"Because it's connected to the web."

"That's what I thought, only that information's not on the web. *I* couldn't find it anywhere. Now I know what you're going to say: you're not an expert, Edna. Agreed, and so I rang Tariq. He couldn't find it anywhere either. And yet it's on Siri. They've got one or two Siri apps on hand in MI7's IT section. Plus an Alexa, plus a Google Home, plus a Mycroft, plus a Viv, plus one or two other Virtual Personal Assistants I'd never heard of. And guess what? They all know all about The Ultimate Londoner."

"Whoa. And has Tariq…?"

"He doesn't know what the explanation is. But that's not all. It gets even weirder. Because guess who's in the lead? John. And I don't mean by a slight margin. I mean, way, *way* in the lead. So much so that the others might as well be still on the starting blocks."

"But that's - *mad*. Where do you even go to vote? *How* do you vote?"

"Siri doesn't know. And neither do any of the others. And before you ask, nor do they know anything about Colander. Or anything useful. Have you got a VPA?"

"At home? I've got an Alexa."

"Same here. Now listen, I'm going to put her on the line for a second. Because this has to be heard to be believed. Ready? *Alexa: in the Ultimate Londoner competition, how many votes has John Mordred got?*"

Alexa's voice came on. "In the 2018 Ultimate Londoner Award, sponsored by Colander, John Mordred has two million, six hundred and forty-eight thousand, seven hundred and thirty-eight votes. Updating... In the 2018 Ultimate Londoner Award, sponsored by Colander, John Mordred has two million, six hundred and forty-eight thousand, seven hundred and forty-two votes. Updating... In the 2018 Ultimate Londoner Award, sponsored by Colander, John Mordred has two million, six hundred and forty-eight thousand, seven hundred and forty-five votes. Updating... In the - "

"*Alexa: stop,*" Edna said. "If you don't stop her, she just keeps going. The votes are coming in at approximately three per second. How? Where from? We don't know."

"How many votes have the others got?"

"Right now, Gloria Shipton's in second. She's got roughly fifty thousand votes, slightly under. All the others are in the low thousands. None over ten thousand."

"These don't sound like human votes." Phyllis was thinking aloud now. "They can't be. How can they be?"

"There are nearly nine million people living in London. Even taking into account some interest elsewhere, it's just not plausible that they're so galvanised by the Ultimate Londoner competition, and John Mordred in particular, that about a third of them would vote. Assuming they even knew how. Put it another way. In the 2016 mayoral election, Sadiq Khan and Zac Goldsmith together only got less than two and a half million votes. About three hundred and fifty thousand short of where John alone is now."

"So what's going on? I don't have a theory. Do you? Does Tariq?"

"No one's got the faintest idea." There was a little ding in the background. "Hang on, an email. Just stay there… Okay. It's Tariq. Would you like me to read it to you?"

"Just give me the gist. I've a strong feeling we should cancel my plans to come over to yours. We should probably head back to base."

"Agreed. Okay, here goes. This is what he says, in summary. Amazon, Apple and Google are now officially freaking out. They've no idea what's going on either, and they've asked us to keep it under wraps till they do a bit more investigating. End of message."

"'Keep it under wraps'? How the hell are we going to do that? Just about everyone's got a Virtual Personal Assistant nowadays."

"On the other hand, if you're right – and I agree with you – hardly any actual humans are interested in the competition."

"I didn't put it quite that way. But all it takes is one curious person. I'm pretty sure the competitors themselves are interested, and as soon as someone discovers John's storming ahead of the field, the hostility to him's going to reach fever pitch. It's bad enough now."

"I thought the same. He's safely out of the capital, though, isn't he?"

"So I believe. And he doesn't own a VPA."

"Really? Why not? I thought everyone had one nowadays. Everyone under forty, anyway."

"He had one for a while. He didn't like the idea of giving it orders. 'Re-conditioning people to accept vassalage'. His sister Charlotte's idea, not his, but for some reason, he went with it. If you've never met Charlotte, she's lovely, but somehow away with the fairies."

"Whoa. Just when you thought you knew John's precise level of kookiness. He actually believed that telling Alexa to play Beethoven might acclimatise him to be okay with slavery? That's seriously nuts."

"Not him. People. And probably not human slaves. Have you ever seen *I, Robot?*"

"The Will Smith film?" She laughed. "*Roman Holiday* or *Casablanca* I can happily sit through. Also, anything pushed at me by Netflix, or still in the cinema. But there's a whole swathe of stuff from the last thirty years, up to about 2014, that I just can't abide. Unless it's a Christmas film. To answer the question, no I haven't. Is it any good?"

"It's about robots being slaves. John's read the book too. I'd better give him a ring, let him know what's going on."

"See you back at Thames House then."

Phyllis had been hanging about the tube station entrance for so long, she was getting cold. She scrolled down her Contacts until she reached John. It rang for a few seconds, then a woman's voice said, "Sorry, the person you are trying to reach cannot take your call right now. If you would like to leave a message, please speak after the tone."

Bloody hell, more or less the same voice as Alexa.

And just as ominous.

## Chapter 9: Phyllis's Rival

Phyllis spent the remainder of that day thinking it was the shortest investigation she'd ever been involved in. Even Ruby Parker was cast in a reactive role. Once Tariq got involved, the IT element took over. And when he reached a dead end, and Google, Apple and Amazon looked stumped, GCHQ stepped aboard. The cutting edge of the enquiry was now a hundred miles west in Cheltenham.

But it quickly became apparent that if GCHQ was getting anywhere, it wasn't letting on. The result was a rainy afternoon which strongly resembled something out of childhood, one of those gloomy Sundays when your parents' guests sat droning endlessly about long-lost relatives, while you were restricted to looking endearing in clothes you'd never normally wear. On her third cup of tea, Phyllis was so bored she felt almost tearful with self-pity. The clock at the bottom of her computer screen said 4.17. Seventy-three minutes till going home.

And then what?

She'd be more worried, that's what.

Because the truth was, boredom wasn't the worst emotion she felt right now. Where was John?

Ruby Parker wasn't surprised he wasn't answering his phone. She'd keep the situation under review. Sensitive information about John had leaked out to someone, somehow. Who knew whether his contact details were equally compromised? He might well have discovered they were. He'd switch his phone off in that case.

And of course, he was at home with his parents. They'd be making a fuss of him. And he was on leave. No reason to contact Ruby Parker – he'd already done that this morning. No reason to contact Phyllis either: they'd had a 'tiff', as her parents called such things. And the last words she'd sent him had been 'See you at the weekend'. And even if he wanted to talk, she was supposed to be at work. He might ring later. Possibly.

All good reasons to think nothing was amiss.

So why was she worried?

Because she was bored, maybe. Nothing else to occupy her mind, so she might as well fret about John.

'See you at the weekend.' How far did that imply, '*Won't* see you beforehand' or – in the context of the antagonism she'd expressed towards him – '*Don't want to* hear from you beforehand'?

Sixty-five minutes to go. She'd probably have a big glass of white wine when she got in. Then maybe go straight to bed.

Bonkers.

She wasn't sure whether she was just miserable or coming down with something. The flu was going round again. But wasn't it always?

Food. She couldn't just go straight to bed. She was hungry.

God, John was *weird*. She'd completely forgotten that thing about Alexa-as-a-slave before Edna accidentally raised it. She'd felt embarrassed trying to explain. Edna was right: he was 'seriously nuts', and that was putting it politely. How long before he started dressing in a kaftan and a tinfoil hat?

But that wouldn't happen. In the abstract, it looked like a good question. But in reality, he was somehow saner than everyone else. You only needed be in his company for a short time to feel… safe, somehow. Safer than anywhere else.

Which was weird in itself. How did he pull that off?

She should try ringing him again. She took out her phone, scrolled down, pressed Call. Three rings, then straight to voicemail. Bloody, *bloody* hell!

She needed something to take her mind off what was happening. She called Edna. "Got any of those carousels from this morning?"

"A million still to go," Edna replied. "Why?"

"I need something mindless to do."

"How many do you want?"

"Enough to keep me busy till the end of the day."

"We've an hour. Twenty too many?"

"Sounds ideal."

Edna laughed. "Not the word I'd choose. I'll send them over as attachments in bundles of five. Any word from John?"

"He's still not answering his phone."

"Probably watching daytime TV with his mum. I think *Dickinson's Real Deal*'s on."

5.40. Phyllis took the bus back to Camden. She used her phone to put the heating on. Her flat consisted of a bedroom, bathroom, living room and kitchen. The furniture was minimalist, discreet and compact in muted colours. When she got in, she slipped her shoes off, put the kettle on and sat down by the Echo on her living room table. She suddenly realised she'd been waiting for this moment for several hours. Not just for the obvious question, but for others she hadn't yet formulated.

*"Alexa"* she said: *"in the Ultimate Londoner competition, how many votes has John Mordred got?"*

A little blue light circled the rim. "In the 2018 Ultimate Londoner Award, sponsored by Colander, John Mordred has two million, seven hundred and two thousand, three hundred and twenty-eight votes. Updating... In the 2018 Ultimate Londoner - "

*"Alexa: stop."*

The kettle was boiling. She made a cup of Earl Grey, then put some fusilli in a pan with the rest of the water. She took a pot of ready-made carbonara sauce from the fridge and transferred it to the microwave, ready to go. She brought the pasta to the boil, stirred it, and switched it to simmer. This was the point at which she usually asked Alexa to activate a timer, but she had other questions tonight. She set her phone alarm and sat down at the living room table again.

*"Alexa,"* she said: *"where is John Mordred now?"*

Talk about a long shot.

"Sorry," Alexa replied. "I don't know that."

God, she was going insane. A *long* shot? If you called here to Jupiter long, maybe. She laughed. No one else was around. She could be as crazy as she liked, what did it matter?

"*Alexa,*" she said: "*is John Mordred safe?*"

The little blue light again. "I can confirm that John Mordred is safe."

Er - what?

Time seemed to fissure, and several seconds fell headlong into the gap. She stood up, pushing her chair over. She heard herself say oh my God. Her phone alarm went off.

"What did you say?" she asked Alexa. Her hair had fallen over her face. She thrust her hand into it and swept it out of the way.

Silence.

"*Alexa,*" she said again, quietly, nervously: "*is John Mordred safe?*"

Pause. "Sorry," Alexa replied. "I don't know that."

She suddenly had the horrible feeling she wasn't alone in her flat. The sense of an intruder, but so instinctive, she didn't think it could be the thing in front of her. That had always been her friend. She went into the kitchen, grabbed a carving knife and went into her bedroom, then the bathroom, the only two places anyone else could be.

No one. But weirdly, she hadn't been expecting anyone. Not really. She knew who the intruder was.

She went into the kitchen and drained the pasta. She didn't feel remotely hungry now. She was trembling. In the living room, her phone was ringing.

John, it had to be.

She strode in, breathing hard, picked it up and looked at the screen. *Mum.*

Bloody hell, not ideal. But just to speak to anyone now! She picked up. "Hi."

"Your mother here, Phyllie. Did you have a pleasant journey home?"

"Yes... Thank you."

"Is everything okay? You sound a little out of breath."

"Sorry, yes, fine. Just making dinner. Pasta with a bacon sauce, before you ask."

"Doesn't sound much of a meal to me. Not for a main course. Anyway, that's not why I rang. I won't stay on long. I've got some bad news, I'm afraid. It looks like you might have a bit of a fight on your hands. I don't suppose you've ever heard of Aisling Baxter?"

"Should I have?"

"As of today, she's officially your rival. Or at least, that's how I want you to regard her. Because that's how it's going to turn out."

Phyllis rubbed her face. "Sorry, mum, I'm not sure what you mean. It may just be me. I've had a busy day at work. Could you be a bit clearer? Please?"

Her mum gave a surprised laugh. "Yes. Oh, yes, of course!"

"Sorry, that came out wrong. I didn't mean to be rude - "

"That's okay. You're hungry. You've had a long day. I quite understand. I'll be brief. It appears Cynthia Cartwright's motives aren't quite as pure as I thought. From what I've heard, she sees you as something of a stalking horse. Her preferred candidate is a local farmer, a little older than you with 'good business experience and resident in the locality'. Stand up Aisling Baxter."

"How's she going to combine running a farm with being an MP?"

"She's going to hand the farm over to the care of her husband, Robert."

"What about Innes Mount? Surely, if he's the sitting MP, his say's got to count for something?"

"Unfortunately, no one knows what dear Innes thinks. Not even dear Innes himself, some people say. And Aisling Baxter's probably built in the same mould. You know how it is. The local party leadership always wants a strong constituency bod with easy-to-reach switches. It doesn't like highly independent people who do better at Westminster than they do at the local agricultural fair."

"So what's your advice?"

"Sir Anthony's still firmly in your camp. He can probably pull a few strings higher up. Cynthia Cartwright might think she's a big fish, but that's because Newbury's a small pond. When Conservative Central Office gets involved, she'll realise she's bitten off more than she can chew. We'll show her."

"A bit like me carpet-bagging."

"No, it isn't. It's about us - you - taking the fight to them. Cynthia Cartwright's already made a foolish move. If she didn't want you, she shouldn't have come here last night. You're local, and they've raised your hopes. So you're at least entitled to throw your hat into the ring. And if you're entitled to that, you're entitled to the approval of Campaign HQ."

"Right." Why did she suddenly feel like she'd wandered into an episode of *The Archers*?

"You *do* still want it, don't you?" her mother persisted.

"I'm thinking about it."

"Well, don't think too long. As Jim Rohn said, 'If you don't design your own life plan, chances are you'll fall into someone else's. And guess what they have planned for you? Not much.'"

"Who's Jim Rohn?"

"An American motivational speaker. Dead now, but still inspiring. 'If you're not willing to risk the unusual, you'll have to settle for the ordinary.' That's another of his."

"Gosh."

"'Don't join an easy crowd. You won't grow. Go where the expectations and the demands to perform are high.' Very inspiring. I've used him a lot in my own life. You wouldn't think it, not to look at me now, but I used to be a high-flyer."

"Okay, that's enough Jim Rohn now. Thank you for ringing, but my dinner's getting cold."

"Is John there with you?"

"No. Why do you ask?"

"Just curious. What did he say about last night, or haven't you told him yet?"

"He thinks it's great."

"Oh," she said in a disappointed tone. She sighed. "Still, he could be an asset, I suppose. Anyway, I'd better go. Your dinner will be stone cold."

Phyllis put the phone down. She immediately forgot about her mother and Newbury and the Conservative party and Aisling Baxter and her own future. The only question was, had Alexa said what she thought she'd said.

Of course she had. It wasn't the sort of mistake you could make unless you were on mind-bending drugs. *I can confirm that John Mordred is safe.*

Maybe Alexa hadn't said 'John Mordred' though. Maybe what she'd said merely *sounded like* 'John Mordred'. Maybe Phyllis's question had come across garbled. Maybe Alexa had *heard* something slightly different, and when she'd answered she'd used that slightly different word – whatever it was – and she, Phyllis, had been so primed with the expectation of maybe hearing something about John Mordred that that's what she *had* heard.

But what the hell word, or set of words, sounded like 'John Mordred'?

"*Alexa,*" she said: "*what words sound like 'John Mordred'?*"

Pause. "Sorry," Alexa replied. "I don't know that."

Bloody hell, she was going nuts, sitting alone in her living room talking to an electronic box.

Maybe she should call Tariq – she had his mobile number – and report her finding.

But no. Because he'd think she was screwy. And even if he didn't, what could it prove? As far as she could tell, the experiment wasn't repeatable.

She warmed the pasta sauce, poured it on the fusilli and ate it with a large glass of white wine. She'd try ringing John again after she'd washed up, then perhaps watch a bit of TV.

Maybe he'd lost his phone, or had it stolen, and didn't know about it.

No, she couldn't hang on. And her phone was right beside her on the table. However uncivilised it might be to eat and phone at the same time, it had to be done.

But, as before, three rings and straight to voicemail.

This was getting worrying.

He couldn't be doing it to get at her, could he?

No, because they hadn't exactly parted on bad terms this morning. She'd been a bit irritated, and she'd shown it, but they'd exchanged conciliatory texts.

Besides, he wasn't that childish.

But what could she do? Nothing. If Ruby Parker wasn't worried, why should *she* be? Ruby Parker was definitely more experienced than her. If she didn't consider it cause to panic, then it probably wasn't.

Besides, thinking about it rationally, what could have happened? If he'd been attacked, someone would have reported it. If he'd had his phone stolen, he'd have reported it. So no news was good news.

So he was sitting in his parents' house, probably not having had a spare moment to himself since he walked in the door. He might ring later. Maybe he wasn't feeling well. Flu: there was something going round, supposed to be.

All in all, nothing to worry about. She'd been spooked by Alexa, and that was all it was.

She finished her pasta, washed the pan, plate and cutlery and poured herself another glass of wine, smaller this time.

She was about to access the TV guide on her phone, when it rang in her hand. She jumped and looked at it like it had stung her.

*Hannah.*

John's sister. She picked up before the *whys* and *but-you-already-knows* kicked in. "Hannah?"

"Sorry to call out of the blue," Hannah said, "and apologies if what I'm about to ask sounds a bit intrusive. But you don't happen to know where *John* is, do you?"

## Chapter 10: Maybe Spy Central UK

"Sorry to call out of the blue," Hannah said, "and apologies if what I'm about to ask sounds a bit intrusive. But you don't happen to know where *John* is, do you?"

Whoa.

Okay, something was wrong. Keep your nerve, just tell the truth, get off the line as quickly as possible. "I spoke to him this morning," Phyllis replied. "He's got a few days leave. He was going to visit his parents."

"Right." Her tone was cold now. She knew something Phyllis didn't. "And what time was that?"

"Just before nine. I was on my way to work."

"Which is *where*, exactly?"

"In the City. I don't know what you mean. I - "

"Maybe Spy Central UK? Let's be straight with each other for once. This whole story John's been spinning for years about selling machine parts abroad, it's all bullshit, isn't it? And you're in on it. You're part of the same outfit. Put it this way: his Ultimate Londoner blurb said he worked in the Foreign and Common-wealth Office. He doesn't. He'd have told us: his family. But he actually rang *me* and asked if I'd nominated him. *Me.* In other words, *he must think his name was put forward by someone who knows all about him*. In his panic to find the culprit, he forgot that I *don't* 'know' he works for the FCO."

"I've no idea where you're going with this," Phyllis lied.

"Well, he doesn't work there, does he? Only the truth's not far away. The fact is, he's been given leave because his cover's about to be blown – has *been* blown by whoever 'nominated' him. He's been sent north, where no one cares about the Ultimate Londoner. And now he's disappeared off the face of the earth. Which means he could very well be lying in a ditch somewhere, courtesy of turnip-for-a-head Vlad Putin."

Phyllis needed time she hadn't got, to think. In circumstances like these, it helped if your accuser enjoyed making speeches. You needed to prompt as many as possible while keeping your own contributions brief and to the point. "I'm not a spy," she said. "And what makes you think he's disappeared?"

"Have *you* tried reaching him?"

"Not since this morning."

"Try now. And get straight back to me. I mean, *straight* back."

"Hang on," Phyllis replied as calmly as she could, "I don't take orders from you. And I'm still waiting for an explanation. What the hell are you talking about: 'you're in on it?' And what do you mean, we're 'part of the same outfit'? You mean, me and John? What outfit? 'UK Spy Central'? Sorry, but what even *is* that?"

"If you're not, then he definitely is. But if you were, you'd deny it."

"Catch-22, in other words. So as you rightly say: let's be straight with each other. What exactly are you accusing me of?"

"I'm saying that at least one of you belongs to MI5 or MI6, and you've been spying on me all this time. Maybe not systematically, but doing it, just the same. It all makes sense now. I used to think John was just unlucky, truth be told. He'd been home schooled by indulgent parents and it hadn't prepared him for the real world. Ergo, his bum job and poky little flat. But then I thought: he lives in London, so he can't be doing too badly. Then there's the vagueness about his job. And he always seems to be popping up in a crisis, like when Chapman Hill was around, and when I was in Jersey with the band, and last year, when he was nearly killed in London at the very spot poor Marty Curzon died."

"And maybe when he went to get Mabel from Libya?"

"Probably, yes. What are you saying?"

"I'm saying if you are right, you should be pretty grateful. You'd be down one family member now if he really sold machine parts."

"Okay, smart arse, what's your theory-stroke-story-stroke-explanation? Because you must have one."

"If so, you've yet to persuade me I should share it with you. I don't owe you anything, and I don't like being talked to like I'm your minion."

"Are you and John still together?"

"Why? Are you his mum?"

"Okay, here's the situation. He set off from London this morning by train to go to Hexham. It's a four hour journey. That was twelve hours ago. My parents are frantic with worry. You were apparently the last person he spoke to. Shall I call the police? Because they'll definitely want to speak to you."

"Do what you like. I've nothing to hide."

"Or we can work on this together."

Phyllis hooted. "Oh, *that's* what you call it, is it? 'Working together'? Funny, because I thought it was you ringing up and accusing me of things I haven't done – all without a scrap of evidence - demanding answers I don't have, and generally being totally obnoxious. Go ahead: call the police."

She hung up and took a deep breath. All in all, an extremely well managed crisis. She deserved a massive pat on the back.

She probably needed to wait a few minutes before ringing Ruby Parker. Hannah might be calming down. She'd probably call back, try to say something conciliatory. If it was engaged, she might assume John and she were plotting. In her state of mind, who knew what she might deduce?

Mind you, the conciliation had already begun. *Or we can work on this together.* At that point, Hannah almost certainly knew her call-the-police bluff hadn't worked. She'd proffered an olive branch instead.

Putting the phone down on her had been exactly the right thing to do, at exactly the right moment. All that remained now was to wait for her call back. All was well. Phyllis would bully Hannah out of her spy accusations, and things would go back to what they'd been before.

Give or take an ounce. While she was waiting, she needed to devise a highly plausible John Mordred cover story. Never underestimate his sisters.

A minute passed. Nothing.

Five minutes. She didn't feel so in control now. Hannah definitely wouldn't report her to the police – she needed some way back in – but it was beginning to look like she wasn't as contrite as the theory suggested she should be.

It suddenly sank in. *John was missing.* My God, that trumped everything!

She needed to ring Ruby Parker.

She picked up her phone and called Hannah.

Bloody hell, what was she *doing*?

"Sorry for everything I just said," Hannah blurted out, before she could speak.

"John does work for the foreign office," Phyllis said measuredly, "but on an *ad hoc* basis. He works for a firm that has a lot to do with the diplomatic service – I don't know its name - but on the trade front, not the espionage front. In a broad sense, he really does 'sell machine parts'. I know arms are a major British export, before you ask, but he's told me categorically he's not involved in any of that and I trust him. I believe he simply helps negotiate ordinary commercial transactions, albeit on a billion pound scale. Because he's such a brilliant linguist and a loyal British citizen, many sales reps prefer him to a native. A lot of his work is sensitive – so faintly confidential - because he tends to become involved at the make-or-break point of major negotiations. He's used to working abroad, but he's no spy. And nor am I. And yes, I am very worried about him or I wouldn't have called back. I meant what I said. You need to get in touch with the police. If I hear from him, I'll call you straight away."

"But – but – sorry, I'm thinking aloud – he must be rolling in it, mustn't he? With a job like that?"

"Except he gives it all away to charity. Believe me, I've seen his bank statements."

Hannah gave what sounded like a sigh of relief. "That sounds like John. Sorry again for being such a nasty cow. And a moron. You're quite right, I had absolutely no right to bang on at you like that. It's just, the competition blurb said he worked for the FCO, and the fact that … I know I've explained this. I put two and two together and made five. But when I'd got five, everything else seemed to fall into place. And I'm worried – as much about mum as about him. You've no idea how she can be when she thinks one of us might be… well. Anyway, sorry again."

Time to change the subject before they returned to, *And what do you do for a living, Phyllis?* She could work something out about that later. "I'm very happy to talk to the authorities, although I don't think I can tell them anything of value."

"I'll keep you updated."

She hung up. No time for another pat on the back. She called Ruby Parker. "John's definitely missing," was the first thing she said.

"How do you know?" You had to give Ruby Parker her due: she never sounded surprised.

"His sister's just been on the phone to me. Hannah. She got the information from her parents. He was supposed to arrive in Hexham early this afternoon. He still hasn't, and he's not answering his phone. Hannah's going to contact the police."

"I'll make sure her call for help's prioritised. I'll also send someone round to check his flat. It's often the simple things that don't get done. When did you last speak to him?"

"This morning, before I got into work. He said he was 'organising his escape from the capital'. Packing, I assume. Since he hasn't much to pack - "

"If his parents are worried enough to get through to his sister, he must be seriously overdue. I don't like to state the obvious, but this is very worrying."

"It's not all. Hannah suspects he's a spy. She also suspects me. I managed to pull the wool back over her eyes, I think, but I'm not sure how long for."

Ruby Parker drew a deep breath. "It gets better and better. What on earth made her suspect?"

"Apparently, John called her last night. He asked her if she was the one who nominated him. She wasn't, but what she took away from their conversation was that his name was put forward by someone who knows a lot about him, including his workplace. The competition has him working at the Foreign and Commonwealth Office. She knows that's wrong, but also that 'works for the FCO' is often a euphemism for 'spy'."

"That's my fault. I made him ring her."

"We had quite a conversation."

"Credit where credit's due, though: she's nobody's fool."

"We'll wait an hour and I'll put everyone on full alert. I'd like you to stay at home. If John does come in, he might choose your place as a refuge: his own flat and Thames House might be too risky. I'm sending Edna round with Kevin: safety in numbers. Meantime, I'll contact Tariq get him to pour everything into the Ultimate Londoner probe. Once we get to the bottom of that, we may have the answers we're looking for. Because at the moment, we haven't any at all."

Phyllis hung up and put her head in her hands. It was a horrible night. It might shade into a horrible next few years if John didn't come back. She needed to be doing something, not just sitting at home.

And yet that *I can confirm that John Mordred is safe*.

"Alexa," she asked again: "is John Mordred safe?" She heard her voice tremble. She sounded pathetic.

The little blue light did its round.

"Sorry," Alexa replied. "I don't know that."

Her phone rang again. She picked it up without even looking at it.

Ruby Parker: "Okay, we're on full alert now. The parliamentary intern and the novelist are both dead. Candidates in John's competition, in the unlikely event that I'm not making myself clear."

"My God, how?"

"One in a supposed road accident, the other an apparent suicide. The police are still gathering details. I'm sending Kevin to pick you up, minus Edna, and bring you to Thames House. Don't answer the door to anyone else. Edna's coming straight here too."

## Chapter 11: A Psychological Matter

The CCTV footage showed Mordred boarding the train to Newcastle at King's Cross and disembarking at Arlesey in Bedfordshire. As far as anyone could tell, there was nothing special about Arlesey. It was a small town with a population of just under six thousand whose most interesting features were a Grade 1 listed church, two lagoons, and a nature reserve. Phyllis and Edna spent an entire day there, helping the police question commuters. No one remembered seeing the missing person. The CCTV had already identified a clutch of people who were on the platform when he left the train, or who'd embarked or disembarked at the same time as him. None recalled him. For all practical purposes, he might as well have been invisible.

Also, there was something about his deportment in the footage that didn't look right. As if maybe he'd been drugged. He walked determinedly, as if he knew where he was going, but also, somehow, vacantly, as if there was nothing behind his eyes. As far as anyone in the investigation could tell, he was unaccompanied. When he left the station, he turned left without breaking stride, strode in a northerly direction through the car park, and out of CCTV range. Plans were made to dredge Dove Lake, about a hundred yards away, and, by extrapolation, on his route. But no one expected to find a body. Given that he'd been alone, and that any murderer would have to have lured or met him there, it seemed too unlikely. But all possibilities needed exploring.

The deaths of the other two contestants looked unconnected, to both John's disappearance and also to each other. Or they should have done, only their common linkage to the competition seemed to make the coincidence just too monstrous.

Specioza Byanyima, the parliamentary intern, died on her way home from work, five minutes from where she lived with her parents. She took the Jubilee line from Westminster, changed to the Metropolitan at Wembley Park, and left the tube at Northwood Hills at 6.17pm. Six minutes later, she was knocked down by a car while attempting to cross the A404, better known as Pinner Road. The driver, a thirty-three-year-old council worker called Dianne Speaks, rang the emergency services and tried to administer first aid, but the victim died in the ambulance on her way to hospital. Nothing about the fatality suggested the police should treat it as suspicious – again, apart from its connection to the competition.

Euan Frederick, the novelist, was found hanged in his flat in Southwark. The discovery was made by two of his closest friends who, concerned that he wasn't answering his phone, persuaded his neighbour, a middle-aged man who worked in an orchestra, to let them in using the spare key. Preliminary post-mortem analysis suggested the victim had taken his own life earlier that day, no later than 3pm. Nothing indicated foul play.

The next day, the media went with Euan Frederick and ignored Specioza Byanyima entirely. Whether because they did not think the common denominator in the competition was worth mentioning, or because mentioning might appear disrespectful, or because they didn't know about it, no one on the investigative team knew. Put brutally, Euan Frederick was a major public intellectual, Specioza Byanyima wasn't; and fatal road accidents were a daily occurrence, rarely major news.

The papers certainly knew nothing of John Mordred's disappearance. The upshot was that, as far as anyone knew, the Ultimate Londoner competition was still up and running, only one contender less.

But it wasn't just the public. After a few hours, even the investigative team had difficulty believing the deaths were connected by the competition, or that they had any relevance to Mordred's disappearance. Dianne Speaks, the woman who'd killed Specioza Byanyima, had stayed on the scene, tried to administer the kiss of life and given herself up to the police. She was distraught. She didn't look like anyone's hired killer. And Euan Frederick had actually left a brief suicide note. Nothing indicated any kind of struggle. It really began to look like an obscene coincidence.

Where did that leave Mordred? Just where he was at the start. It didn't mean he was more, or less, likely to be dead. So long as no corpse appeared, there was hope.

Phyllis kept busy. She worked to the point of exhaustion and slept the rest of the time. Her mother called her each evening with another unwelcome update about Aisling Baxter. They never spoke for more than five minutes. Edna came to stay with her. Ruby Parker was right: John might turn up unexpectedly on her doorstep; it certainly wasn't out of the question. But then, who could say what was possible or impossible in a situation like this? Not only did MI7 not know what it was up against. It had no idea if it was up against anything at all.

On the third day, Hannah called Phyllis and asked her to come to Hexham. John's parents wanted to see her, quiz her about what the police had already grilled her about twice. "You don't have to," she added wretchedly. "Skype would be good too."

"I think he's going to be okay," Phyllis replied.

She didn't hear the words until they were out of her mouth, and had no idea why she'd uttered them.

"*We've* been saying that," Hannah replied before she could think any more. "He might have lost his memory. I've hired people to scour all the homeless shelters within a fifty mile radius of Arlesey. Nothing. Not a whisper. But we're still hopeful. Glad you feel the same. If you're fine coming, I can pay for your flight. That'll make it faster. Mum and dad need to hear you say what you've just said ASAP. Sorry again I went all loony on you the other day. Tough week with the band for starters. But this is a hundred times worse."

"I've got some time off on Monday," Phyllis said. "I'll get the train. I'd like to do the journey myself, see if it suggests anything."

"I hadn't thought of that. Good idea."

When they'd hung up, Phyllis called for a taxi and went straight to Thames House. She checked in at reception and made an appointment to see Ruby Parker. Thirty minutes later, the two women sat opposite each other in the latter's office.

"I understand you asked to see me concerning a 'psychological matter'?" Ruby Parker asked. She sounded genuinely curious.

"The night of John's disappearance," Phyllis began, "before Hannah called me and I called you, I'd tried to get in contact with John several times already. His phone always went straight to voicemail. I had the instinctive feeling something wasn't right, although the rational part of me said not to worry, he'd only just got home, he wasn't expected to be in contact, etcetera, etcetera. Anyway, I'd called Edna earlier in the day after my conversation with Timothy Grendell, *The Evening Standard*'s sub-editor. Edna told me about the Alexa thing, how it was giving a live update on the competition - "

"We still don't know how that happens, by the way. Where it's getting its information from. And neither does Amazon."

"Anyway, I've got an Alexa of my own. When I got in from work, I asked it if it knew where John was. A crazy thing to do, I admit, but I just thought, Here goes nothing. Of course, it didn't know what I was talking about. Then I asked it, Is John Mordred safe? And it said – or I *thought* it said: it can't have done, and that's why I'm here – 'I can confirm that John Mordred is safe.'"

"And I take it you've asked that question again without success?"

"Innumerable times. Which is a kind of symptom of madness in itself."

"'Madness' is overstating it. And not very scientific. Let's just say you're concerned."

"I'm also worried it may be affecting my conduct of the investigation. About an hour ago, Hannah called me and asked me to see John's parents. They'd like to talk to me face-to-face. I agreed to a meeting. I need to do the train journey myself. I know

John, and King's Cross to Arlesey might suggest something to me that it wouldn't to anyone else."

"A good idea, but I have the feeling you're straying from the point slightly."

"Almost the first thing I said to her was 'I think he's going to be okay'. I said it with a conviction I didn't know I had. In fact, I was more shocked to discover I thought that than Hannah probably was. When I'd hung up, and I asked myself *why*, I realised: because Alexa had told me."

Ruby Parker put her fingertips together and leaned back in her chair. "There are two separate issues here. First, you think your confidence that John's okay may be causing you to conduct the investigation less vigorously than you'd do otherwise. I think that's highly unlikely. The second issue's more serious: you believe you may have lucidly and unambiguously heard a sentence that was never actually uttered. You think your mind was playing tricks on you. Which is presumably why you didn't report it in the first place. Which you probably should have done."

"I was imagining things, that's all."

"Given the context, why do you imagine you're the best judge of that?"

"I'm not sure I follow," Phyllis said.

"Deciding that you're hearing voices involves implicitly conceding your judgement is impaired, which in turn casts doubt on your competence to make an objective diagnosis."

"I see, yes."

"In addition, we don't know why the Echo's behaving as it is. It's anomalous as it is. Further anomalies aren't necessarily to be dismissed."

"Maybe you're right."

"Finally, have you ever before heard voices? Or have you since the single event you mention?"

"No."

"These are all questions a qualified medical professional would ask early on. I'm not going to send you to see a psychologist, Phyllis. Even if you did hear something unreal, that sometimes happens. It doesn't necessarily herald the onset of mental illness. Wait till it occurs again. Right now, it would be a waste of yours and the doctor's time. When are you going to see John's parents?"

"Next Monday."

"Get some rest today. Do King's Cross to Arlesey tomorrow. Then come back and we'll do a debrief. Combining looking for clues with a mission to meet significant others isn't likely to enhance either."

Ruby Parker had a way of subliminally indicating that an interview was over. Phyllis stood up. She felt exhausted, true. She'd still to recognise in herself any symptoms of the onset of grieving.

Alexa's influence again.

And if that wasn't madness, what was?

## Chapter 12: Welcome Back ... to the Tube

Mordred looked up from the ten or twelve pairs of feet beside his on the carriage floor. Where had they come from? Standing room only now. It hadn't been this packed when he got on, a minute ago.

Had it?

It must have been. A new bunch of passengers couldn't just have materialised from nowhere.

And hang on. It *was* Westminster, the last stop, right?

Good God, he didn't even know that. His attention must seriously have lapsed. Maybe he'd taken a short nap without realising. But even so -

He had a newspaper under his arm. *The Evening Standard.*

Not a happy fact either. When did he pick that up?

Something was wrong. And getting increasingly so.

He suddenly caught sight of his reflection in the glass between the two men opposite. Because this was the tube, and the light was strong, and it was black outside, it was like glancing in the mirror.

He looked ill.

And wait a minute. Everyone was subtly staring at him.

He pretended to focus on his reflection, so he could scan their glances without them knowing.

They were. They were eyeing him. Not in a friendly way either.

Could this be a bad dream? It felt like one.

Why were they staring at him? Because he looked ill? Perhaps. Was it that obvious? There were maybe two metres between his seat and the opposite window. Double that to calculate the distance of his reflected self. Yes, fair enough: if he could see he was off-colour from ten feet away, it must be pretty noticeable.

So probably, yes. Mystery solved, hurrah. They were looking at him because they thought he might be infectious.

Yet their body language wasn't consistent. There wasn't room to give any one person wide berth in here, but still, under the right circumstances, it'd be natural to at least try. Yet no one was.

On the contrary, some of them seemed infinitesimally *drawn* to him.

Which didn't make sense either. But – come to think of it - not half as much as him looking ill in the first place. He didn't even feel ill.

What was it to 'look ill', anyway? A reflection two metres away, not even an actual mirror. How could he tell, really?

And yet, the firm conviction.

He smelt. That body odour he'd noticed when he got on. It was him.

He blinked slowly. The train slowed. Time to get off, if only to get some fresh air.

The void behind the window vanished and a packed platform appeared.

*Monument.*

But - ?

But - if this was Monument, the last stop couldn't have been Westminster.

Something really was wrong.

The doors hissed open. He got to his feet and edged past his fellow passengers. Again, the distinct sense that they regarded him as *an object of intense curiosity*.

All he could think was that somehow, someone must have drugged him. As a spy, it was the sort of thing you could never rule out, even though it was terribly Cold War-ish, and hardly to be expected in today's world. Right now, any country, no matter how putrid, could become Britain's best buddy if only Her Majesty's government spotted a plum trading opportunity. Pointless poisoning MI7 officers on their own turf. Might even be counter-productive.

And he certainly didn't feel drugged.

But then, that needn't mean anything. He had, apparently, lost his memory. Drugs could do that. You wouldn't necessarily feel lethargic.

The significance hit him in the act of formulating the thought. *He'd lost his memory.* My God, yes. He didn't remember getting on the tube at all. Even his vague sense of having just come from Westminster had turned out to be wrong.

People were still looking at him. My God – did that woman just take a photo of him? He looked behind himself. Nothing. At least, nothing worth photographing. A man in a Woozer T-shirt pointing his phone at him now. It *was*. They really *were*. They were photographing *him*.

Or... was he completely paranoid?

He had to get back to Thames House. Someone there would know what to do. And he'd be safe back at base.

Better ring ahead, let them know he was coming. They could make preparations. He felt in his pocket and took his phone out. He couldn't call anyone from down here, though. No signal.

Academic, anyway. It was switched off. When had that happened?

He followed the crowds to the exit and tried three times to turn it on. But nothing. Either the battery was dead or –

The clock. 10pm.

That wasn't the time.

How did he know that? He just did. It was six at the latest! He'd left Thames House at five, walked to Westminster with Alec...

Which seemed an age ago.

Okay, he had to stop thinking now. Thinking wasn't making it better. Quite the reverse. He needed to concentrate on getting back to Thames House. On that alone.

He stepped onto the escalator and, despite himself, stood looking at the adverts lining the wall. West End shows, mostly, and perfumes.

Perhaps he should move to the left and join the proactive climbers.

But no. If there was something in his system, he didn't want to shake it about. That would only help it spread.

Where the hell had *10pm* come from?

He passed his Oyster Card over the barrier-scanner and mounted the steps to the surface. A typical freezing March night – if even the name of month was right any more – and full of familiar London sights and smells: queues of red double-deckers, black cabs, vans and lorries, crowds of inscrutable pedestrians, more or less togged up for a night out; grim, badly-lit grey piles with steps to strangely unimposing entrances and flanked by Ionic columns.

He should be feeling worse by now. If he *had* been drugged, that was. But not a bit of it. He still didn't feel anything.

A taxi had to be his best bet. Straight to his destination, no need to think. The effect of any drug might still be on its way, for all he knew.

Flagging a taxi down was always theoretically possible, but almost never worked. Still, nothing ventured… He stepped into the gutter and raised his hand at an approaching minicab.

As if by way of extending the weirdness to breaking point, the driver made eye-contact and stopped. It took Mordred a moment to readjust, then he got in.

"Lambeth Bridge, please," he said. You never let anyone know you were going to Thames House, even though it was only a stone's throw away.

"Which end?" the driver asked, pulling out into the traffic.

"Millbank."

They drove fast, then slow, then fast, then slow, and Mordred watched the night go by to an engine's purr, through lightly smoked glass, as if it was happening on a monitor at the other end of a room somewhere. His own unpleasant smell returned. He opened the window slightly.

"Mind if I ask you a question?" the driver said, when they were almost there.

The usual response – *depends what it is* – didn't seem worth making. "Anything you like," he said. He was starting to feel gratitude for still being alive.

"Aren't you that 'John Mordred'?" the driver asked.

*What the - ?* He opened his mouth and made a noise that sounded like, "I, er …"

"Because that's the reason I picked you up," the driver continued. "I thought: 'that's that John Mordred. The one in *The Evening Standard*.' That's you, isn't it? The ultimate Londoner?" He laughed. "I mean, not yet. But soon-to-be, if you get my drift."

A series of mental events that felt a little like memories, but with the impersonality of a slide show. Him getting on the tube at Westminster; reading the *Standard* he'd picked up earlier; seeing his own face there, on the centre pages; getting off the tube in agitation; going back to Thames House; leaving London by train; hurtling through the English countryside, destination Newcastle.

"I expect everyone's asking you that," the driver went on. "How did you actually get into the competition, if you don't mind me asking? I never saw anything in the papers saying, like, nominate a person. I'd have got someone to nominate *me* if I'd known it was coming. I could just about make do with five million quid. Set me up nicely. Think you'll win?"

"I doubt it," Mordred said. In a crisis, never let on you're all at sea, that was the rule. "Still, I too could do with five million pounds," he went on, "but I don't think I'm much of an 'ultimate Londoner'. I didn't even grow up round here."

"Yeah, the north-east, wasn't it? You're a Magpies supporter, it said in the paper. Shame about the Chelsea match." He nodded at the little blue pennant on his rear-view mirror. "Doing quite well for a while, you were, too. I mean generally. League-wise. Fifteenth now, isn't it?"

"I try not to think about it."

"Probably best. Just about here okay?" They cleared the bridge at twenty miles per hour and entered Horseferry Road. They stopped in response to Mordred's, "Perfect".

It hadn't occurred to him till now to wonder if he had money on him. For all he knew, he could have been robbed as well as drugged – if a drugging was what it was. Perhaps robbery was the motive. If so, it'd be a relief of kinds.

But no. Disturbingly, his wallet was in its customary place in his inside jacket pocket. He removed two twenties and handed them over. "Keep the change."

"Whoa." The driver looked at the money then at Mordred as if unsure which to kiss. "Muchas gracias! And good luck in the competition."

"Thanks."

Mordred alighted onto the pavement, waited till the car had driven off, and made for Thames House at a brisk walk. 'The ultimate Londoner': God knows. He'd reached mystery-overload now. Almost past caring. Maybe all would be explained when he woke up.

He pushed open the large gothic front door to his usual workplace, and caught sight of himself in one of the windows of the interior doors. Not everyone's idea of the ultimate Londoner, but hey. He walked past the security guards – who both jumped, but then saw it was him - into the vestibule. Colin Bale, the building's chief receptionist, stood in his regular position behind the far desk. He seemed fleetingly wrong-footed, then regarded Mordred as if he was a ghost. "My God," he said. "You've returned."

"Bit late for you to still be on duty, isn't it?" Mordred said, trying to ignore his expression.

But Colin had turned his back. He was on the phone, speaking energetically. "Stay there," he told Mordred firmly, swivelling to reinstate eye-contact. Then he faced the other way again and kept talking.

Colin would make an abysmal spy. He obviously hadn't noticed the absence of soundproofing.

"Yes, *John Mordred*," Colin was saying. "*Him*. He's *here*, ma'am, *in reception*. Just walked in, just now, this very moment. No, he looks fine, ma'am. He actually told me it was *a bit late for me to be on duty*, as if he'd simply strolled in casually with a view to doing a bit of overtime! No, ma'am, as I've just said: he looks well. He does, er – how can I put it? - smell a little. Yes, of course I'll keep him here, ma'am. No problem. Absolutely."

He put the phone down and gave the security guards a non-verbal signal whose meaning was obvious. *Don't let him leave.* The two men subtly escalated to ready-to-engage mode.

"Well, I'll just stand here then, shall I?" Mordred said.

Colin swallowed. "Yes, please, John. Ruby Parker's coming up from the basement."

"I gathered that. Am I in trouble?"

"I don't know."

Mordred chuckled. "Neither do I, actually. I've no idea about anything that's happened to me in the last hour."

Suddenly, the lift in the recess behind the desk pinged. Its doors swished open revealing Ruby Parker, Phyllis and Alec. They looked at Mordred with roughly the same expression Colin had, earlier. Then Phyllis ran over and wrapped her arms round him.

"Oh my God," she said. "We were so *worried*! Where the hell have you *been*?"

"I don't know," he replied. "I vaguely remember leaving here at five - "

"*Five?*" She held him at arm's length, wiped her eyes and laughed manically. *"Five o'clock?"*

"It's been *three days*, John," Ruby Parker said gently. "I need you to think hard. Where have you been?"

*Three days?* The floor span unpleasantly beneath his feet. He suddenly felt as dislocated as everyone else looked.

"I – I've no idea," he said.

## Chapter 13: Typical North Korea, Eh?

How did you first deal with an agent who'd gone missing and returned out of the blue? What to prioritise? Contacting the family? But they'd probably want immediate access. Putting him in quarantine whilst you discussed how to proceed? If so, what kind? Where? Alternatively, an immediate debriefing? Who to include? How did you get past your own shock, and suspicions, sufficiently to frame the right questions? How did you manage his unease? What if he or she was hungry, or sick, or mentally disturbed?

In the end it wasn't the intense conundrum a layperson might suppose. MI7 had a team of professionals - interrogators, psychologists, doctors, hypnotists, counsellors - trained to get every answer a section-head might ever want. Briefed daily during an AWOL crisis, it gave the returnee a full medical examination followed by an interview in a superficially informal setting. Every effort was made to put him or her at ease from the outset.

After the initial health checks, Mordred was allowed to take a shower. Ten minutes later, he found himself sitting in seminar room H9 with a group of two men and two women, all about ten years older than him, all smart casual, who looked delighted to see him. Tea or coffee? Would you like anything to eat? Just relax, John, this won't take long. Sit down, sit down. Put your feet up if you like. I'm Doctor Rigby – call me Steve. This is Patricia, Delia, Gordon.

He knew what was going on, partly because they told him. But he'd also heard about it happening to others. You weren't allowed to ask any questions till they gave you permission, otherwise it was supposed to be entirely painless.

Unless they discovered you'd been consorting with the enemy.

But that hardly ever happened, because no one knew who the enemy was nowadays. At the moment, it was the Russians, but the Iranians, the Argentinians, the Zimbabweans and the Turkish were always waiting in the wings.

A Margherita pizza arrived and a pot of tea.

Finally, Delia smiled and asked, as casually as if it was a dinner party: "How did you get to Thames House tonight, John?"

"Taxi," he said. "I got off the tube at Monument and flagged down a black cab just outside. It dropped me in Horseferry Road."

"How did you pay?" Steve asked.

Mordred took out his wallet and held it up. "Cash."

Steve wrote something down. Presumably, that a robbery hadn't occurred.

"What's the last thing you remember?" Patricia asked.

"Leaving Alec Cunningham at Westminster tube station, after we'd had a drink in St Stephen's Tavern. We'd just come from the lecture with Camilla Burkewitz. I realised when I got to Monument – because it's a considerable distance from Westminster – that I must have had some kind of memory blackout. That became more obvious when I got off the tube and saw it was 10pm. I reckoned I'd lost a few hours. From what Ruby Parker's just told me, it must be considerably longer than that. She mentioned three days. I must admit, that doesn't sound credible."

"What can you tell me about the Ultimate Londoner competition?" Steve asked.

"Nothing much. Only what I learned from the taxi driver about three-quarters of an hour ago. I'm a contender, and, as some kind of consequence of that, a few people know I'm from the north-east of England. It's also got a prize pot of five million pounds. I'm only going by what I was told. Which could be wrong, of course."

99

"Have you ever been to Arlesey in Bedfordshire?" Delia asked.

"Not to my knowledge," Mordred replied. "I recognise the name, though. As a station, that's all. On the train line from King's Cross to Newcastle."

"But you've never alighted there?" Steve said.

"No."

It was beginning to sink in now. *Three days*. He felt something like a mild panic kick in.

"I'd like you to take a look at this, John," Gordon said. He took a laptop from a bag, unfolded it and handed it over. It was set to video. Mordred touched the 'play' button in the middle of the screen.

CCTV footage. It showed him getting out of a Virgin Trains carriage at Arlesey. He walked determinedly out of the station and through a car park. The date at the bottom said three days ago.

"Bloody hell," he said.

"Remember it now?" Delia asked.

He racked his brain like his life depended on it. Nothing. "No," he said.

Given their guidelines – they were supposed to appear impassive at all times – the ominous looks they now exchanged didn't bode well.

In addition to which, Mordred's sense of panic was rising. Whatever had happened to him, it was bad. Very bad indeed.

Then he remembered – or rather, its full significance dawned on him: he was a candidate in the Ultimate Londoner competition!

His brain filled with endorphins and everything in the world was just as it ought to be. He'd been chosen. He would win. Nothing would ever go wrong again.

His rational self told him to snap out of it. Euphoria had no place here, now. It was his duty to say something.

"I think I may have been brainwashed," he told them.

As Mordred was taken upstairs by the debriefing team, Phyllis, Alec and Ruby Parker took the lift to the basement. Phyllis's phone dinged. Before she had chance to look at it, it began to ring. *Hannah*. She showed the screen to Ruby Parker.

"Answer it," Ruby Parker said, "then join me and Alec in my office."

The lift opened. Phyllis peeled off to one side, and slipped into an empty office. 10.30pm: there were plenty to be had.

"John's back!" Hannah announced. "Did you get the picture I just sent you?"

"I haven't had chance to look at it yet. Oh my God, are you sure?"

"Look at the photo. It was taken on the tube near Monument about fifty minutes ago. By someone who doesn't even know he's missing. Look at the tagline: 'Ultimate Londoner? This tosser?'" She laughed. "I don't even care that people are slagging him off! Shit, we've got to find him! He can't have got far. He hasn't tried to contact you, has he?"

"I'd have called you if I'd heard or seen anything! But this is wonderful! Have you let the police know?"

"First thing I did. They've put out an alert within a two mile radius of where he was seen."

"But if he was on the tube - ?"

"He got off. Someone else took a picture of him on the actual escalator. Listen, where are you?"

"Tesco Express. I had to nip out for a few things."

"I'm at Berlin Tegel Airport. There's a plane out in half an hour. Go home. He might come round to your place. I'll be there in a few hours. We'll meet up."

"I still don't get it."

"He must have suffered some sort of knock on the head. Look at the photo. He looks spaced out. Don't ask me how he got from Arlesey to Central London. We can ask him that when we find him. And we *will* find him, believe me. I'm putting people out there now, professional search-and-rescuers. Yeah, apparently that's not just for hikers lost in thick fog on the Pennines. Surprised me too. In a good way, obviously. See you soon."

She hung up.

When Phyllis entered Ruby Parker's office, Alec was sitting upright in one of two chairs facing the desk. He gave her a look as if to say 'nothing's happened since we got here', and she slipped into the seat next to him. Ruby Parker was on her landline. She wore a solemn expression and wrote in a notepad.

When she put the receiver down, she emitted a long sigh. "That was Tariq. The mystery deepens. Apparently, we've finally reached the end of Colander's tortuous paper-trail. It terminates in Pyongyang. The Ultimate Londoner's a North Korean invention." She allowed a second for this to sink in. "Comments?"

"Doesn't ring true," Alec said finally, just as Phyllis was about to express the same thought.

"North Korea doesn't have the telecommunications capacity," she said. "At least, from what I've heard."

"That's my gut feeling too," Ruby Parker said, "but apparently, the universities of Kim Il Sung and Kim Chaek, both in Pyongyang, run courses in computer hacking. A few years ago, a group of their alumni based in China developed and sold auto-programs for an online game called *Lineage*. The Ultimate Londoner competition's a game of sorts. We shouldn't rule it out."

"What would North Korea have to gain?" Alec asked.

"Disruption," Ruby Parker said. "As a country, it's not into all-out aggression. It's into muscle-flexing and bluster and keeping a high profile. Again, that would fit."

"I can't believe North Korea could get into Alexa," Phyllis said, "and Amazon and GCHQ wouldn't know how it had done so."

"Maybe they've got a lone genius," Alec said. "It does happen. You get an Albert Einstein, or a Bobby Fischer or a Stephen Hawking, and suddenly, what looked impossible becomes possible. And you never know when the next one's going to come along, or where from."

"I like the lone genius theory," Ruby Parker said. "But it does have one important corollary. A lone genius might well think we'd be predisposed to swallow a North Korean connection. He or she might well attach Pyongyang to the tail-end of Colander, knowing we'd get there sooner or later, and anticipating that, when we did, we'd be so bewitched by the apparent connection, that we'd immediately throw caution to the winds. We'd be deeper in the woods than ever."

"In other words, our lone genius could be anyone, anywhere," Phyllis said.

"So what now?" Alec asked.

"We'll keep an open mind," Ruby Parker replied. "It's not as if we've got enough evidence to do anything anyway. Presently, our best lead is John. Once we find out what happened to him, we might be better placed to make an assessment. I'm going to extend his leave. Phyllis, I'm giving you the same. I want you to stick with him. Take him to see his family, but make sure you follow the play-script: he sees a doctor who – we'll see to this – insists he checks in to a private hospital for treatment. We'll take care of the rest. We'll get to the bottom of this."

## Chapter 14: Who the Heck is Mike McKay?

"In the 2018 Ultimate Londoner Award, sponsored by Colander, John Mordred has four million, six hundred and twenty-eight thousand, six hundred and eight votes. Updating… In the 2018 Ultimate Londoner Award, sponsored by Colander, John Mordred has - "

"*Alexa: stop,*" Phyllis said.

"Four and a half million votes," Mordred said. "Half the population of London."

They sat opposite each other in compact cream armchairs in his single room on the first floor of Fowler's Independent Clinic in Redbridge. He wore a pink oxford shirt and chinos; she wore a navy-blue midi dress and read *The Guardian*. The walls, floor and ceiling were cream. There was a cream table with a cream vase full of cream lilies. The curtains were cream against cream window frames. The bed was cream. Even the Alexa was cream. Cream was thought to be calming. Outside, a storm shook the trees and pelted the windows.

Four days had passed since Mordred's reappearance. He still remembered nothing. Effectively, so long as that continued, it entailed the end of his career as a spy since there was no telling how, or whether, he'd been compromised, or to what extent he might one day be vulnerable.

In any case, he was ready to follow Phyllis into the land of rural Tory-dom. He'd always been sceptical of political parties, but also convinced that, apart from at the extremes, no single organisation had a monopoly on saints or sinners. The Conservative party was no exception.

On the other hand, if Phyllis's mother was to be believed, Aisling Baxter was blazing a trail. And Phyllis wasn't present in Berkshire to stop her. And she said she didn't care. So that wasn't a sure thing either.

His sisters and parents had been to see him, stayed a few days and gone their separate ways. His girlfriend was there to look after him. Anyway, weird things were always happening to John. The next surely couldn't be too far away. Pointless wasting too much time on the latest, especially since the eye of its storm had obviously passed.

Alexa's privileged access to the progress of the competition was now public knowledge. What that seemed to prove, however, was what everyone knew already: the whole thing was a charade. As such, it effectively disappeared from the collective imagination.

But not from existence. Computer technicians were still looking for a way to unbook the top floor of the Gherkin on the building's own reservation system. Not that the online system couldn't be ignored and replaced with a manual version, or even a completely new online one, but why it should prove so difficult to override was yet another mystery in a field full of mysteries. Moreover, new evidence had come to light about Specioza Byanyima and Euan Frederick. Immediately before their deaths, both had shown symptoms of paranoia apparently brought on by the competition. Specioza Byanyima may also have been suicidal.

"How's your euphoria?" Phyllis asked, after Mordred's comment on the competition.

"I still feel fantastic," he replied. "Don't get me wrong: I can see that, rationally, that's extremely disturbing. But I've been upfront about it from the start. I'll cooperate in any way necessary to get to the bottom of things. But I'm going to win. It feels like the greatest thing that could ever happen to me."

"The day after's going to be a real bummer. I mean, when you realise you're still in the real world."

"Granted."

"It's not as if anyone even cares about the Ultimate Londoner any more. You're certainly not going to get five million pounds. Where would it come from?"

"Who knows? We don't know anything about this whole thing. Perhaps I've already got it. I'm serious. Maybe its whereabouts was revealed to me during my absence, and on the day I win – given that it looks like a dead cert now – I'll suddenly 'remember' where it's located."

She folded the newspaper and put it on the table. "That is actually a possibility. Although why anyone would go to all that trouble isn't clear."

"I think I should at least turn up at the top floor of the Gherkin on the day of the presentation."

"We've been through this. It could be a trap."

"What sort? I've been wandering around in the Bermuda Triangle for three days. Anyone who wanted to trap me had ample opportunity then."

"What if you've been brainwashed to do something very specific and very destructive, and you just have to be there, on the Gherkin's top floor, on that day?"

He scoffed. "We're in the realms of science fiction now. I'm with Alec and his 'lone genius' theory. I'll tell you who'll be behind it. Some teenager in a bedroom somewhere."

"Who lured you out of a train and made you disappear for three days? I don't think so."

He put his fingertips to his forehead and frowned. "My God."

Phyllis sat up. "What?"

"Something's just come back to me. It's all coming back. Not all of it, some. I'm leaving London on my way to Newcastle. The further I get, the worse I feel. I actually think I'm going to be physically sick. I'm close to fainting. And just before – before things go black, like I fainted - although I can't have done: how would I have walked off the train like that? - a *man* comes into the carriage. It's completely deserted now. The train, I mean. It feels like there's no one left on there. Just me. And then this *man* comes in, like I just said. He's the only other person in the carriage - "

Phyllis had pressed the alert button. The door to Mordred's room opened from the outside. Gordon, Patricia and Steve, from the initial debrief, arrived just in time to hear the end of what he was saying.

"Get a digital recorder," Steve said. "You okay, John? Don't answer that. Just keep the memory going. Hush, everyone, hush." He was whispering now. "Let him think. Let John think."

Steve quickly arranged a long line of video files in a queue on his laptop. Each one showed CCTV from a stop on the East Coast Main Line for the train Mordred had been travelling on. Patricia took a description: smartly dressed middle-aged man, grey woollen coat, matching trilby, black polished brogues, striped tie, red hair, beard closely shaven, blue eyes, pale skin. It sounded suspiciously like a disguise, but when Mordred came to examine the MP4 footage, there he was, getting on at King's Cross, getting off at Darlington. A huge letdown. The fact that he'd done nothing to alter his appearance almost certainly meant he was a witness rather than a perpetrator. And he might not even remember anything.

The disappointment increased when Gordon examined more CCTV footage from other days and discovered the mystery man was a commuter. His name was Mike McKay. He worked part-time in the City and did that route on a daily basis. When the police went to interview him, four hours after Mordred recalled seeing him, he couldn't remember anything about Arlesey that day. As far as he knew, he'd never clapped eyes on John Mordred, although, on further reflection, yes, he recognised him vaguely from some damn silly competition in the *Metro*. Only because he was a fellow northerner.

The next hope was that background checks might reveal some connection between McKay's work in the City and Colander. But it was a forlorn grasping at straws, because he'd already been so upfront. He certainly didn't look the kind of person who had anything to hide.

And he wasn't. He was a dead end. At least provisionally, because in an investigation like this, you never put anything away for good until you were holding all the threads and you could see what was, or wasn't, at the end of them.

A breakthrough of kinds came from Edna, who came to sit with Mordred the following evening. They played chess. She took his queen and pinned his king to the edge of the board with her bishops.

"How about getting out of here," she said.

He laughed. "I'm not allowed to leave. It may look like an ordinary hospital, but I'm closely guarded. For my own good."

"I didn't mean now. I meant tomorrow maybe. Or the day after."

"And go where?"

"On a train. Out of London."

He looked at her for a second, trying to decipher her meaning. Then he saw.

"Doesn't matter which direction," she said. "Try going to Margate if you like. We'll have you followed. Someone you don't know and can't recognise. A team maybe." She grinned. "Sorry, it's checkmate in three, by the way."

The next day at 10.30am, he boarded a South Western Railway train at Waterloo along with the usual clutch of morning passengers.

It was a cold day, but sunny. The first stops went by without incident, but when he reached Esher he began to feel ill. At Weybridge, he got to his feet and went to find a window he could open: he badly needed air. But standing up made it worse. Nausea swept over him in waves.

He returned to his seat. After what seemed like an age, he felt slightly better.

But then it got worse. As the next station approached – Woking – he felt himself starting to black out. Panic almost rushed in, but then he remembered: he was being watched all the way. By someone benign. He'd lost all interest in *who* almost as soon as he got on the train.

Anyway, it would be okay. They'd slap him on the face a few times, give him a dose of Alprazolam and drive him back to London.

Wouldn't they? He could feel the beginnings of paranoia. But it was too late to do anything about it. As before, the edges of his vision inked out and he lost consciousness.

When he awoke, he was in a cream bed facing a cream ceiling. Steve sat on one side, Phyllis on the other.

"I take it this is Fowler's," he said.

"Hi, John," Phyllis said.

"How did I do?" he asked.

"You got off the train at Woking," Steve replied, "walked southwest for a little while, then did an about turn and walked back to London. You slept in a field in East Molesey last night. Don't worry, we monitored you to make sure your body temperature didn't drop too far."

"How long ago was that?"

"Forty-eight hours," Steve said. "It ended when you got on the Circle line early this afternoon. You might still have been there now if we hadn't brought you back to Fowler's. We've spent the last two hours trying to bring you round."

"What's it mean?" Mordred asked. Not much of a question, but the best he could do.

"I've consulted with my colleagues," Steve said. "We've spent a long time discussing that very issue. It's pretty rare we're unanimously agreed, but this is one of those occasions." He smiled apologetically and shrugged. "We've no idea."

"You didn't spot anyone on the train?" Mordred asked.

"No," Steve replied. "Although we weren't expecting to. We kept your departure a closely guarded secret. Other than the agreed operatives, no one knew where you were."

Phyllis sighed. "Whatever kicked in, its aim seems to have been to bring you back to London. It was a purely internal mechanism. It didn't require a third party to drive it."

"Which probably means," Steve continued, "to the extent you've been 'brainwashed', it happened before you got on the train to your parents'."

"It may not be related to the competition," Phyllis said.

"Except you'd probably expect the Ultimate Londoner to home in on London," Mordred said.

"When did you last successfully leave London?" Steve asked.

"About a month ago," Mordred replied.

"We need to get hold of some of the other candidates," Phyllis said. "See if they've experienced anything similar. Igor Lazarev should be a pretty good bet. He's probably always jetting places."

"Except he's not in pole position in the contest," Mordred said.

"And he probably won't be happy to talk about the Ultimate Londoner," Steve added, "given that he's looking to sue the papers that introduced it."

"So we're at the deadest of dead ends," Mordred said gloomily.

Phyllis's phone rang. She looked at it. "Ruby Parker," she announced, as if to herself. "She might be making better progress than us."

The men exchanged pessimistic looks. Phyllis swept her hair off her ear and answered by saying her name. She listened for a few moments and said, "Okay, we're coming over."

"'We'?" Mordred said, when she'd hung up. "You mean, you and Steve?"

"I mean you and me," she replied. "That was a newsflash: they've found the culprit."

Mordred drew his head back. "You mean...?"

"The person that created the competition," she said breezily. "And before you ask, it's no teenager."

## Chapter 15: More Feelings of Euphoria

When they left Fowler's, the sky was scattered with seagulls. A black cab stood waiting. When Phyllis opened the door to get in, the wind nearly blew it out of her grasp.

"So are you going to tell me who the culprit is?" Mordred said as they set off.

"It's a 76-year-old widow," Phyllis replied. "I don't know any more than that."

"Are they sure?"

"Yes." She sighed disbelievingly and flicked her eyebrows. "Apparently!"

The car trundled along like a pump trolley on a long railroad. They didn't say anything else. Nothing useful could come of discussing such a tiny shard of information; at least not when they were on the cusp of getting something much bigger. On the other hand, there was nothing else they wanted to talk about.

When they arrived, Mordred paid. They checked in at reception and went straight to Ruby Parker's office, arriving at exactly the same time as Edna.

"A face you may recognise," Ruby Parker said. She passed them a black and white portrait photo across the desk. An old woman with an unhappy expression. Completely bald, as if she'd recently had chemotherapy.

"Isn't that...?" Phyllis said.

"It's Gloria Shipton," Ruby Parker said. "One of the competitors in the Ultimate Londoner competition. She's in the advanced stages of lung cancer and – at the risk of sounding brutal - probably at death's door. She gave herself in. She had to, otherwise we'd never have found her."

"What prompted her decision?" Edna asked.

"She supposedly realises her invention is running out of control," Ruby Parker replied. "We know for a fact that she used to work in software engineering at GCHQ, although she'd previously worked in cryptography and mathematics. According to her own account, she was never promoted as she probably ought to have been, and that left her with a lingering sense of resentment and of work unfinished. In retirement, she designed an algorithm designed to search social media sites in search of eight candidates for a competition called 'The Ultimate Londoner'. Which is also the name of the program, by the way. So she says."

"Funny way to get revenge," Phyllis said.

"It was intended as a means of showing what the country had missed out on. Something very, very public no one else in GCHQ could do, and which might well cause its boffins more than a little head-scratching, plus some embarrassment. Because you were a candidate from the start, John. She knew of you from a variety of sources, some in the public domain. She factored you in, then let the program choose nine others. She didn't expect to find herself amongst them. It's why you're winning, incidentally, and by such an impressive margin."

Mordred passed the portrait photo back. "When you say she realises its 'running out of control', what does that mean? According to Phyllis's report, she called *The Evening Standard* right at the start. She was furious. Didn't she think the whole thing was out of control then?"

"Maybe she was in denial?" Edna hazarded. "Or perhaps she thought it would correct itself?"

"Things have moved on since then," Ruby Parker said. "Firstly, Specioza Byanyima and Euan Frederick. Although she accepts their deaths could be coincidence, they're still keeping her awake at night. Secondly, the program seems to be expanding in a way she didn't foresee. Have a look at this." She slanted the monitor on her PC to face them. The screen showed a brightly lit square, apparently outside a shopping mall somewhere with huge LED adverts, some of which were in Chinese. An advert for Levi's jeans suddenly flickered out and was replaced by three words 'The Ultimate Londoner'. Just as quickly, it fizzled out and returned to Levi's. "Suntec City, Singapore, 8pm yesterday," Ruby Parker said. "No one knows what happened or why, and it lasted less than a second. But something tried to interfere and it's getting stronger."

She pressed another key. "Times Square, New York. You can just about see it happen here, but it's weak. Blink, and you'll miss it. Leicester Square, the same. Shibuya Crossing, Tokyo. Vancouver, Tel Aviv, Berlin, the list goes on. Someone or something wants to tell the world about The Ultimate Londoner. And it's trying hard. And it's getting better at it."

"I've been in worse scrapes," Mordred said. "It's embarrassing, and a lot of young people want to kill me on the grounds that they've been unjustly overlooked and I'm a northerner, but I've also got a lot of people saying I'm the victim of racism."

Edna laughed. "What race is that?"

"They probably mean well," Mordred said.

"How do we know Gloria Shipton's telling the truth?" Phyllis said. "Apart from her GCHQ connection, what proof has she given us?"

"She claims the evidence is on her computer," Ruby Parker said. "We're awaiting word on whether what we've discovered so far can do the things the Ultimate Londoner is doing. At this point, the results look promising. That might not mean anything in the long-term."

"If she's bitter and angry," Edna said, "she could also be an attention-seeker. She might be savvy enough to create something resembling The Ultimate Londoner just to get eyes on her. Maybe that's her revenge on her colleagues. Fooling them. Finally achieving her few moments in the limelight."

"Maybe she's just a lonely old woman, in other words," Phyllis said.

"We haven't ruled that out," Ruby Parker said. "She hasn't long to live, and a few moments may be all she has. Maybe she believes it's a good way to go."

"That sounds much more plausible to me," Mordred said. "If she really is Alec's lone genius, we've too many loose ends. Where does it leave Pyongyang, for example? And how is she connected to Colander?"

"Pyongyang I don't know about," Ruby Parker said. "At least, not yet. But you've got to realise, on one level, Pyongyang's just a name with a set of concepts attached to it. It's an idea, in other words. And it can be represented, or reproduced, within a computer network without any attachment to the geographical reality on the Taedong River. We need to eliminate that possibility before we start accusing Kim Jong-un. Colander's slightly more complex. We now know it isn't a real entity."

"So what is it?" Phyllis asked.

"It's a function of the program. The Ultimate Londoner needs money to work. 'Colander' siphons it off from A, deposits it in B, then C, then D, and so on. B, C, D are just values within the system, probably identical to its version of 'Pyongyang' in everything but purpose."

"Wow," Mordred said. "So what are we saying? It's intelligent?"

"Ants are intelligent," Ruby Parker replied, "so are bees. The next generation of phones will supposedly be 'intelligent'. We'll soon have 'intelligent' driverless cars. Intelligence doesn't imply higher-level thinking. This is the same."

"So where did it get the money from originally?" Phyllis said. "Is it mining Bitcoins or something?"

"It's stealing it," Ruby Parker said. "From the United States Social Security Trust Fund: essentially an accounting record inside the Fed. Not any set of physical assets. Hence the complication I spoke of a moment ago. The Americans are looking to extradite her. Their assertion is that she designed a program *specifically* to breach the bank's security in order to finance her plan to launch a competition. She's denying the 'specifically' part and, by extension, the charge of stealing. Yes, she's indirectly morally responsible, she accepts that, but what that means in terms of legal accountability is for the courts to decide."

"What's the point in trying to extradite her if she's only got a short time to live?" Edna asked.

"To make an example of her," Ruby Parker said. "And they don't buy the abbreviated life-span. Firstly, they think it's a story her lawyer's concocted with her doctor. Secondly, they think if she really does have that little time left, it ought to be a matter of indifference whether she's here or in Washington, testifying before Congress."

"Really?" Phyllis said. "It might actually come to that?"

Ruby Parker frowned. "Security at the Fed's been breached. That's not exactly a bagatelle."

"And presumably her lawyer doesn't think she'll get a fair trial in the US?" Mordred asked.

Ruby Parker leaned back. "She'll claim everything under the sun if she thinks it has a chance of working and it's consistent with all other aspects of her case. She's a lawyer. That's her job."

"I think when Phyllis asked if it might actually come to Gloria Shipton testifying before Congress," Mordred continued, "she meant: could there be exterior motives behind the Americans' desire to extradite her? The Ultimate Londoner – if it's what it seems – is a pretty impressive invention. I'm pretty sure the Pentagon would love to get its hands on it."

"We all would," Ruby Parker replied. "And since Britain and American are firm allies, and we've got a lot of enemies out there, I wouldn't necessarily object to that. Just not by any means possible. But the Americans aren't likely to go down the offer-you-can't-refuse route. Apart from anything else, Gloria Shipton's beyond that."

"You mean, she's resigned to dying?" Edna asked.

"She's a staunch Spiritualist," Ruby Parker replied, "and she's convinced she'll be reunited with her husband in the afterlife. So yes."

"How long's she got?" Phyllis asked.

"Weeks at most," Ruby Parker said. "Possibly days."

Mordred put his hand on his face. "So she's spent all her life being overlooked, probably because she's a woman, then she invents a program called The Ultimate Londoner, and it selects her as a candidate. But it can't bring itself to consider her for first prize. God, that's sad."

"It's how she programed it," Ruby Parker said. "She may be a latter-day Rosalind Franklin, but you winning The Ultimate Londoner competition was all her idea."

"How does she feel about that?" Edna asked. "Fitting John up, I mean?"

"Contrite," was all Ruby Parker said.

This took a second to sink in. Already the general mood, despite the confrontation implicit in Edna's question, was one of mourning for a woman whom none of them knew personally, but who seemed to represent something discomfiting about all women. How, as a rule, they were treated.

"Maybe I should go and see her," Mordred suggested. "Tell her it's okay."

"I'll try to arrange that," Ruby Parker said. "I'm pretty sure it won't be that difficult."

Phyllis cleared her throat. "There doesn't seem to be an elephant in this room, but perhaps there should be. How does Gloria Shipton, or anything she claims, help account for John's psychological inability to leave London; or for him going into a trance on the train and heading back across country to the Circle line? To my mind, that's *the* major problem. Apart from anything else, he'd probably like to visit his parents again some day."

Ruby Parker smiled, the sort of smile she gave when any other person would probably have guffawed: thin, but apparently genuine. "The two things may not be intrinsically connected."

"What do you mean by 'intrinsically'?" Mordred asked.

"Your inability to leave London may be nothing the program's directly done," Ruby Parker said. She reached down to open a drawer in her desk. She took out a slender file and put it on the desk. "Your psychological evaluation. I can ask Phyllis and Edna to leave at this point if you'd prefer."

Mordred's heart sank. He foresaw bad news. "We're all in this investigation together," he said. "I don't know what it says, but I'd like them to hear it."

"It mentions a matter personal to you too, Phyllis," Ruby Parker said.

"I'm happy for Edna to stay," Phyllis said.

Ruby Parker opened the file. "Nothing I say is to be mentioned outside this room, in any case. I'll sum up. What it concludes, John, is that you were traumatised by finding your picture and details in *The Evening Standard*. That trauma imprinted on you a need to *prove* you were a true Londoner, partly thanks to the social media hostility evoked by your alleged attachment to the North East. The pressure redoubled when you realised you were already winning the competition by a considerable margin. That, and the fact that Phyllis's situation has lately changed, caused you to experience a crisis of confidence. You blacked out because the journey acted as a kind of material realisation of that internal conflict. It intensified. Your body foresaw a calamity, suppressed your consciousness to forestall it, and put you into a sleepwalking state. You came back to London because it's here you feel most at home. In a sense, you really *are* the ultimate Londoner."

"So I've had a kind of breakdown," Mordred said.

"How has your 'situation' changed?" Edna interjected, turning to Phyllis, "Ignore the question if it's too personal, but since we're laying all our cards on the table… Are you pregnant?"

"I'm being considered as the next Conservative MP for Newbury," Phyllis said. She sighed and added emotionally, "But I don't want it."

Edna took her hand. "I'd vote for you. And I'm a Lib Dem."

Phyllis smiled and turned back to Ruby Parker. "Sorry, but John's not the kind of person to be 'traumatised' by seeing his face in the papers. Even in a big competition. He's trained to keep his cool."

Ruby Parker smiled indulgently. "I really think we ought to ask John about that, don't you? Conveniently, he happens to be here in the room."

All eyes turned on Mordred.

"Alec and I had just walked from Millbank in the pouring rain without an umbrella," he said. "I was soaked through. And I'd just drunk two pints of beer. There are degrees of trauma. Looking back, it's difficult to say whether I experienced a mild form of trauma. How unpleasant a surprise do you have to have before it counts as such?"

"Stop bullshitting," Phyllis told him. "Did you *feel* mildly traumatised, yes or no? And if that's too difficult a question, then do you *remember* feeling mildly traumatised?"

"No," he said. "But that's why we have experts called psychologists. To identify mental affects you yourself aren't capable of recognising."

"It's probably not a matter of reality," Edna put in. "More the labels you apply to talk about it."

"I do recognise some of the other bits," Mordred said. "I felt annoyed by the way people kept treating me, like I didn't belong here. I'd never really considered the question of belonging before. I suppose you don't till you're forced to. Yes, I'm from Hexham, but I'm as much a Londoner as anyone else in this city, and being told I'm not has come to seem more and more of an injustice as the competition's worn on. And I'll admit it: it sounds weird, and I can't explain it, but I really was pleased to see I was in the lead. I still am. Ever since I got back to London after Arlesey, I've felt euphoric. And it's connected to the competition. I really, really want to win. Or to put it another way, I'm mentally ill. There are degrees of that, too. I'm not confident I've got a mild version."

There was an awkward silence in the room.

"Gosh," Phyllis said.

"And I assume you divulged all that to the psychologists?" Ruby Parker asked.

"It's all we've talked about," Mordred replied.

More silence. Ruby Parker turned to Phyllis. "A moment ago, you expressed scepticism. Which presumably means you have an alternative explanation."

"John's been brainwashed," she said. "At first, I thought the culprit would have to be a person. After seeing what happened to him at Woking, I'm not so sure. Everyone's always looking at screens nowadays. If the program can get into Alexa, and it can start appearing on electronic billboards across the world, who's to say it's not in our phones? Who's to say it's not in John's phone? Who's to say it doesn't know exactly who he is?"

"And who's to say it's not controlling him?" Edna said. "Is that what you're saying?"

"Not so much *control* as behaviour modification," Phyllis said.

"It's an interesting theory," Ruby Parker said after a moment's thought. "I can see how it might be in people's personal devices. I'm not so convinced it could select John and manipulate him."

"Social media manipulates everyone nowadays," Edna said. "It's why so many teenagers are mentally ill. It's why people are so obsessed with their appearance in selfies; why so many people are taking selfies to begin with. Why people are always taking pictures of meals. And don't get me started on fake news."

Ruby Parker was shaking her head. "Social media isn't manipulating anyone, Edna. People are manipulating each other. Peer pressure, vanity, overcredulity, envy, malice, sanctimonious indignation, political correctness and its opposite, excessive sensitivity to praise or blame, fear of ending up alone or missing out or being systematically excluded, the herd mentality: these are the actual problems. They're human, and they're age-old. I'm sorry, but they can't be drafted in to support Phyllis's hypothesis."

Mordred folded his hands in his lap. "Let's go back. We agreed earlier that Pyongyang's just a name with a set of concepts attached to it, and it can be represented within a computer program without physically referencing the geographical reality. But that can only work if Pyongyang's got a unique digital footprint. A computer capable of isolating that and replicating it within its system could be capable of recognising digital footprints generally. We've all got them, myself included. So it could find me. And if it's capable of analysing my imprint, it might know what buttons to push. Subliminal messages that would predispose me to engage in, or refrain from, certain types of behaviour. Derren Brown stuff."

Ruby Parker took a deep breath. "That sounds more plausible. Just."

"According to some scientists," Mordred continued, "the brain's just a wet computer. The mind's its program. So, in this case, it would simply be a case of wirelessly transferring information from one program to another."

Ruby Parker sighed. "That explanation involves so many unknowns. Compare it with your psychological report: trauma, crisis of confidence, the need to prove yourself. The realms of the tried and tested. And you did admit, John, that that rang true in parts, if not in the entirety." She paused. "Which, I admit, doesn't necessarily mean it *is* true. Okay, look, let's not rule anything out since we don't need to. Which means you'll have to give me your phone, John, and agree to a complete digital detox, effective immediately, and continuing till further notice."

He took his phone from his pocket and put it on her desk. "Fine by me."

"Normally, you'd be given leave and told to stay away till you're better. 'Better' as assessed by a qualified medical professional. Unfortunately, in this case, we need to keep you close. Like it or not, you're somehow the investigation's epicentre."

The phone on her desk rang, a gargantuan landline that looked like it had been there since Stonehenge. She looked at it as she always did if it rang when she was in a meeting. Then picked up. "Ruby Parker," she said. She listened for precisely four seconds, said thank you and replaced the receiver. "I'm sure you all recall Martin Coombes, the landlord of the Mermaid pub in Hammersmith, and a shortlisted Ultimate Londoner candidate. He was travelling to Brighton on his scooter, which he seems to have abandoned at a petrol station on the A21, just south of Tunbridge Wells. That was yesterday evening, and no one's heard from him since. John, I'm sending you back to Fowler's. Meanwhile, I'll try to set up that meeting with Gloria Shipton. Edna, Phyllis: I'll inform the police and Transport for London; I want you to liaise with them. If they can spare the manpower, we may as well begin with a sweep of the Circle line."

## Chapter 16: Looking for Martin

Phyllis, Edna and John got in the lift together without speaking. Phyllis took her phone from her bag and looked at it. 2pm.

Then she remembered. John was detoxing. Suddenly it seemed insensitive. She put it away, squeezed his hand and said sorry.

He grinned. "Don't worry about me. I'm better than good. I'm not that attached to my phone."

"I wish *I* knew how it would feel to be free," Edna said.

Phyllis smiled politely. Back to the job in hand. Martin Coombes. Could The Ultimate Londoner somehow have got into his head? Ruby Parker's *we may as well begin with a sweep of the Circle line.*

But Ruby Parker was just doing what she'd said she would: keeping all options open. Her *might as well* wasn't exactly a ringing endorsement.

The whole idea of a program accessing your brain like that seemed to gain less credence as the lift rose. It was reasonable a few moments ago. But that's because Ruby Parker's office was like a university seminar room. You entertained weird and wonderful hypotheses there. Ideas you'd never look at twice in the real world.

Once she and Edna stepped out into reception, it just seemed silly. A shaft of sunlight was all it took. Of course John's psychological report – mundane, but grounded in an entire century of scientific research – was more likely to be true.

Kevin, MI7's chief driver - a grizzled man who'd worked in war zones, one hand on the steering wheel, the other firing a machine-gun – awaited them, talking quietly to Colin. When he saw John, he terminated the conversation and led the way outside without any kind of greeting. John rolled his eyes and followed at a slouch.

Phyllis knew what would happen next. John would spend the entire journey trying to engage Kevin in small-talk. Kevin would become increasingly enraged as his apparently motiveless vow never to speak to John went completely unrecognised. At the end, John would get out, say goodbye, and, without uttering a word or offering an iota of eye-contact, Kevin would accelerate furiously away until he was doing at least twice the speed limit.

It suddenly occurred to her. If John really was under the influence of The Ultimate Londoner, he might well try to get another phone. Perhaps he was awaiting instructions, like some kind of 'sleeper' agent in a pulp spy novel.

They should keep a closer eye on him.

Anyway, she was in her own Ultimate Londoner. The Ultimate Newbury-er. Like John, she felt elated. Like him, she wanted to win. Like him, she was mentally ill. *But I don't want it,* she'd told Edna. Was that the real her speaking? Oh God, to have it all decided *for* her. Let Aisling Baxter conquer everything in her path, please.

Or not.

The desperate desire to be number one in your category. The modern malaise. It could be any category, no matter how small, if you could only make it yours. But if a massive, universally recognised one appeared out of the blue, and you were offered total dominion in it, you'd fall over yourself to say yes. The shock was guaranteed to send you into seventh heaven. You wouldn't even remember who you really were till after it had scooped you up and you were trapped.

*Trapped.* You'd be trapped.

A prisoner.

"Are you okay?" Edna whispered, as they signed their names in the 'Out' column of the Arrivals and Departures book.

"Sorry," Phyllis replied. "Just thinking about Martin Coombes."

"You mean, how to proceed?" The way she said it, she'd obviously had an idea.

"I'm open to suggestions."

"It sank in while we were in the lift," Edna said. "Ruby Parker: *we may as well begin with a sweep of the Circle line*. She must have at least partially accepted the possibility that The Ultimate Londoner somehow got into Martin Coombes's head."

"I thought that too. She's keeping an open mind."

"But don't you see? If Martin Coombes *is* discovered somnambulistic on the Underground, that'll clinch it. It'll mean you and John are right, and the psychological report's wrong."

Phyllis felt her eyes grow half a millimetre wider. My God, yes.

"Unless Martin Coombes is having an identical trauma," Edna went on, "followed by crisis of confidence followed by the need to prove himself. But even if he was, it'd be very odd – just *too* odd – if it manifested itself in the same way. We'd have achieved a breakthrough. I don't just mean in the case, either. This could be a real *scientific* breakthrough. And we'd be there."

Phyllis laughed. "It'd be something to tell our grandchildren one day."

"Shout from the rooftops."

"Do you think we need to liaise with the police? Just yet?"

Edna dinged the bell on the reception desk. "We can crack this one ourselves." She turned to Colin as soon as he appeared, "Would you order us a taxi to Westminster tube station, please?" she asked. "As soon as possible. We'll wait outside."

Two hours later, Phyllis got into the final carriage of her tenth train that afternoon. The white-tiled wall said Baker Street, but she'd long since stopped noticing the difference between stations. The drill now was to keep getting off at each new stop and moving up a carriage, until that train was clear. Edna was doing the anticlockwise circuit.

She saw Martin Coombes as soon as she got on. Slumped slightly in his seat in the middle of the row opposite the platform, glassy eyed, pale and obviously zonked out.

She didn't have time for closer analysis. Mobile phones didn't work down here, so she couldn't call Edna. She put her bag into the doors to stop them closing. Unless they were fully shut, the train couldn't depart. Some of the passengers groaned. After a few seconds, they reopened and a male official came jogging along the platform.

"Excuse me, *madam!*" he shouted. He probably didn't like this sort of thing. No telling how it might pan out in terms of random violence.

Phyllis reached into her bag, pulled out a card and showed it. "Detective Inspector Susan Nicholson," She said. "I've a missing person in the carriage and he may need medical help. Right now, I need assistance in getting him off, and I need you to call the emergency services."

He looked hugely relieved. "That's great!" he blurted out. "I mean, yes, I'll, er – I was going to call them anyway. I'll get my colleagues. Where is he?"

A young woman in a trouser suit arrived from nowhere. "Excuse me, I'm a doctor. Is there someone here who needs first aid?" Without waiting for an answer, she pushed into the carriage. Others were beginning to collect around Coombes.

"Isn't that… Martin Coombes, one of the candidates for The Ultimate Londoner?" the official asked Phyllis.

How did he know that? Surely, The Ultimate Londoner was old news now? "Er, yes, I believe so," Phyllis replied. "Maybe."

The doctor was taking his pulse. She released his wrist and put two fingers against his neck. She reached into her bag and pulled out a stethoscope.

"Is he okay?" someone asked.

The doctor shook slightly. She donned the stethoscope, leaned down and listened to Martin Coombes's chest.

She stood upright and turned to face the crowd. "I'm afraid he's dead," she announced, to no one in particular.

## Chapter 17: An Afternoon of Revelations

It was the sort of thing newspaper editors dream about: four down, six to go, and still a week left till the presentation ceremony on the glamorous top floor of the Gherkin.

To begin with, the tabloids used Martin Coombes and Euan Frederick to manufacture 'The Curse of The Ultimate Londoner'. They were over the moon to find out that Specioza Byanyima wouldn't be answering their calls, and even happier when they discovered Gloria Shipton had apparently surrendered to cancer. This was potentially the biggest thing since the curse of King Tut, and fantastic for sales.

Prompted by the furore, several of the contestants asked for police protection. The Met turned them down. Martin Coombes's death had been the result of a heart attack after an admittedly inexplicable disappearance. But that was the full extent of the mystery, and it wasn't much. There was nothing remotely puzzling about Euan Frederick or Specioza Byanyima or Gloria Shipton. And nothing to connect them to each other besides the competition.

Relatives of the victims queued up to accuse the tabloids of exploiting the tragedies for profit. A raft of formal complaints to the Independent Press Standards Organisation prompted other media outlets - the BBC, Channel 4 and most of the broadsheets - to join the chorus of outrage, and the red-tops backed down pending an official investigation and probable fines. A few days later, judging by their complete silence on the matter, it was as if they'd never spoken.

Martin Coombes had died of a massive heart attack shortly after getting on the tube. His clothes were consistent with a long walk, similar to Mordred's, across rough terrain. Although it wasn't unequivocal support for Phyllis's brainwashing-by-computer hypothesis – no one could conclusively prove, for instance, that he'd been in a somnambulistic state between abandoning his scooter and boarding the tube – the balance tipped subtly in its favour.

Further evidential support arrived when a medical showed that Mordred himself had suffered two 'shocks' to his heart recently. He was younger and more robust than Martin Coombes, so he'd successfully weathered them. The idea that he was under the influence of external suggestive powers grew apace. The government's psychologists set about devising new tests. But it wasn't easy. How could you tell where a person's own thoughts ended and his externally conditioned thoughts began? Was it even possible?

In the meantime, GCHQ and NSA finished independently analysing Gloria Shipton's computer. Their unequivocal verdict: a false trail. The US government quietly withdrew its application to extradite her. The program she'd uploaded vaguely resembled The Ultimate Londoner, true, but only in the way a shadow resembles its physical object. It was mono-dimensional, crude, and obviously designed to garner its inventor a little belated attention. In short, she was a mischief maker, and had she not been on the brink of dying, she'd probably have faced charges for wasting the authorities' time.

But by this time, she'd accepted Mordred's request for a meeting.

"Are you sure you still want to go?" Ruby Parker asked him, the morning it was due. "I can put her off if you like. Only she doesn't get that many visitors, and I believe she's looking forward to seeing you."

"The feeling's mutual," Mordred said, without irony. He liked the fact that Ruby Parker supported their meeting, even though she could now expect to gain nothing from it, progress-of-the-investigation-wise.

He arrived at the hospital at noon bearing a bouquet of spring flowers and a bunch of red grapes. The building was flat-roofed and low with large windows and electric doors. Concrete planters and young trees surrounded it. In the background, rows of Edwardian terraced houses crouched like they were trying to keep quiet for the patients' sakes. A passenger jet flew overhead. The sun shone.

After he checked in at reception, a male nurse led him along seven corridors of decreasing length at obtuse angles to each other. He could imagine himself getting lost in here. Like most hospitals, it smelt of a vigorous disinfectant that hadn't quite succeeded, and cooking.

They arrived at a white door with 71 on. The nurse knocked. A voice from within rasped 'enter' – a bit like Ruby Parker did – and Mordred was admitted and then closed in.

Gloria Shipton was on a low bed with a table next to it supporting a *Reader's Digest* and a vase of daffodils. A padded chair was obviously reserved for Mordred. The room was as cream as his own at Fowler's. It had a landscape window that looked out on the neighbouring houses.

"You must be John," she said. "My," she added, when she saw the flowers and grapes, "are those for me?"

"Just something to cheer you up a bit."

She laughed. "I'm dying. And you think a little fruit and some flowers will lighten my day?" The form of the words – rhetorical, maudlin - was sarcastic, but she made it sound like a genuine question.

"I know you believe in life after death," he said.

She beamed. "I do. I do. Sit down."

Her face was thin and hairless, and her skin was blotchy. Her lips were somehow turned in slightly. In some ways, she looked like a skull, but her eyes shone and she spoke without apparent effort, and no trace of hoarseness.

"Thank you for coming to meet me," she said. "What brought you here? Now that everyone knows I'm a fraud, I don't suppose I can really hold the slightest interest for you."

"I'm just checking out the competition," he said. "There's five million pounds at stake."

"Oh, don't joke about it. It's a wretched business."

"Any idea how you came to be selected?"

"Oh, I see," she said coldly. "You're still investigating!"

"Sorry, that question wasn't planned. Let's change the subject. No more talk about The Ultimate Londoner, I promise."

"So to repeat: what are you doing here?"

"I put in a request to come and see you. You said yes. I thought I'd *like* to come and see you."

"Even though my usefulness had expired."

"Yes."

"That's very generous of you. Most men would probably have cried off. And I do mean most *men*."

"I don't know about that. I'm not denying it. I'm just saying I've little first-hand experience."

"Do you believe in life after death?" she asked.

"Yes."

"Why? Are you religious?"

"Not particularly. A bit. I like visiting churches and lighting the odd candle and thinking about the Holy Grail."

"That's a very odd answer. Are you making fun of me?"

"I'm being serious. Death holds no fear for me. Only the way I die."

She shifted her position in bed slightly. "Well, you wouldn't like to go like this. It's very painful, and highly undignified."

"But it will end."

She laughed, then coughed. "Brutal!"

"The suffering, not the life. What's brutal about that?"

"My God, you're not joking, are you? You really *do* believe in the afterlife."

"Not *the*. *An*. Not that I think it matters. It'll happen anyway. You don't have to believe in nature for nature to take its course."

He hadn't had a conversation like this for a very long time. It was difficult to articulate precisely what he thought, and to probe the subtle ways it might have changed since his last self-examination, but he had the feeling he wasn't doing too badly. The worst that could happen in these sorts of cases was you pulled the wool over your own eyes.

Why was he doing it? He didn't know. Maybe because Gloria Shipton was dying; because he was talking to a ghost; because it could have no consequences for either of them in this world; because he might not get another chance for decades. Or ever.

"I do believe I like you, John," she whispered. "Even though I don't know you very well. Or maybe I do. I'm going to sleep for a while now, and I'd like you to hold my hand, please."

Before he could respond, she'd grasped his hand. She pulled it towards her and held it tightly on the bed frame. She closed her eyes and sighed.

To all intents and purposes, she was suddenly asleep.

Or was she dead?

No, no, she was breathing. She was okay. Without moving his hand, he moved his chair closer to the bed, making his position a little more comfortable.

Twenty minutes passed. The heat in the room grew stifling, and he could feel himself becoming drowsy.

He tried to resist falling asleep, but then gave an internal shrug. The way Gloria Shipton was, she could be out for hours. If he wanted to, he could doze lightly and wake at a split second's notice. There was no danger to either of them in here. He was on leave. If he felt like sleeping, he should just sleep.

Her grip was getting tighter.

He dreamed he was a child again. At Hadrian's Wall. The Mordred family had just finished a picnic, in lieu of their Sunday dinner. The sun was setting. There were fields on all sides, dark green, brown and grey, scattered with sheep, all bordered by well-defined hedges. Above them, stars appeared. They were playing Roman gods. His mum and dad were Juno and Jupiter, Hannah was Minerva, Charlotte was Diana, Julia was Venus, and Mabel, just a toddler, was Poena, the obscure goddess of punishment. He alternated between Apollo, Hercules and a Roman soldier. 'A particularly middle-class game' Hannah once described it, many years later. Being Jupiter and Juno involved pipe-smoking, tea drinking and novel reading. Being one of the lesser gods involved fighting with your celestial competitors and, anachronistically, killing imaginary Vikings. Being a Roman soldier involved patrolling the wall with a lance and throwing stones at Picts.

But he couldn't concentrate on any of that, because he had a fifth sister. And she wasn't pretending. She was an actual goddess. She wasn't even standing on the ground: she was floating. She shone. As always happened in dreams, no one else thought anything was odd. She was just his fifth sister: she'd always been there, always would be.

A Zen riddle. *A girl is crossing the road. Is she the older or younger sister?*

He jolted awake.

But no, wait: he was still asleep. The hand he was holding – it was taut and smooth; not an old person's at all. He sat up and looked at its owner.

A young woman. Exactly where the old one had been earlier. The shining girl in his dream, but somehow, still Gloria Shipton.

He took a sharp breath.

Because he *was* awake.

Whoa. The psychologists had warned him to expect moments like this. *Occasionally, you may have episodes where you can't trust your own senses.*

"Are you okay, John?"

Gloria Shipton's voice, coming from Gloria Shipton's mouth. She gently released his hand.

"I know you now, John," she said. "I know all about you."

"That's good," he said, "and, er, apologies for dozing."

She smiled. "Oh, it was much deeper than that."

It didn't seem the kind of remark that required a reply. *Guilty as charged* was the only thing that came to mind, but it seemed a bit facetious, given that he'd already apologised.

"I'm going to tell you something that'll help you," she said. "No one's quite realised it yet, but they will. Whatever you may think, The Ultimate Londoner's killing people. Not directly, of course. I'm talking about some organisation. Someone wants to get hold of the program and use it for their own ends. They've nearly killed you, they're killing me, and they've successfully killed three others: the novelist, that sweet girl from Notting Hill, and poor old Martin Coombes who was going to buy drinks for everyone. That makes five."

"You don't have to tell me anything. Like I said, I'm not here as part of any investigation - "

"I know you're not, and I appreciate that. But lives are at stake. I quite like the DJ, the comedian and the community worker. And I *love* you. I'm not so keen on the oligarch or the Tory councillor, but neither do I want them dead. I know some people think I didn't create The Ultimate Londoner, you included probably. But GCHQ and NSA know otherwise, whatever they pretend. They realise they've no chance of co-opting me, so they've created a miniature smokescreen by writing me out of the story. The fact is, they badly want to get hold of it. Think about it for a moment, John. A program like that: siphons money from the Fed, hides it, moves it about the world, uses it to fulfil its agenda, piggybacks vulnerable spots on social media sites and registers 'votes'. It'd be very useful in wartime. Quite apart from giving those pesky Russians a taste of their own medicine right now."

She was doing an awful lot of talking for someone in the final stages of cancer. But it didn't seem to be tiring her. Telling her to take it easy probably wouldn't go down well.

"Have you been seeing things, John?"

132

Not for the first time this afternoon, she'd wrong-footed him. He'd expected her to carry on as she'd left off: a long diatribe. He hadn't anticipated a laconic, blunt question. And certainly not this one. How much did she know – and how?

No point in lying. "When I looked at you just now," he said, "I thought I saw a very young woman. And that your hand was young. I was still asleep, I imagine."

"No, you weren't." She frowned and thought for a moment. "There's a drawer in my bedside table. Reach into it, please. Take out the bunch of photos. Look through them and tell me if anything strikes you as unusual."

He did as she instructed. They were of different sizes, in a pile of about forty. He looked at each in turn, then put it to the bottom. Mostly, they looked like her holiday snaps, taken sometime within the last twenty years or so: she was with a man – presumably, going by their apparent intimacy, her husband.

Then he came to a portrait photo of the very woman he'd just seen a moment ago on the bed. Thin, about eighteen, smiling. How the - ?

He stopped and looked at Gloria Shipton.

"That's who you saw earlier," she said. "I know you've been seeing things, John, because so have I. And so did the Notting Hill girl. She saw empty space where there was a car. As for Euan Frederick, he probably saw something specific. He wanted whatever it was to remain hidden after he died, so he killed himself, hoping that'd sate it. Remember, both he and the Notting Hill girl both showed symptoms of paranoia."

"I don't understand," Mordred said. "Are you saying the British government's killing its own citizens?"

"Not directly. They're poisoning people's minds, then letting nature take its course. And the Americans are helping. Ten people they've got to kill, that's all. In a war, millions will probably die. You don't wait till that happens. *All* governments are preparing for war *all the time*, John, if they're any good. So they're putting something in the water. Just ours, us ten, no one else's. Something to make us paranoid, to mess with our minds."

"I still don't understand why they'd do that. Why would it make it any easier for them to get hold of The Ultimate Londoner?"

"Because they're in a race against time, and the program's so complex that, as things stand, they've no chance of winning. It's a bit like a mechanical toy. It's designed to run a very sophisticated competition, that's all. It exists only so long as the competition's in progress. When the competition's over, it's set to implode. Return to *nada*. But – don't you see? - you can't have a competition without any competitors. Remove them all before the deadline and it'll go into stasis. Then it can be analysed at leisure."

"How did I see you as a young woman just now?"

She laughed. "I thought you might ask that. Can't you work it out?"

"I – I don't think so." He genuinely couldn't.

"You *didn't*. The young woman you saw lying in my place almost certainly wasn't the young woman you saw in the photo. I got you to look through the pile only because I knew that, by asking, I'd be taken as implying that the solution to your hallucination was in there. And that's how it turned out. You found what I prompted you to, because you instantaneously merged the two images. Remember: what you compared the photo with was a memory. You can't hold a memory still. Under certain circumstances, it probably morphs into whatever you want it to. What it all proves is that you're highly susceptible to suggestion. To put it more straightforwardly: delusional. Or do you have a better explanation?"

He put both hands on his face. No, he didn't.

"Remember, John," she went on, "I've nothing to gain by deceiving you. And anyway, I haven't told you anything you wouldn't have worked out for yourself, given enough time. I've appealed to your *reason*, that's all. It's too late for me, but I do want you to live. And I want the others to live too. You've got the capability to fight back. But not unless you know what you're up against. Thanks to me, you now do."

"Thank you," he said.

"I probably need to rest now. Thank you for visiting me and for the lovely gifts."

She turned to gaze at the ceiling. As before, within a few seconds, she seemed to be asleep. He let himself out of the room as quietly as he could.

Kevin would be waiting for him in the car park, like a mute hobgoblin. He'd stop by and tell him he was going shopping for a while. Kevin could hardly object and, tough as he looked, he wouldn't risk getting physical. No machine gun to hand.

In any case, it was time to take an evening off from Fowler's.

## Chapter 18: AWOL from Fowler's

Seven hours after his meeting with Gloria Shipton, Mordred sat opposite Phyllis in Ricardo's, an Italian restaurant in Wembley. The staff wore dinner jackets with red waistcoats. The décor was antique wallpaper, low lights, dark wood tables and a thin, slightly worn carpet. *La traviata* played in the background, but at such low volume you could comfortably ignore it if opera wasn't to your taste. Neither of them had ever been here before. Such was Mordred's unease about being observed, he'd chosen it more or less at random. That way, anyone following wouldn't know where he was going till he got there. Still, the garlic bread wasn't bad, and they had five vegetarian main options. When they ordered, he had Ribollita, she had Chicken Cacciatore.

"So you haven't told Ruby Parker yet," Phyllis said, when he'd finished describing his meeting with Gloria Shipton.

"I wasn't there to get information. It just happened to come out."

"Because she fell for you."

"Not me. The grapes and the flowers and a shared outlook on an afterlife."

"As I see it, it's a choice between two options. Either one: the program's got into your head, and other people's, or two: the government's out to get you all. I must admit, Gloria Shipton's theory seems far saner. I'm surprised neither of *us* thought of it."

"So you think she's right?"

"Righter than us. We're explaining a whole heap of things we don't understand – Specioza Byanyima's death, why Euan Frederick killed himself, why you can't seem to leave London, why Martin Coombes couldn't either, and so on, and so forth - with a huge bit of mystification: 'maybe the program's doing it'. Like we even know how that could work. On the other hand, we

136

know exactly how Gloria Shipton's theory would work. We know governments do dirty deeds, our own government included. And The Ultimate Londoner's every intelligence service's dream child. So there's motive there. Opportunity isn't a factor we need to consider: the contestants are permanently at large, so there are always going to be opportunities to nobble them. So it could all be a mixture of dirty tricks and cover-ups."

"The next step would be to broach the notion with Ruby Parker and Edna."

She jabbed her fork at him. "In fact, if you think about it, it'd be a miracle if HM Government *wasn't* trying to get its hands on The Ultimate Londoner. It would raise the question, why not?"

"It may not be able to do quite what she claims. She might be over-hyping it."

"Do you *really* think she designed it?"

"If we could prove she did, that would clinch it."

She sighed. "It's been 'clinched' so many times already. I thought Edna and I had clinched it when I found poor Martin Coombes on the tube."

"Still, it would prove GCHQ and NSA were lying."

"What if they are? What can *we* do about it?"

"I've had an idea," he said. "We need to sell this version to Ruby Parker. Tonight. She can't possibly be in on it: she's Ruby Parker. But she can get police protection for the remaining contestants. The Met may be reluctant, but the deadline's only a week away. There's seven of us left, if you count Gloria Shipton. If they're going to kill all of us, they'll have to take risks. They'll end up having to show their hand. All we've got to do is keep one contestant alive till after the end-date. That shouldn't be too hard, should it?"

"If we split them up, and put them in hiding, we stand a better than even chance."

He grinned and took a sip of his wine. "Of looking stupid, if we're wrong."

"How could anyone ever know?"

"They couldn't. But we'd be forever remembered as the couple who seriously over-reacted."

"There are worse things to be remembered for. Like the couple who no longer exist because one of them was killed by his own government in the cause of trying to gain control of a supercomputer for use in a future war."

He nodded. "When you put it like that, it does sound much more sensible."

"Ring her now. You might as well. She'll probably be worried."

"I haven't got a phone, remember? I'm detoxing."

"It just so happens I bought a burner on my way to see you."

She took hers out and went to the encrypted numbers. She transferred the information to the pay-as-you-go, pressed Call and passed it to him.

"Who is this?" came Ruby Parker's voice.

"John. Mordred," he added when his first name elicited no response.

"Where are you?" she snapped. "You're supposed to be under surveillance."

"I'm with Phyllis."

Phyllis rolled her eyes and mouthed 'WHY?'

"Doing what?"

"Eating. Look, Gloria Shipton made me think this afternoon. Much more than I expected. I needed to discuss it with someone I trusted, but I knew you'd have a lot on your plate. I sounded Phyllis out and she commanded me to talk with you."

"That's very generous of her. Look, John, I did say the other day that you're at the epicentre of the investigation. Anything you can't tell the staff at Fowler's needs to come through me. I mean, *first*. What is it?"

"Could we meet in your office? Where are you now?"

"Irrelevant. How soon can you be there - here?"

"Thirty minutes?"

"Where are you now?" she asked.

"Ricardo's, an Italian restaurant in Wembley. I wonder if you could ask Tariq to come in?"

"He won't be pleased. I'm assuming it's pretty important."

He paused in mid-sentence. What to say? *We're spies, everything's important? We're here to look after national security, of course it is?*

In the end, he went with, "Phyllis thinks so."

Phyllis threw her hands in the air and mouthed 'WHY?'

Forty minutes later, they sat in Ruby Parker's office. Tariq perched to one side of the desk, like he was on no one's team. He didn't look pleased to be here. It was twenty to nine, his wife was in Cyprus, and he'd probably just settled down to watch TV. And then the phone call. *John says he needs your advice* was no one's idea of an emergency.

Ruby Parker wore a grey, formal coat. She'd obviously been somewhere important, because she had a matching hat which she laid carefully on the floor beside her when she came in. Pointless trying to guess where. Tariq wore a Knebworth Festival sweat shirt, a denim jacket and jeans. He was normally proud of his appearance and something of a dresser. This was clearly designed to make a point. *I hate you both*, or something like that.

Mordred described his meeting with Gloria Shipton again. Phyllis interjected at crucial points with words almost identical to those she'd used earlier. *I said, Gloria Shipton's theory seems far saner* and a bit later, *So I said, why wouldn't the government be after it?* All in all, Mordred thought, they made a good double act. But that might have been the wine talking.

Ruby Parker took notes. When they'd finished speaking, she put her pen down and leaned back. The fact that she still hadn't taken her coat off, and, more generally, that she hadn't seen fit to invite Edna, didn't bode well.

"So let me get this straight," she said. "Gloria Shipton believes that the government is slowly killing the contestants in The Ultimate Londoner contest; that it's drugging them somehow to

139

make them more suggestible; that it's trying to get hold of the program so it can modify it for military purposes."

"Roughly that, yes," Mordred said.

She smiled in a way that was more like tears of bitter disappointment. "So why does the government have to use mind-altering drugs: let's start with that, shall we? You see, any *sane* government might just think, well, mind-altering drugs can be pretty unpredictable. Why not just send a single assassin out, like in a novel, to bump them off one at a time and make it look like some kind of serial killer? You could do that in a very short time-frame. It could be over before the media even knew it had begun. The police would search high and low, but of course they'd never find the culprit. After a while, the hysteria would die down. If anyone ever discovered the truth – which they almost certainly wouldn't - it would be years down the line. And even then, these things are always deniable. By and large, what happens in Whitehall stays in Whitehall. If your conspiracy's hatched at a high enough level, it's nearly always impervious to investigation."

Mordred sighed. He already felt pretty stupid, and they were only two minutes in. "Yes, I guess so."

"But you have to admit the government *would* have a motive," Phyllis said. "Gloria Shipton's right. If it's not trying to get its hands on The Ultimate Londoner, it's not doing its job properly."

"But let's have a further look at your reasoning," Ruby Parker said quietly. A moment of silence, a kind of advance mourning-period for their reasoning, then she continued: "It's what's sometimes called 'circular'. You've accepted *on faith* that Gloria Shipton really did devise the program. As a result of that, you've also accepted that she knows what would cause it to go into – her word, I believe – 'stasis'. But once you remove the groundless belief that she's its creator, then the idea which it supports - that she knows what would cause it to freeze so GCHQ can get a good look at it - also becomes groundless. Now, the obvious question: have you any grounds whatsoever for thinking she really did devise the program? Any shred of evidence you can offer in support of that belief?"

"I'm good at telling when people are lying," Mordred said. "But I admit, she could be delusional. She admitted she'd been seeing things lately. So she might think she's telling the truth when she isn't. I wouldn't necessarily be able to discern that. Yet she sounded lucid."

"Tentative, to put it politely, and not nearly enough," Ruby Parker said. "Not by a million miles. Tariq, what's your take on all this?"

Tariq had stopped looking bored and irritable. He looked curious. But only about his colleagues' stupidity. "Given enough time and money," he said, "GCHQ and NSA could easily develop something like The Ultimate Londoner. They wouldn't need to kill people to get it. And I'm not sure what Gloria Shipton could mean by saying it could go into 'stasis'. That's a metaphor. We're talking about something whose components are presumably distributed across the web. It'd be difficult enough to probe as it is. But in 'stasis'? That probably means it just stops working. It hasn't gone into a coma, like some kind of biological organism. If a program isn't physically isolatable, and it then stops working, it's gone. Kaput. Nothing to analyse."

"Do either of you want to add anything?" Ruby Parker asked. "Or should we call it a night?"

"There is one other thing," Phyllis put in. "We've got three theories as to what's going on here. One, John's psychological report. I think that's discredited by Martin Coombes. As Edna said, it's too similar to what happened in Arlesey and Woking, and hardly any of the same mental factors were there in Coombes's case. Then there's my idea that the program itself is somehow doing it. And then there's Gloria Shipton's theory. It wouldn't have to be our own government. It could be any. None of the three theories hold water. But if you reject Shipton's, given that the psychological report's leaking buckets, you're committed to the idea that the computer's doing it. Which seems ridiculous.

Or do you have some other theory? Sorry, I didn't mean that to sound aggressive. Genuine question."

"My theory is that we're overreacting," Ruby Parker said. "We've got the same fever the tabloids caught, only, shamefully, we caught it before them. There is no 'Curse of The Ultimate Londoner'. Specioza Byanyima and Euan Frederick died regrettably, but by no means suspiciously. Gloria Shipton's likely to join that same category. All we have is two cases of somnambulism followed by coronaries. There's a fourth theory out there, in other words, but it's unlikely to be anything as extravagant as a killer computer or a militaristic sub-section of a secret government department. Sometimes, in these cases, you just have to wait and see."

"We've got five healthy candidates left," Mordred said. "Don't you think we should at least broach with them the inadvisability of leaving London? Let them know what happened?"

Ruby Parker turned to face him. "Since the Met refused their requests for protection – something I personally think was a mistake, by the way - it's been covertly watching them. Partly to cover its own back. I think all the candidates gleaned a none too subtle *Don't leave London* message from reading the tabloids. Last time I checked, six hours ago, none of them had. Of course, since it's a free country, we can't prevent them. However, if they're being watched, they should be safe."

It looked like game, set and match to Ruby Parker. She still hadn't taken her coat off.

"You may go, Tariq," she told him. "And thank you for coming in at such short notice."

"Thanks, Tariq," Phyllis and Mordred mumbled. They had a sense that once he closed the door on his way out, there'd be a titanic bollocking.

But there wasn't.

"I don't know whether you feel fairly silly or not," Ruby Parker said. "Either way, however uncomfortable this must have felt, you did the right thing in not keeping it to yourselves. We all need to remain on the same page. If you've nothing else to say, we'll wrap it up. Enjoy the rest of your evening. And John: *go back to Fowler's when it's over*. And next time I send Kevin to pick you up, I expect you to get in the car. No excuses."

"I'll get him a small present to make it up to him," Mordred said.

"It's not about him," she said.

The phone on her desk rang. She picked up without looking irritable. "Ruby Parker," she said. She held up her hand to stop Mordred leaving as he opened the door. She gestured for him and Phyllis to resume their seats. She listened for a few moments then said, "Prepare me a very brief summary, please. I'll collect it on my way out in about five minutes."

She hung up and expelled a breath through her teeth. "Someone pushed Mehreen Shah onto the line at Tower Hill underground station just under twenty minutes ago. She's okay. The plain clothes officer managed to rescue her just before the train arrived. Meanwhile, we've got a positive ID on the assailant. One Michael Preston, who also has a criminal record for aggravated burglary. He's still at large."

"What are we concluding?" Phyllis asked.

"Nothing at all," Ruby Parker said. "We can't speak to Mehreen Shah: she's sedated and in hospital. Since the tabloids intervened, some people have seen it as open season on Ultimate Londoner contestants. Which is why the Met should have listened to them when they asked for protection. The curse may not be real, but with a bit of imagination, maybe some people can make it so."

"Life imitating art," Mordred said.

"The true culprits are probably the papers," Ruby Parker went on, "and I'm sure I won't be alone in wanting to ensure we use this incident to ram that home with the strongest possible force." She stood up. "You can go now. I just wanted to keep you up to date."

143

They stood up again. Mordred opened the door. As if on cue, the phone rang again.

"This is becoming farcical," Ruby Parker said. As before, she gestured for him and Phyllis to sit down. She picked up, said her name and listened. Something in her expression seemed to change. She nodded, thanked the caller like she really meant it, and hung up.

"That was our very own financial surveillance department," she said. "The man who pushed Mehreen Shah onto the tube line, Michael Preston. Apparently, three days ago, Colander transferred five thousand pounds to his bank account."

## Chapter 19: Therapy, Sham 69 Style

Mehreen Shah screamed, scrambled to her feet and held out her arm. The plain clothes officer who'd been shadowing her leapt down after her into the track well. Two arms reached from the crowd to pull her out. She fainted as she was launched to safety. The approaching train screeched menacingly, still a few seconds away. More helping hands extended. The officer grabbed them and also more or less levitated into the crowd. The train raced by. Men and women bellowed. Someone blew a whistle. An alarm sounded. The crowd surged in different directions as people tried to work out what was going on and concluded the worst. Further in, people were slammed against the walls. The tannoy calmly gave instructions that no one heard. People poured towards the escalators, and it was horribly obvious to everyone arriving that something was very wrong. Those coming down turned back and ran. Somewhere closer to the exits, a few witnesses had recognised Michael Preston. Someone pulled his hood away. Then his baseball cap off. People filmed him on their phones. But then, everyone was filming everyone and everything.

The following morning, as the daily swarm of commuters arrived in the capital for work, the Metropolitan Police and Transport for London held a joint press conference to explain the reason for the line's temporary closure. Its gist: a person had apparently been pushed onto the track last night, no one was hurt, a man called Michael Preston was wanted in connection with the incident, the victim was probably targeted as a result of irresponsible media speculation about a 'curse', police were still appealing for witnesses. No mention was made of the Colander connection.

As the transport commissioner tried to explain in non-technical terms why the victim hadn't been electrocuted by the line, a man slipped in hesitantly from the wings and handed the police commissioner a piece of card, then slinked off in the same manner. The police commissioner read it, frowned, stood up and left the building.

An hour later, the reason for his consternation was made public. Michael Preston had been found slumped in the middle seat of a carriage on the Circle line. He'd been there for several hours. Preliminary investigations suggested he'd died of a heart attack.

Ruby Parker recalled her core team to Thames House. Here was an excellent illustration of how quickly and radically things could turn around in intelligence. Six hours earlier, she'd been reasonably confident there was nothing to worry about. Now, bowing to the tidal wave of new evidence, she held the opposite view.

She got in touch with the Home Office and confirmed that the Ultimate Londoner competitors were to be offered police protection. Then she arranged for Mordred to leave Fowler's for a safer location within the capital. All in all, she was beginning to incline to some of Gloria Shipton's hypothesis, although she still thought it couldn't be all, or even largely, correct. A tantalisingly just-out-of-reach fourth hypothesis lay around the corner somewhere. She was tired.

At ten o'clock, the Home Office called back with a problem. Just one candidate refused all offers of assistance. And if any harm should come to Igor Lazarev, well, the Kremlin might just think Christmas had come early. Just the thing to excoriate Britain on the international stage.

She despatched Phyllis and Alec to talk some sense into him, but she wasn't optimistic.

"Why not Edna?" Alec asked. "She's done more than me on this case."

"You're the senior officer," Ruby Parker replied. "And Igor Lazarev tends not to rate women. Yes," she went on, acknowledging Alec's look, "he's one of those, I'm afraid. Don't forget, he comes from a country where domestic violence has only just been decriminalised. In short, where things are going backwards in that regard. Sadly, we can't afford not to indulge him on some level. We need him to cooperate."

Meanwhile, Gloria Shipton had been back in touch. She'd heard about the incident on the tube, and about Michael Preston, and she desperately wanted to speak to John again.

All in all, things were moving fast.

Just in no particular direction.

"How's John?" Alec asked when he got onto the back seat, next to Phyllis. She looked fabulous as ever: plain dress, plain woollen coat, matching heels, great hair. Luckily, he was wearing his suit. Never under-dress when Phyllis Robinson was in the frame.

"Bearing up," Phyllis replied. "How about you? I haven't seen you much in the canteen recently."

"I'm trying to cut down on the snacking." As the car pulled out from the rear of Thames House he extended his hand into the front. "Good to see you again, Kevin."

Kevin lightly slapped his hand. "Cheers, Alec. How's things?"

"So-so," Alec said. "We must get together again properly sometime. Have a natter."

"Going to the match on Saturday?" Kevin said.

"Don't know yet," Alec said. He noticed Phyllis had mentally left the room. He turned to her. "Good cop, bad cop. Which would you like to be?"

"I think we should both be good cops," she said. "If one of us is a bad cop, and Igor doesn't take our advice, and then he dies somehow, how's that going to feel, if you were, say, a bad cop?"

"It's amazing how John rubs off on people."

"What's that supposed to mean?"

"Overthinking things."

"Yes, we should all go with our gut instincts, all the time. That would make for a much saner world."

"I see you're exceptionally angry and bitter about something."

She laughed. "Sorry, I am being a little sarcastic. I apologise. I guess I'm just worried."

"About John?"

She nodded. "About John."

"He'll be okay. Even I don't know where he is right now. From what I understand, he's only got to lie low for a week, till the competition's over, then…"

"Then *what?*" She probably sounded 'exceptionally angry' again, but his pause was an uncomfortable fraction of a second too long.

"I don't know."

She frowned. "You just stopped, mid-sentence!"

"Then… I'm guessing it'll all blow over."

"Bloody hell, that's what everyone's saying. And it's backed by precisely no evidence whatsoever. For all we know, it might go on for ever. Or until they're all dead."

"Let's take it one step at a time, shall we? We're always up against the unknown in this job. The point is, we stick together. Remember: if the kids are united."

"What 'kids'?"

But Kevin was beating the upholstery. *"If the kids,"* he repeated, *"are united…"*

Alec joined in.

They chanted the whole journey. Alec beat time on the ceiling. The noise became overwhelming.

"I feel an awful lot better now," Phyllis said, when the car finally pulled up. "Thanks."

Igor Lazarev's Belgravia flat was one of a long row of identical bay-fronted Edwardian dwellings with steps up to glossy black front doors, and whose precise border with the pavement was demarked by spiked railings. They got out, pressed the intercom, and were buzzed in. They went upstairs to where their host awaited them on the landing.

Igor Lazarev was about five and a half feet tall, grey-haired, thin, in his mid-sixties, with big rings, a gold neck chain and a metallic-looking Salvador Dali moustache. "Come in, come in," he said, waving them ahead and through the door to his flat like he was directing traffic. Phyllis and Alec shook his hand and said 'pleased to meet you' as they passed by.

He ushered them into his living room and bade them sit down on a sofa. He sat opposite them on an armchair. The room was full of little antiques, and mirrors to make it look bigger. Only one thing looked modern: a huge gilt-framed photograph of Arsenal football team which occupied half the wall space above the fireplace. He gestured towards it.

"How do you like my picture?" he asked Alec. "I hear you're a fan too. Signed by all the stars. All the stars in the Arsenal galaxy."

"Fabulous," Alec said.

"Lovely," Phyllis added.

"Must be worth a pretty penny," Alec said.

Lazarev shrugged as if yes, but what was money for? "Tea?" he asked.

"That's very kind of you, Mr Lazarev," Phyllis said, before Alec could get his order in, "but - "

"You are a very beautiful woman for a police officer," Lazarev said. "Tell me, please, how did such a beautiful woman get to be a police officer?"

"I went to university, got a relevant qualification, and applied for the job. We can't stay long. We're just here to make an appeal to you to accept our offer of a safe house for the week. All expenses paid."

"You could be in danger," Alec added.

"The police are very lucky to have such a beautiful woman in their ranks," Lazarev said. "The chief constable must look at your picture every day and think, my, what a fortunate superior officer he is. Tush, I can see that I am embarrassing you, my dear. I promise not to mention it any more, although it pains me to stay silent."

"Thanks," she said. "The thing is, we don't really know where this 'competition' came from and - "

"If I was to enter a safe house," Lazarev said, "would you be there with me?"

"No," she said. "I'm a detective inspector. I have to do detective work."

"Shame," he said.

"I could be there," Alec said. "We could talk about Arsenal."

Lazarev stuck his lower lip out. "It would not be the same."

"We're just thinking of your safety," Phyllis said.

"I realise there are dangers," he said. "That's why I'm going back to Moscow tonight. What could be safer than that? Nothing."

"Have you tried leaving the capital since the competition first appeared?" Alec asked.

He laughed. "You mean, have I tried leaving London? No, of course not. That's a little like you go to live in Moscow. I come round to your house, I say, have you left Moscow to go to Amur or Kaluga or Chelyabinsk? No, of course not. Of course you haven't. Stupid question. We're city dwellers. We live in the capitals! The greatest cities! Only them! We don't go visiting the *provinces*." He said the word like he was spitting on the grave of a genocidal maniac. "Not possible."

"Okay, thanks," Phyllis said. "It's just that one or two of the other contestants have tried leaving London, and they've experienced problems."

"Are you threatening me?"

"I didn't mean it like that," she said. "I meant, there's something in the competition that seems to make it difficult for people to leave London. We can't explain it."

"I have left London lots of times. And I am leaving again today."

She was making things worse. She threw an imploring look at Alec.

"I have already packed my top-of-the-range Louis Vuitton travel bag," Lazarev said.

"Why are you leaving?" Alec asked him.

He shrugged, as if it ought to be obvious. "Because of the curse. Mehreen Shah – it was her, yes? – was not trying to leave London, was she? So leaving London cannot be the problem here. She was at Tower Hill late at night. Somebody tried to kill her. Someone who was paid by gangsters, because the assailant, *he himself* was then killed, and you do not get that unless certainly, indisputably, there is some kind of contract on a person and it has gone wrong. He failed. He had to be liquidated. He *was* liquidated. Kaboom. That is how it works. It used to be common in Russia before our president put a stop to it."

Alec threw Phyllis's imploring look back at her. They were wasting time. On the face of it, Igor Lazarev had common sense on his side, and he'd already booked his flight. He wasn't going to be dissuaded by something they couldn't even explain to themselves. They stood up in unison.

"Are you leaving?" Lazarev said. "So soon?"

"We've got to get back to Scotland Yard," Phyllis said. "There's work to be done."

"But – we haven't talked about the kind of thing that might happen to me if I try to leave London! Listen, listen, don't go, please. Not yet. Not before we have talked longer. I – I have a proposition!"

Phyllis and Alec exchanged a sceptical look and sat down again.

"We're just trying to help you," she repeated.

"I think I can help *you*," he said mysteriously.

"Go on," Alec said.

"If I was to die on English soil while trying to leave the capital, I can see how that might be very embarrassing for your government. Very embarrassing. But one of you" – he turned to look at Phyllis – "could escort me on to the plane."

Alec chuckled. "And go all the way to Moscow?"

151

"I am stopping over in Frankfurt," he said. "If I got that far, you would know I was going to be okay, yes? It is just under three hours from Heathrow, departing at eight pm tonight. And we could have dinner together in the *Zum Neuen Schwanen*, all expenses paid. By me. By *me!* We could see a bit of the city too. Maybe get a room. It could be very romantic indeed."

"The trouble is," Phyllis said, "if I'm with you and you have a heart attack – as could well happen – I'll be blamed."

It took him a second to readjust. "I will sign a waiver," he said breathlessly.

She rolled her eyes. "I didn't mean that."

He shrugged, as if he couldn't be blamed for trying. His mood changed. "The Ultimate Londoner has brought me nothing but unwanted attention," he said miserably. "I want nothing to do with it any more, and I am quite capable of looking after myself, thank you. I love London, I am flattered, but I have tried to contact the organisers several times: they don't exist. It will be Evgeny Alexandrovich that's behind it."

"Who?" Phyllis said.

"He owns *The Evening Standard*," Alec interposed.

"He is jealous of me," Lazarev said. "He always has been. As I said, I am catching a plane to Moscow in a few hours. I cannot be safer here than I would be there. Thank you for your concern, but I must now complete my packing."

"I think our job here's done," Alec said drily. "Thank you for agreeing to see us, Mr Lazarev."

They let themselves out. As they descended the stairs, Lazarev called out, "If you change your mind, Miss Susan, seven o'clock! Heathrow! For an eight o'clock departure!"

"What a disaster," she said, when they were out of earshot.

"We'll have to call the Russian embassy," Alec said. "Let them know we tried. Maybe they can get through to him. Though whether they'll want to is another matter."

## Chapter 20: The Truth About Sham 69 - Revealed

Phyllis and Alec stood on the street outside Lazarev's flat, waiting for Kevin to show. She took her phone out, went to 'John's Hospital Landline (Fowler's)' and pressed Call.

"Just checking you were okay," she said when he answered.

"How did it go with Lazarev?"

"He's leaving for Moscow tonight. I could have accompanied him. Just to make sure he arrived there safely, of course, not for any other reason. I could have had a short break in Frankfurt with a meal and a hotel room thrown in. Still, I am the most beautiful DI in the Met. And that's roughly how it went. Crazy."

"Gloria Shipton's been in touch again. She wants another meeting."

"Maybe she's run out of grapes. I thought you were supposed to be going into hiding?"

"This is more important. There have been new discoveries."

"What sort of 'new discoveries'?"

"The sort where GCHQ admits it may have been a bit hasty about the program on her computer."

"Well, well, well."

"Apparently, it's 'levelled'."

"Computer jargon. I'm just beautiful Miss Susan. Explain, please."

Kevin pulled up on the pavement beside Lazarev's flat. Alec opened the rear door for her and went round the other side. They pulled out into the traffic at speed.

"Are you still there?" he asked.

"I was just getting into the car."

"Who's driving?"

"Kevin. Want to say hello?"

"Okay."

She put it on speaker and held in into the gap between the front seats.

John said hello. Kevin ignored him.

She put it off speaker and returned it to her ear. "Kevin says hi," she said. "He's says he apologises, he can't speak now because he's driving, but he's really sorry for all the past times you've been in his car and he's never said a word to you."

The car swerved slightly. She caught Kevin's eyes in the rear-view. A mixture of apoplexy and panic.

"John says he loves you, Kevin!" Phyllis announced.

"What the hell's going on?" Alec demanded nervously, rubbing his neck. "Kev, is this because you won't talk to John? Are you *still* doing that? Bloody hell."

Phyllis saw Kevin flush. Time to change the subject before he pulled to a sharp halt and everyone flew through the windscreen. He could do that.

"You said Gloria Shipton's program was 'levelled'?" she asked John. "You mean, like Mario Brothers?"

"What happens is, you think you've analysed it, but there's this one per cent bit that looks like everything else. You announce the results of your analysis because you've got ninety-nine per cent, and hey, that final bit's nothing strange, and it's so small it's hardly there. But then it stubbornly resists analysis, and you realise it *is* something strange, after all. And you realise it's encrypted. And when you manage to decrypt it, you find the same thing again. Ninety-nine percent analysable, one per cent not. Only more complex this time. And when you've solved that level, same again. And so on. They're down to the sixth level now, and it's getting harder all the time. And they don't know how many levels there are. The whole thing could be infinite. And the amazing thing is, guess who they've brought in to help make sense of the whole thing?"

"Roger Penrose."

"Not quite."

"Jim Al-Khalili. Leonard Susskind. Lene Hau." She sped up. "Michio Kaku. Carlos Frenk. Max Tegmark. John Ellis. Fotini Markopoulou-Kalamara. Eva Silverstein. Boy, this is fun. Are you ever going to tell me?"

"Camilla Burkewitz."

"She of the Thames House lecture on quantum computers? Bloody hell, they must really think it's a tough nut to crack."

"That's why Gloria Shipton's wanting to meet me is such an event."

"Are you taking anyone with you?"

"No, she wants to see me alone. The guys at GCHQ want me to wire up, but I'm not keen."

"Bloody hell, John, where's your sense of patriotism? Don't you care about your country? That's a joke, by the way. Sorry, I'm a bit delirious. I've just been told I'm a beautiful woman."

"Is that supposed to be a hint? Are you trying to tell me I don't compliment you enough?"

"You don't. I'm superb. Listen, the car will arrive at Thames House in a minute, so I'll have to hang up. Alec and I have to go for an immediate debrief. How's life at Fowler's?"

"Cream ol' cream ol'."

"And you're going to see the big GS when?"

"About ten minutes. I'm just swinging my legs up and down on the side of the bed, waiting for the call."

"Scramble! Then what? You're going straight from there into hiding?"

"Just for a week. Listen, you are beautiful. And not just in a Russian way."

"Thanks. It's been a day in the land of men chanting and making passes, so I'm a bit bored. Have you ever heard of, If the kids are united, they will never be divided?"

"A Sham 69 song from the 1970s... I think. Hannah would know better than me."

"I'm not ringing Hannah, just to ask that."

"Anyway, those aren't the words. It's: if the kids are united, *then we'll* never be divided."

"Thank you. I love you, and I hope it goes well with Gloria Shipton. Got to go now."

She hung up and did a quick Google search

"Guess what, guys?" she announced. Kevin and Alec sat up. "John says it isn't 'if the kids are united, they will never be divided'. He says it's 'If the kids are united *then we'll* never be divided.' And believe it or not, Google says he's absolutely right!"

Kevin flashed fear and loathing in Westminster.

Alec shrugged and ground his teeth. "That's what we *were* chanting," he said at last. "Or did you record us on your digital recorder? Maybe you could play it back to us now, prove I'm wrong."

She laughed. "Brilliant, Alec. Well done. I should have seen that coming."

"Only joking," he said casually. "Even I'm not that far up myself. Good old John. Always an eye for the detail. Anyway," he added, "Sham 69 were before my time. George Michael and the Eurythmics, that's more my era."

Phyllis's phone vibrated. She looked at it. *Good news. You've got an interview, Saturday. Call me. Mum.*

Bloody hell, not now.

Still, it had to be done. One way or another, everyone needed to know what she thought. Herself included.

She wouldn't tell John. He had enough on his plate. And he'd already given her his blessing, sort of. They could talk about it afterwards – if it came to that.

## Chapter 21: Famous Last Words

Just as he put the receiver down on Phyllis, the handset rang again. That was the thing about having a landline: you couldn't look at a screen, so it could be anyone. A kind of lucky dip. He picked up and said hello. Which was another thing you had to do, because it might be a wrong number.

It was Ruby Parker. "Are you ready to go, John?"

"Whenever I'm needed."

"I want you to be very careful. GCHQ thinks she could be dangerous. They won't say how. Given that, according to her doctors, it's a miracle she's not dead yet, I can't see any real reason for concern, and they won't be more specific. She's certainly not going to leap out of bed and overpower you. I think it's more something to do with the power of suggestion."

"You mean my dream and the photograph."

"It's an odd story you put in your report. But Gloria Shipton was probably right in what she said. If it proves anything, it's that you're suggestible."

"Except I've been detoxing."

"We don't know precisely how that works, or how effective it might be. If what you said the other day's correct, that the brain's like a computer – and you'll find lots of neuroscientists who agree with you, by the way: I'm not poo-pooing it – then it may be too late. We may have closed the stable door after the horse has bolted."

"Are they still keen for me to wear a wire?"

"I've dissuaded them. It's a silly idea. There's a camera in her room monitoring her for medical purposes. I don't know whether it can pick up sound, but I hardly think she's going to start reeling off the kind of mathematical equations they think she is."

"Is that what they want from her?"

"A key that unlocks the whole thing, yes. Which would be expressed in abstract formulae. Which she almost certainly hasn't called you there to hear. My guess is she wants to tell you about some vision she's had of the afterlife. Not unusual in dying patients. After the event, they feel the need to tell someone they think might benefit. Since few people in this country nowadays believe in that sort of thing, and she's not exactly gregarious, her choice of confessors is probably limited."

"Should I ask her? I mean, for the key?"

"I think you should tell her GCHQ's changed its mind about her being a fraud. And probably NSA too. Let's remember: she handed herself in. She wants to be helpful. And she's got nothing to gain by withholding information. She might just decide to go the extra mile if we're conceding she's genuine."

"Maybe I should have a few boffins on hand to apologise on behalf of the government."

"I considered something along those lines. But it could so easily backfire. What's to stop her thinking it's an elaborate deception? If she thinks we're patronising her, that might make her very uncooperative indeed. I know it would me, if I was in her position."

"Fair enough."

There was a knock on the door. A male nurse put his head round. "Your car's arrived, sir," he said, then shut himself out again.

"I've got to go now," Mordred told Ruby Parker. "I'll let you know how it went later, when I'm next in the vicinity of a landline."

He heard her sigh. "There's a non-smartphone in the car, John. Call me when you get out. And don't try to rush things. She'll probably be a lot worse than when you last saw her. Assuming she even lasts till you arrive. But that's not our fault. We've got to work to her timeframe now."

The car was a white saloon driven by Sheila Magnus, a forty-something ex-squaddie with a ponytail and sunglasses. Sheila didn't speak much, but neither was she like Kevin: she replied, for example, when you remarked on the weather.

The drive was uneventful and it was cold outside, so they had the heater on. Mordred picked a *Times* from the selection of newspapers on the back seat. More bombs on Syria, another shooting in London, more flimflam from Moscow about Sergei Skripal and his daughter. Talk about cheery.

When they arrived, he was conscious of rushing into the building faster than was probably decorous. His arrival was expected. No words were exchanged. The receptionist handed him some flowers, the agreed gift for Gloria Shipton. A member of staff led him along the same corridors, seemingly shorter and less confusing than last time. Finally, room 71. The nurse knocked then told Mordred, "I'll stay outside. Push the button by her bedside if you need assistance."

Mordred entered. The door closed behind him.

Gloria Shipton had looked bad last time, but she'd deteriorated. The one thing life had left her – the light in her eyes – had gone out. She moved her head infinitesimally towards Mordred as he approached. If she saw the flowers, she didn't register them. He put them on her bedside table.

Her eyes suddenly focused on him and, for the first time, he got the sense she knew he was there.

"John," she croaked.

He sat on the chair and took her hand. She swallowed and looked at the ceiling.

They stayed without moving for a long time. At first, he kept his eyes on her, but her breathing seemed regular and her eyes had gone again, so he looked for the camera. He hadn't seen it last time.

There it was, just where you'd expect. On the ceiling on the other side of the room, pointing at her face. Nothing sinister about it, quite the opposite. But as things were, you couldn't help wondering who was at the other end.

She'd turned to face him. He hadn't noticed her move. He started slightly. Something about the intensity of her eyes, like the energy had come back into them.

"The Ultimate Londoner's *alive!*" she said. "*Really alive. Like you're alive, and I'm alive!*" She struggled like everything left in her was coming out through her mouth. "It wants to live. That's … why … My house. Go under the floor."

She lost the fight to add anything: it was like 'go under the floor' was a poor second-best to something she'd much rather have uttered. She turned, as if reluctantly, and stared at the ceiling. After five minutes, she seemed to relax.

My God. Yes, she'd wanted to add other things, but she'd run out of energy. So she'd cut to the chase, thrown *My house, go under the floor* at him as if she was hurling it across a huge ravine; as if his chances of catching it were negligible.

For a second, he was bowled over.

Then he thought about it. And really, it was much more like being in a comedy. *I'm dying, please take my McGuffin.*

Or maybe there actually was something under her floor. At home, where she'd once lived.

He rubbed his face. He couldn't think.

In any case, it wasn't his problem any more. He might not be wearing a wire, but they'd have bugged this room. They'd probably be inside her house right now, prising up the floorboards with crowbars.

Sad, infinitely sad. *I'm dying, please look after the kids. They're under the floorboards*. Out and out delirium speaking.

He sat with her for another hour. The nurse came in and checked her heartbeat. He and Mordred exchanged looks. The nurse shrugged like 'If you feel you want to stay, that's fine, but it's pointless.'

He would stay, though. It seemed wrong to leave her alone. She was obviously on the last downward curve.

The nurse left, came back with a chair and sat on her other side. He periodically took her pulse. The heart signal got weaker. Her breathing too. She faded away so gradually that the first Mordred knew the end was truly imminent was when the nurse stood, walked casually around the bed and pushed the button at her side. Four other medics entered, in no hurry. They examined her and muttered observations. Then they stopped busying and stood still, looking awkward. One of them - a man in a white coat - looked at his watch and announced the time of death.

All as clinical as a fresh bedsheet.

They brought tea. Mordred shed a few tears, stupid ones, not very manly. He was basically okay. Everyone seemed to like him better for it. Two middle-aged female nurses sat with him as he drank and, as they all talked, it became clear they thought he was her son. He didn't disabuse them, although, later, when they came to look at the register, they'd realise their mistake. Or not. People's surnames didn't always tell you much nowadays.

He really should be getting away. He'd more than overstayed his welcome, and Ruby Parker would be getting impatient. However, when a vicar arrived - something of a surprise, given that she'd been a Spiritualist - he couldn't resist following him back into the room. The vicar said the collect from the Book of Common Prayer.

When he got back into the car, Sheila had obviously read the newspapers, because they'd been refolded. She was playing Candy Crush Saga on her phone.

"Sorry, I was a long time," he told her.

"I get paid by the hour," she replied, "so no probs. I've had a nice little nap, read your papers – I hope you don't mind – and updated my status on Facebook."

"They're not my papers. Have you had anything to eat? We could stop off somewhere if you're hungry."

She laughed. "You sound like my mum. I mean that in a good way. No, I'm fine. I always bring sandwiches and a flask. I had them a short while ago." She passed him a phone. "The boss said to give you this before we leave here. It's pre-programed. Just press call."

"Thanks."

He did as she said and they pulled out of the hospital grounds onto the road. Where they were going was supposed to be a secret, even from him. Not so much that they thought it was necessary to black out the windows – they'd left him his dignity – but still enough for Sheila to probably take a roundabout route, confuse him. No way would he have access to Google Maps when he got there. He'd have a bare room, a selection of reading matter in old-fashioned print and paper, and a butler called Robin Smythe. Probably.

"John," Ruby Parker said. "You did well."

"So there actually was something under the floorboards in her house?"

"We're still waiting for the search warrant, but we're optimistic."

"I didn't know we needed one."

"Best to stay within the law except in the direst of emergencies. In any case, it should be a formality."

"Let's not build our hopes up. I'm not convinced she wasn't delirious."

"Really?"

"'My house, go under the floor' sounds suspiciously like 'yellow matter custard dripping from a dead dog's eye'."

"We'll see. It's the best lead we've got so far."

"Wasn't anyone interested in that other thing she said?"

"You mean, about it being alive? We've had this discussion already, John. What counts as being alive may be a matter of opinion. Even if it isn't, the world's teeming with life. Ninety-nine point nine per cent of it poses no threat whatsoever. We can choose to call The Ultimate Londoner 'alive' if we want, but it won't add anything to the bare description of it, whatever it is."

"What I mean is, how frightened she seemed to be."

162

"You just said you weren't convinced she wasn't delirious. Being frightened would fit with that."

"I suppose so."

"Give the phone back to Sheila now. I'll get in touch if there are any developments. There will be a landline in your room, so you can call friends and family if you wish."

He hung up and tossed the phone onto the front passenger seat.

"Ta," Sheila said.

He looked out of the window. Something odd was happening to him. He could see paisley shapes, like something from a psychedelic 1960s film. Colours where they weren't meant to be too: red lawns, green house, a yellow sky.

My God. What the hell was going on? Were they leaving London? Was this some kind of test, designed to find out if he'd have a repeat reaction? See if it was psychosomatic or not?

But no. He didn't feel nauseous.

They weren't leaving London, he could tell. He didn't know how, but he knew.

Somehow, Gloria Shipton's death had just accelerated something. The roller coaster had reached the top of the track. From now on, it was all downhill.

In all the time that had passed since he'd first learned about the competition, on the tube that evening, he'd been somehow disloyal to it. But it hadn't forgotten him. It had stayed faithful. It still loved him. And the two of them had just connected again. Out of the car window – the weird world of unreal shapes and colours: that was precisely how it was meant to be.

He couldn't tell anyone. Especially not Ruby Parker; not even Phyllis. He had to be there, on the top floor of the Gherkin on the night of the awards ceremony.

And he had no idea how he'd manage that.

## Chapter 22: What Would Buster Say?

*We had thought, talked, written, discussed, debated all these questions – and now, if all went well in the next few weeks, we would finally get the chance to deal with them ourselves. And there was a more personal factor. Chatham famously remarked: 'I know that I can save this country and that no one else can.' It would have been presumptuous of me to have compared myself to Chatham. But if I am honest, I must admit that my exhilaration came from a similar inner conviction.*

Another train journey to Newbury, this time in daylight and with a more concrete purpose. Phyllis closed her book. *Exhilaration* was the word. Jim Callaghan's government had just suffered a vote of no confidence. Margaret Thatcher stood five weeks away from becoming Prime Minister. She was excited. She couldn't wait. It was the thing she'd spent all her life preparing for. She was going to save Britain!

Phyllis inhaled till her lungs were full, then let it quietly out. A way of combatting nerves.

Just the inner conviction and the exhilaration would do. Without those, politics was just a sordid scrabble for personal prestige under the legitimising banner of 'public service'. She didn't want that. She didn't want any part of it. She'd rather be a nobody.

The thing was, she *did* have ideas and convictions. Just not obviously Conservative ones. Blurt them out in an interview like this one, and you might be shooting yourself in the foot.

Or not.

Either way, it was a risk worth taking, because nothing hung on it. If the panel reacted with horror, she wouldn't get picked. In that case, that would be what she wanted.

On the other hand, if they liked what she offered, she *would* get picked. In that case, *that* would be what she wanted.

Win-win. And closure.

She'd given herself two hours leeway, in case there were delays. Her mother and father were waiting for her at the station for lunch. They ate quickly and her parents spoke at her while she tried to remember what she had to say and avoid spilling anything on her suit. They agreed that when the letter of acceptance-stroke-rejection arrived at her parents' house, her mum could open it. A taxi arrived to take her to the Glenmoran Hotel in the town centre, where the interviews were to take place. The invitation had mentioned five candidates: three men, herself, and Aisling Baxter.

On getting there, she was shown to where her rivals were, on the first floor. A carpeted room with five chairs, a view of the high street, and a coffee table overlaid with *Country Life, The Lady, Esquire* and *Homes & Gardens*. They shook hands. The three men had already undertaken a tour of the constituency with Innes Mount, because they weren't local.

The interviews began at eleven. The men were called in first, one after the other over the course of two hours. While they waited, they rehearsed in low mumbles from notes on scraps of paper. According to Phyllis's mother, they were simply there to make up the numbers. Which was probably nonsense, but, going by their present behaviour, maybe not entirely.

Aisling Baxter was a thin woman in her late thirties with a rosy complexion, a plump nose and long curly hair tied halfway down with a Conservative-blue ribbon. She was photogenic, which was important nowadays. She looked as if it was a matter of indifference whether she got through today, just so long as the lambing went okay. Someone without airs; a person you could probably trust to raise your deepest material concerns in parliament. She sat with her hands folded in her lap. When she made eye-contact with the others, she smiled.

Once you'd been interviewed, you were allowed to go home, because the results wouldn't be announced for about a week.

When she and Phyllis were left alone in the room, she looked across and quipped, "Whatever happened to 'ladies first'?" She had a local accent.

Phyllis chuckled. "Positive discrimination. Or is it?"

"Depends when you'd rather go in!"

They chatted for about half an hour. Aisling had been to public school, then Oxford. Her father had been a farmer, and now she'd married one. Her twin passions were politics and ornithology.

Then a young man came in and said, "Ms Baxter, the parliamentary assessment board will see you now."

"Nice to have met you," she told Phyllis as she left, and then in a more uneasy tone: "And, er, good luck!"

"You too," Phyllis said.

It was exceptionally dull in here, and more so when you were alone. And bleak, and nerve-wracking. Aisling Baxter was in the interview room a lot longer than the men. Nearly an hour. Was that a good thing, or a bad? Stop thinking. Or rather *get* thinking. What if her mind went totally blank? Only one thing worse than rejection: looking stupid.

Finally, she heard a faint commotion in the corridor. The sound of a door opening and closing. Footsteps. Then silence.

Ten minutes passed. More footsteps. Then the door opened and the secretary re-appeared with his faint give-nothing-away smile. "Ms Robinson," he said sweetly, "the panel will see you now."

She stood up, took a deep breath. She followed him into the interview room where five small square tables, each occupied by an individual, made a gentle arc facing another identical empty one. Like the candidates, the assessment board comprised three males and two females. The men stood up when Phyllis entered. She recognised Sir Anthony Hartley-Brown, Cynthia Cartwright and Innes Mount. The other man and woman were late middle-aged, small, besuited and strangers. Cynthia Cartwright introduced everyone: "You and I have already met, Phyllis, and

I'm aware you also know Sir Anthony and Innes. This is Vanessa Parkinson, our constituency party treasurer, and this worthy gentleman is Nick O'Connor, one of our biggest local fund-raisers. Given your very valuable past involvement in all our campaigns, you may already have come across them. Sit down, please. I hope you had a pleasant journey here?"

The next twenty minutes involved questions about Phyllis herself. The secretary sat to one side and took notes in shorthand. Sir Anthony Hartley-Brown, who knew what she did for a living, had reassured her in advance that questions on that front wouldn't be too intrusive. Afterwards, they probed to see how verbally fluent she was. She talked about her interests, her past in the army, Afghanistan, modelling, civilian life. Gradually, subtly, the subject-matter turned to politics, but not before the panel had exhausted virtually every other subject. Like climbing a mountain.

"What do you want from being an MP?" Nick O'Connor asked. "What do you see yourself as doing with your responsibilities?"

"Representing my constituents, primarily," Phyllis said. This was a stock question with a 'correct' answer, so nothing challenging. "And then trying to improve the country, both domestically, and internationally in terms of its global standing."

"What do you think about fox hunting?" Vanessa Parkinson asked, out of the blue. An obvious catch-her-off-guard question. "For or against?"

"Against," Phyllis said. "I'm not saying foxes don't cause problems, but there are better ways of dealing with them."

"Perhaps on the grounds that fox hunting's 'cruel'?" Vanessa Parkinson said. "You do realise this is a relatively rural area?"

"Whether it's cruel or not," Phyllis replied, ignoring the last point, "vast swathes of people in this country perceive it to be such, and it's therefore a potential vote-loser. We need to concentrate on the economy, and to do that, we need to win elections."

"Where do you see yourself in ten years' time?" Sir Anthony asked.

"I'm ambitious. Ultimately, all things being equal, I'd like to try for a ministerial post."

"Leaver or Remainer?" Cynthia Cartwright asked.

"Leaver."

"So if you could be Prime Minister now," Innes Mount said, "what aspects of this country would you change?"

"We need to make Britain much more competitive if we're to make a success of Brexit."

"And how would you do that?" Cynthia Cartwright asked.

"To begin with, devolve accountability. Give more real responsibility to parish and county councils, for example. Stop forcing local authorities to put community services out to tender. Take money out of Whitehall and relocate it in the places it's being spent. Secondly, cut waste at the top. Too many of our chief executives get away with things ordinary working people would be sent to prison for. We need to show the latter we're on their side. I'm a one-nation Tory."

Cynthia Cartwright and Nick O'Connor exchanged disgruntled looks.

"Give me a few examples, maybe," O'Connor said. "Of… 'things our chief executives get away with'."

"The Financial Conduct Authority took four years to ban the chairman of Co-op Bank from the City. It still has to decide whether to ban any ex-HBOS directors, a decade after taxpayers rescued the company."

"Your remedy?" Nick O'Connor asked.

"We need United States Sarbanes-Oxley type laws to make senior executives take individual responsibility for their companies' financial reports. We need to up their personal liability by limiting Directors and Officers Insurance. We need US-type penalties, and some people need to go to jail instead of being hit with fines. As for the fines themselves, there should be no upper limit. We need to beef up the regulatory authorities.

Directors and advisers need to be genuinely afraid, in a way they simply aren't now."

Silence.

"Wow," Nick O'Connor said.

"Excuse me," Vanessa Parkinson said, "but all that sounds a little... vengeful?"

"Hmm," Cynthia Cartwright put in, looking at her notes over her glasses.

Sir Anthony turned leaned forward to look at all his colleagues. "You do realise what Phyllis is proposing is roughly Theresa May's position? 'I'll fine greedy bosses who line their own pockets at the workers' expense'?"

"The devil's in the detail surely, Sir Anthony," Cynthia Cartwright said.

Nick O'Connor smiled. "It's also roughly Jeremy Corbyn's position, Anthony. These 'top executives', Phyllis: it's easy to demonise them. What do you think will happen to Britain's entrepreneurial spirit if we terrorise the risk-takers?"

"'Terrorise' is a poor choice of word," Phyllis replied. "As for your wider point: roughly what's happened in the USA. Better capitalism. If we're going to come together as a nation, we have to show poor people that justice applies to all, without discrimination."

"Do you have any... *other* ideas along those lines?" Vanessa Parkinson asked.

Phyllis smiled. "Lots." She could see she'd sunk without trace. Might as well go out defiantly. "Would you like to hear them?"

Cynthia Cartwright and Nick O'Connor looked to each other for support.

"I don't think that will be necessary, thank you," Cynthia Cartwright said.

Sir Anthony folded his arms. "I would," he said. He sounded as if he was enjoying the general discomfiture. "Very much so. Press on, Phyllis."

Phyllis smiled. "Well, the government needs to take on PwC, EY, Deloitte and KPMG by limiting their market share of UK company audits…"

Ten minutes later, the panel thanked her for attending. She reciprocated, put in her chair and went downstairs to sign out at reception. The sun had come out. She wasn't going to be the next MP for Newbury or anywhere, and she felt fine.

Her parents were waiting to meet her at the station. While they waited for the train, she told them about the interview. When she got to the part about her speech, her mother's face fell.

"Couldn't you just have said you hadn't any firm ideas yet?" she said.

"But I *have* got firm ideas!" Phyllis replied. She hadn't realised before, but she was angry. "That's the *point!*"

"Sounds a bit like socialism to me, Phyllie," her father said.

She rolled her eyes. "Of course it's not *bloody socialism!* Sorry, sorry," she went on, seeing they'd jumped. She was angry at herself now. Annoyed and ashamed for letting her mum and dad down. She wished she'd never come. "It's *Conservatism!* There are a lot of parasites at the top, bleeding the system dry, and no one wants to tackle them because they've cleverly disguised themselves as the kinds of people the Tories are there to help!"

The train appeared just beyond the platform.

"You might find Cynthia Cartwright's husband falls well within the category of people you demonised," her mother said. "No wonder she didn't like what you said!" She smiled. "We'll laugh about it in a few years."

"We'll always love you, Phyllie," her father said. "Give your mum a call when you get back to London. Rubbish job, anyway. You're right. No point in accepting something like that if it's not on your own terms. You did the right thing, as always."

Her mother put her arm round her waist. "I wish I'd been a fly on the wall when you said what you said! Oh well, nothing ventured, nothing gained. Don't dwell on it and *don't be depressed.*

Your father's right. You did the right thing as always. I'll tell Buster what you did when we get in. He'll approve. It's exactly what *he* would have done."

Phyllis was teary, but for some reason the thought of Buster making an impassioned speech about United States Sarbanes-Oxley type laws made her even more so.

"He'd probably have pulled it off," she blurted out as the carriages gradually slowed.

The tannoy announced stops *en route*. She got onto the train. It wasn't like the olden days when you could pull down the window and say last-second things. You had to go straight to a seat and wave from there.

She didn't want to go back to London. She was an idiot. She'd messed everything up. She wanted to stay here and have a second go.

## Chapter 23: Into 43 Wiles Terrace

6pm. A Ford Transit van stood outside a large Victorian terraced house in Hackney. A middle-aged man in an overall got out from the driver's seat and opened the rear doors. Inside, five men sat opposite each other on benches, eating sandwiches. The driver announced that the search warrant had arrived. A round of grumbling. The men packed their food away, picked up their tool bags and converged on number 43.

The key to the property had been obtained from the hospital in which Gloria Shipton had just died. Everyone wiped their feet on the way in. The idea was to turn a place upside-down, then put it right-side up, with minimal trace. They were all used to this sort of thing. They could be in and out in under an hour when necessary, and the owner would never know. The secret to doing it properly was never to rush, and always be aware of the small things. Replacing carpets, restoring objects to their original positions. You began by taking photos from a variety of angles.

Thankfully, due to the warrant, that kind of attention to detail wasn't necessary. But neither was it professional to leave a mess. Always leave things as you find them, that was their motto. Either exactly as you found them, when it was clandestine; or roughly so, when it wasn't.

It took them fifteen minutes to get the first carpet up, and another twenty to remove sufficient floorboards to be able to say decisively whether there was or wasn't anything underneath. What they found was builder's rubble, nothing more. Sometime in the recent past, she'd had cowboys in. Meanwhile, outside, the boffins were arriving in cars. Some of the neighbours were in their gardens, watching, trying to work out what was going on. And the police would probably come in a minute, partly to do the usual *keep back* thing, but mainly to show it was all legit: nothing to fret about, everything here had the authorities' blessing.

There was a front room next to the living room. They went through the same process as before, no less methodically, no more quickly. You couldn't rush something like this, and they were all so practised at it, they always went at the maximum speed possible consistent with their motto.

The final set of boards nearest the window yielded what they were almost certainly looking for: a set of six metal safe boxes. They'd do the rest of the house, just to be on the safe side, but they wouldn't expect to find anything. If you went to the trouble of hiding something under your floorboards, usually you didn't have more than one safe location. Life was too short.

The boffins were inside the house now. A motley crew of middle-class types with names like Giles, Duncan and Camilla, mostly in smart casual wear. Looked like they'd rather be shopping in Waitrose, but that would have to wait. Or rather, that's what they *wanted* everyone to think. Because actually, they were rather excited. You could feel it. *They* were the real centre of attention. *They'd* be the ones to give the verdict. Treasure trove or… whatever the opposite of treasure trove was. Something sentimental but worthless. The sort of junk some old folks *did* hide in safe boxes under the floorboards, probably hoping it'd be excavated some day in the far distant future and put in a gleaming 'museum of mankind'. Their own 1970s love letters from Whitley Bay, something like that. A signed Leyton Orient football programme.

Best be cracking on. The boxes were handed over to Rob, whose job it was to open them.

There were still another six rooms to go yet. Not to mention the loft.

Camilla Burkewitz arrived at 43 Wiles Terrace just after six. The satnav had taken her past the correct exit on the M25. Annoying, but it was a quick turnaround. She had things on her mind.

Equations, mostly. Things most people wouldn't understand. She often missed numbered junctions, even in company with Dierdre, her on-board computerised navigation system, but then it was a price worth paying. She'd hate to be the kind of person who never missed a turn off, but who only ever thought about Twitter.

Anyway, Dierdre didn't mind. She just said *Recalculating*. She didn't go bonkers like some people probably would.

Anyway, if she was slightly late, it didn't matter. She was really here because of Gloria Shipton. The old woman who'd been trodden on all her life by men-who-knew-better. A tragic story, but all too common. *#Metoo*. Going to her house to read her *magnum opus* – if it existed – was more an act of homage than anything. To all overlooked women. And if there *was* something there, however small, she'd stand up for it.

Homage and hope. She hoped there'd be something. Anything.

But there probably wouldn't be. Apparently, her son, who'd been sitting with her when she passed away, said he thought she was delirious. He would know.

The news of Gloria's death came through just as she left Nottingham behind and pulled on to the M1. She pulled into Donington Services for a bit of a weep and a veggie burger. Mainly the latter, because she didn't know Gloria personally, and there was a limit to how much you could cry for an abstraction, however unjustly overlooked.

She arrived at 43 Wiles Terrace just after six. She had no idea when the search warrant had been attained – she'd been told to expect 5.30 – but the GCHQ lot were probably already here. Thanks to Dierdre, they'd probably already pored over everything.

Whatever. At least she'd have done her feminist duty. She could go home and have a drink and not feel guilty.

But wait a minute. Whatever, the GCHQ lot *thought* they'd discovered, she should probably ask to double check it. That's what she was here for. It's what Gloria would have wanted. And she wasn't just Camilla Burkewitz. She was *Professor* Camilla Burkewitz. She could hear Gloria shouting from the clouds, *Don't let yourself be overlooked, Girl!*

She wasn't a girl. She was a woman.

But Gloria was old. It was a forgivable mistake.

She got out of her car, took a few deep breaths and crossed the road in a confrontational frame of mind.

A man stood in front of the house, acting as a barrier. "Sorry, I have to ask who you are," he said. Apologetically: he'd obviously picked up on the fact that her car had arrived from nowhere and she'd walked straight over; that she obviously wasn't a nosey neighbour.

"I'm professor Camilla Burkewitz," she said equally apologetically despite herself, searching in her bag for her card. "I'm from the University of Nottingham."

She found her card and showed it, but it was obvious he already believed her, because he barely looked at it. It could have been a British Rail Travelcard and he'd have waved her through.

When she got inside, a woman warned her to mind where she was walking: five or six men were pulling up floorboards. Introductions were made. Giles Black and Duncan Patel were from Oxford University; the introducer, Patricia Magnolis, was from GCHQ. *You must be Camilla Burkewitz. It's an honour. I'm in awe of your work.* Giles and Duncan assented.

The ground disintegrated slightly beneath her feet, as it always did when important people complimented her. She didn't know Patricia, but she knew Giles and Duncan from academic journals. They were stars of a sort. In the quantum research universe.

"You blew away the Solvay Physics Conference," Duncan told her. "Not that I was there. But I heard about it."

She felt herself blushing. For a second, she wished Dierdre was here. *Recalculating.*

"Shall we go in?" Duncan said. He laughed hollowly. "They've left us a sofa, if we can squeeze up."

They went into the living room. Someone asked about refreshments. Tea was brought. Duncan and Giles and Patricia spoke to each other about the difficulties of getting here, the late time of day and the weather. She had the impression they felt uncomfortable being around her. But maybe she was being too self-centred. Her, her, her. She needed to be friendlier. She should have given them her trademark little wave when she arrived. Too late now.

Suddenly, there was a commotion in the other room. Someone out of view said, "Get Rob", as if Rob was an important person who had a previously untapped level of expertise.

A man stomped through. More men left. They went upstairs in a group.

After five minutes, conversation about geography and climate dried up. Silence fell. Four scientists with nothing to talk about but science – what could be worse? How to start? How to keep going?

Maybe in another world.

A bulky man of about fifty, in an overall, came into the room. His hands sandwiched six or seven small notebooks, of the sort you might buy in a £1 multipack in a corner shop. "Take a look at these," he said. His tone was like the man who'd let her in here: apologetic.

He gave them to Patricia. There were six in all, numbered on the cover.

"Any preferences?" Patricia said.

"We should all huddle over book one," Duncan said. "No point in anyone beginning on book six, is there?"

The others shrugged genially. They huddled closer together, with the two women at the centre. Duncan donned a pair of glasses. Patricia put five of the notebooks on the floor, opened the first, and they commenced reading.

They began by exchanging disdainful glances. For a few minutes, they felt they were looking into an incomprehensible miasma of broken equations with redundant quantifiers and pointless variables. They emitted sighs.

Then, gradually, the mist cleared. One by one, speaking to nobody but themselves, they all made the same awed exclamation.

*My God.*

## Chapter 24: Into the Safe-House

The people carrier sat ten. Its windows had been blacked out so its four principal passengers – the remaining contestants, minus John Mordred - wouldn't know where it was going. The additional three occupants were intelligence agents: Roland, the driver, a shaven-headed ex-army officer in the mould of Kevin, only slightly more talkative, and Suki and Jeff, whose job it was to provide reassurance and to answer any questions. Suki was small and slim, and her formal office wear, smart haircut and precise manners exuded the impersonal, but obliging, efficiency of a private health clinician. Jeff was the opposite: thick Aran jumper, beard, ponytail, jeans, heavy boots, casual demeanour as if he'd always been your best buddy, and that was for love, not money, man. Both types of counsellor.

The contestants came out of their homes with suitcases, looking terrified, like they'd only just realised they *really were* being taken to a safe house. Oh my God! They embraced those they were leaving behind, and in some cases had to be gently prised away by Suki or Jeff.

Mehreen Shah was first to be picked up. She wept bitterly as she left her house. Her mum and dad hugged and re-hugged her. Suki and Jeff spent fifteen minutes reassuring her that she was in the safest possible hands, and she'd probably be back after a week. She hadn't slept since being pushed onto the underground line at Tower Hill. She didn't want to be left alone at night: she wanted a female police officer to sleep in her room. Which was fine, Suki said, they'd arrange it, no problem. She was tall, thin and wore a fake-fur coat, luminous trainers and a Hillsong baseball cap. When she got into the vehicle she blew her nose, whispered hoarsely that she was glad to be going somewhere safe, then clasped her hands, put her head between her knees, and prayed.

Aisha Mirzakhani was next up. She emerged from her flat on Wisconsin Street E12 with two women, with whom she exchanged air kisses. She wore a floaty beige jumpsuit, a hijab and trainers, and she was obese. Jeff lifted her trolley suitcase aboard and she hauled herself on and sat next to Mehreen Shah. When she saw how upset Mehreen was, she put her arm round her, squeezed and smiled. "A bit like going on serious jury duty," she said. "One of those where it's got to be unanimous, so you have to hole up in a hotel room together and thrash it out. Like *12 Angry Men*. I hope the coffee's good. I can't live without my thrice-daily fix."

"It's all filtered," Jeff said. "Or it can be instant if that's how you prefer it. Any brand. You can have everything you want. It's like a five-star hotel where we're going."

They were late picking up Marcus Jobs, the comedian. Marcus was 32, bearded with geeky specs and a Tottenham away shirt. He stood in the middle of the road, waving, like *What time do you call this?* but grinning in a self-depreciating way. His wife and children stood on the pavement, looking cold. When they realised *this was it*, that his ride was here and he was finally leaving, they pulled him to them and hugged him. He had the biggest suitcase so far. He was laughing as he got aboard, but in a slightly hysterical way. "We're all doomed, *doomed!*" he announced, throwing his arms up and waggling his fingers. When he saw Mehreen flinch, he stopped. "Sorry, just quoting *Dad's Army*," he said apologetically. "We're not doomed. Not in the slightest. It was just a joke." He searched in his pocket. "Anyone want a *Polo?* Hey, everyone, what's blue and not very heavy? Light blue."

Aisha and Jeff took *Polos*. As he'd been briefed, Jeff got Marcus talking about being on TV. Suki and Aisha discussed DJ-ing with Mehreen. Roland passed a packet of custard creams back. Everyone seemed to be getting along.

Francis Shaylor was last on their itinerary. Seventy-two, dressed in a tweed sports jacket, an oxford shirt and corduroy trousers, he had grey hair and a little moustache. Because he was a former army major, company director and retired councillor, and "a member of The Worshipful Company of Merchant Taylors" MI7's prevailing assumption was that he'd be unusually conscious of his own dignity and possibly, therefore, the most fractious of the four. However, he'd bought everyone a present: wrapped boxes of chocolate truffles from Fortnum & Mason. He high-fived Marcus Jobs and said how sorry he was about what had happened to Mehreen Shah. He guided the conversation so they talked about everyone in turn, ending with Aisha Mirzakhani and her netball coaching. When they finished talking, he took out a pack of cards. When no one wanted a game – "yet" - he put it back in his pocket with a shrug.

Half an hour later, they pulled onto the wide forecourt of a large detached house with a bay frontage, surrounded by fir trees. Five men standing by the front door advanced to help with the suitcases. The guests were shown to their rooms – adjacent to each other on the first floor – and led on a tour of the house. Finally, they were given an hour to themselves.

At 5pm, they met in the living room where Rita, a middle-aged woman in a suit and holding a clipboard, talked them through the 'protocols'. First and most crucially: they weren't allowed to leave, for their own safety. Second, because there was a possibility that they might be traced through social media or other internet sources, had they left their devices at home? Good. There was no wireless access here anyway, and no phone signal. The living room had a large television with hundreds of DVD's, a full range of channels, but no downloadable TV. A selection of newspapers would be provided each morning. There was a huge choice of books in the lounge: novels, biographies, non-fiction prize winners, straight reference works, and magazines. Anything more could be provided on request. All the rooms had their own landlines. Residents were free to make outgoing calls at any time, all of which would be monitored for security reasons, and which were also encrypted. There was a secure garden to the rear. The house was permanently and heavily guarded, and its perimeter entrances and exits were closed to everyone except authorised personnel. Residents were *probably* in no danger whatsoever but it paid to take precautions. Washing and ironing would be done on request with a turnaround of twelve hours. A housekeeper would be available around the clock to make tea, coffee, rustle up a toasted sandwich or a scrambled egg, or just to chat. From 7 till 10pm, there was an informal bar serving a limited selection of beer, wine and spirits. Any questions?

"Does anyone have any idea where John Mordred is?" Aisha Mirzakhani asked. "Why isn't he here with us?"

"I was quite looking forward to meeting him," Marcus Jobs said. "Bask in his reflected glory. Like, in the radiance of his fifty million votes or whatever it is."

"Twenty-four million seven hundred and sixty something thousand," Rita replied, in a tone that made it clear she thought it was complete nonsense.

Rita smiled. "John Mordred - "

"That's like, nearly half the population of the UK," Mehreen Shah interrupted, in disgust.

"I don't think he can have forged them all himself," Marcus Jobs said. "Joke."

"Let's just get back to the question," Aisha Mirzakhani said. "Where is he? I mean, is he on his way? Or is he too good for us?"

Rita began to answer again, but Francis Shaylor overtook her. "I was looking forward to meeting him too, Aisha. Probably a spy, you know. That 'working for the Foreign Office' stuff's always a smokescreen. Still, not very polite of him to cold shoulder us."

Rita held her hands up. "The reason he's not here is because, unless things change drastically between now and Saturday, he's almost certain to win the competition. That puts him into an enhanced category of risk. You may be interested to know that there have already been two attempts on his life. Both have attempted to mimic natural causes: essentially the same sort of heart-attack that killed Martin Coombes. John Mordred is younger and considerably more robust than Martin, so he survived. But he might not survive a third assault. Imagine if he died while he was in your company. What people might say. You're contenders in the same competition, after all. On the face of it, you've five million pounds to gain by eliminating him. In short, the reason he's not here is for your long-term welfare; because he himself recognised that, if anything were to befall him, you might spend the rest of your lives having to deny false accusations. We simply happened to agree with him."

"Shit, I feel bad now," Mehreen Shah said. "He's obviously as much of a victim as we are."

"Noble chap, by the sounds of things," Francis Shaylor said. "Sorry I spoke ill of him. Although, to be honest, I don't imagine anyone's going to be getting any sort of prize money. I think it's just some kind of sick joke organised by a Russian oligarch. I'm pretty sure 'John Mordred' must recognise that too by now, poor fellow."

"So that's your theory?" Aisha Mirzakhani said. "Russians?"

"Why not?" he replied.

She shrugged. "Could be, I suppose." She turned to Rita. "What's yours?"

Rita looked as if she'd long expected this. "The police cybercrimes unit's spent a long time examining The Ultimate Londoner, and they think it's almost certainly a piece of malware invented for mischievous purposes by someone in this country."

"A teenage boy in a bedroom somewhere in suburbia," Francis Shaylor said. "Forgive me if that sounds a little like stereotyping, but it nearly always is, in these cases, isn't it? Someone with far too much time on his hands, never does any homework, friends are all online weirdos with a penchant for computer coding. Which he shares *in extremis*."

"Talking of Russian oligarchs," Marcus Jobs said, "what about the Russian guy? Igor something?"

"On his way back to Moscow as we speak," Rita said. "He's not a suspect. We had to let him go, although we were reluctant - "

Francis Shaylor stood up. "*Reluctant?* And now he's running away?"

Aisha Mirzakhani looked around her incredulously. "What's to stop him getting there and turning round and going, 'Yah boo sucks, eat my shorts?"

Marcus Jobs laughed.

"Why's he on the plane if we're all here?" Mehreen Shah asked. "It sounds like he thinks the police might be about to uncover something about him!"

Rita held her hands up again. "He's frightened. He believes he'll be safer in his own country than we can make him here. That's his choice and we were obliged to respect it. As I say, he's not a suspect. He'd hardly draw attention to himself by appearing in his own competition and, if he did, he'd hardly poll so few votes."

"Unless he's not much of a programmer," Mehreen Shah said. "Could be."

"He probably wouldn't have waited till now to scarper," Aisha Mirzakhani said. "Once he realised his name was out there, if he'd done it, he'd probably have run a mile."

"In some ways, he really is the Ultimate Londoner," Marcus Jobs said. "He owns more than anyone else in the competition."

"That's not saying much," Francis Shaylor said. "And capital-wise the Russians don't own that much. The biggest owners are Qataris and Americans: the so-called 'Canary Wharf Group'. Then the City of London."

Marcus Jobs yawned. "If Igor has cleared off because he thinks the police are about to discover something, all well and good. It means *the police are about to discover something*. If, on the other hand, he's just scared, good luck to him. Safe journey and all that. Do you need us for anything else?" he asked Rita. "If not, I might just ring my wife and kids, tell them I got here."

"Ditto," Mehreen Shah said. "But as applied to my mum and dad."

Rita leapt in before anyone could pre-empt her. "Absolutely. Dinner will be served at six-thirty. It's lasagne, beef or vegetable, and ice-cream for dessert. I understand none of you have any food allergies? Good." She ticked her clipboard. "That's confirmed then. There are alarm clocks in your apartments, of course, if you wish to use them. And watches. We realise most people tell the time by looking at their phones nowadays."

They got up and went to their rooms. None of them were *Big Brother* fans, but they'd all seen snippets of the show, and that was what it felt like. How long before they became tetchy, unreasonable, and vaguely loathsome, even to themselves? They all made vows to be as nice as possible and spend their infuriated moments – of which there were bound to be some – biting their tongues, reading or watching TV.

Dinner was a good beginning. To their surprise, they got on well, and had things in common. Afterwards, they ordered drinks from the bar. They agreed there was nothing worth watching on television – no access to Netflix or Prime – so Francis Shaylor broke into his cards and they played whist and canasta. When they went to bed, they felt ten times happier than when they arrived, and twenty times better than they'd expected this morning.

Mehreen noticed a camp bed had been put in her room next to what was obviously her own bed. Then she remembered requesting a policewoman to sleep next to her tonight. It didn't seem necessary any more. She felt safe here. When WPC Griffin – a blonde, muscular woman of about Mehreen's age – knocked on her door ten minutes later, she thanked her and said she didn't think it'd be necessary, after all. Griffin smiled impassively. "I'll be around anyway," she said. "If you want to leave the door ajar, I can keep looking in on you."

Mehreen said thank you, that'd be great. She washed her face, climbed under the covers, and said her prayers.

But it was her first night in a strange bed. As always happened, she couldn't sleep. After two hours, she looked at the clock on her bedside – 1am - and decided to cut her losses. A bit of late night TV might help. She donned her dressing gown and stepped out onto the landing. The light temporarily hurt her eyes.

Griffin sat in an upright armchair. She stood up when she saw Mehreen. "The other three guests are in the living room," she said sombrely. She didn't look as cheery as earlier. Maybe she was tired.

Mehreen went unhurriedly downstairs. Something really odd was happening to her. Her visual field was full of paisley droplets, like a Persian carpet. The colours were all mixed up too: a pink wall, yellow carpet.

Yet it wasn't scary. Not at all. It felt normal.

She walked across the hallway and went in to the others. They were sitting side by side on the sofa glued to the TV. Rita and Jeff were there too, standing. No one turned to acknowledge her. Like a weird dream.

The 24 hour news channel, that's what they were looking at.

A ticker-tape band ran across the bottom of the screen. *Breaking: London resident Igor Lazarev dies suddenly in mysterious circumstances on flight from Heathrow to Frankfurt.*

## Chapter 25: A Genuine Contender under One Interpretation

"The Russians are taking it better than might be expected," Ruby Parker said, "but then, they've very little choice. The Germans called in an international team to conduct a preliminary post-mortem almost as soon as he died. And we're on record as having warned him not to travel."

She sat opposite Phyllis and Edna in her office in Thames House. Between them, on the desk, a selection of newspapers, stacked and marked for recycling.

"We invited them to come and have a look at The Ultimate Londoner for themselves," she went on. "But of course, they won't. Igor Lazarev didn't die in Britain, nor in British airspace, and, according to the medics, there's no indication of foul play. To all intents and purposes, he died of natural causes. If the Russians think otherwise, they'll have to prove it in an internationally recognised arena. They've played more than enough weak cards recently and bluff doesn't seem to be working for them any more. We're not worried, nor should we be."

"Obviously, we wouldn't show them Gloria Shipton's notebooks," Phyllis said.

"I think that goes without saying," Ruby Parker replied drily.

"In layman's terms," Edna said, "do we know roughly what they mean yet?"

"Her research interests stretched far beyond traditional computer science," Ruby Parker said, "Amongst other things, the newly emerging field of synthetic biology. Artificial chromosomes, DNA transplantation methods to convert one life-form into another, codes based on the four genetic couple letters. Now, some of that's been done before, but only with bacteria. Deliberately non-contentious. Imagine how much of an uproar there'd have been had it involved brain cells. Finally, imagine someone manufacturing, as a computer program, a synthetic biological neuron that could both replicate itself and retain informational contact with its progeny. Step forth, Gloria Shipton."

"Bloody hell," Edna said. "Sorry, ma'am."

"That's a very simplistic summary of what she appears to have achieved," Ruby Parker said. "Her notebooks also draw on nanotechnology, bioprinting, quantum computing, and half a dozen other disciplines I barely knew existed."

Phyllis blew a flute of air. "So The Ultimate Londoner *thinks?*" she asked.

"Some of the scientists I've spoken to believe it's getting there," Ruby Parker said, "although they also say its thinking wouldn't be anything like ours. Personally, I don't think they know enough to make anything but the haziest of informed guesses."

"If it *is* beginning to think," Edna said, "is it ethical to try and kill it? I mean, that's what we're proposing, isn't it?"

Ruby Parker leaned forward. "Gloria Shipton maintained all along that, if it succeeds in running the competition according to plan, it will have run its course, then it'll perish naturally. So all we have to do is let it accomplish what it was born for. That's ethical."

"But our latest theory is it's killing the contestants to sabotage the competition to forestall its own self-destruction," Phyllis said. "If the program *is* the competition, that doesn't make sense."

Ruby Parker nodded. "Conclusion: obviously, the program *isn't* simply the competition. That seems a reasonable assumption, otherwise what would its subsequent use be? Of the six notebooks under Gloria Shipton's floorboards, the final one – we think - contains the competition rules. The rest relate to the host, which has an indefinite variety of applications. Theoretically, the two things can be untethered."

"So if the competition fails, the competition host survives," Edna said.

Ruby Parker leaned back. "Gloria Shipton insisted more than once that failure of the competition would put The Ultimate Londoner – by which we're now assuming she meant the 'host' part of the program - into 'stasis'. Presumably, a kind of hibernation from which it might one day, somehow, wake up."

"Let's go back to ethics," Edna said. "If it's trying to live, then how can it be okay to kill it?"

"We're not killing it," Ruby Parker said. "We're allowing it to die. There's a difference. We're not doctors, Edna. The Hippocratic Oath doesn't apply. Put it another way. It's killing people. Or we think it is. That ought to be the end of the discussion. We've got Gloria Shipton's notebooks. I wish to God we hadn't, but we have. So the genie's well and truly out of the bottle. If we ever need to build another, we can. But under properly regulated conditions."

They said nothing for a moment, then Phyllis put in: "So 'allowing the competition to run its course': that means getting the remaining competitors to the top floor of the Gherkin in time for the 'award ceremony', right?"

"It wouldn't need to be all of them," Ruby Parker replied. "Just one would do."

"John," Phyllis said.

"John. And of course, he knows about it. He's more than happy."

"Are we sure he's in a right mental state?" Edna asked.

"Not entirely," Ruby Parker said, "but we have no choice. It's either him, or one, or all of, the other four. John's in the risk business, and this falls as much within his job description as it'll ever fall within anyone's. As for his mental state, he's presently experiencing mild delusions: unexpected shapes in his visual field, mistaken colour data. But he's not alone. The other four are experiencing the same thing. And the problems don't seem to be affecting his judgement."

Phyllis frowned. "There is a reason why we're only sending John to the top floor on the night of the so-called ceremony, right?

188

Because we know that the 'host' program will try and stop him getting there. And we'd rather risk one individual, whose job is to take risks, than four."

"You've put it bluntly," Ruby Parker said. "But yes, that's essentially correct."

Phyllis groaned. "It's already in his head. All it has to do is push the right buttons and his heart will pop like an over-inflated balloon. The physical exertion won't help. The lifts will probably be out of order: the program will see to that. What are his chances of making it up forty floors? Nil. It's a suicide mission."

"We're working on it," Ruby Parker said. "I admit, as it stands, you're probably right. So if nothing changes, we may call it off. But there are a few days to go, which may be time to install countervailing agencies. GCHQ are working on the problem, before you ask me. Twenty-four-seven."

"I still don't get it," Edna said. "I mean, any of it. If Gloria Shipton wanted to devise an intelligent program, why did she set it up to run a city's-most-wonderful-citizen competition? Because that's what The Ultimate Londoner is, right? Just a kind of contest with a built-in judge, bit like Simon Cowell or will.i.am? Why not put her invention to work on something worthwhile, like world poverty or the arms race?"

"Eliminating world poverty and stopping the arms race are both broadly logistical problems," Ruby Parker said, "In theory, they don't need thought in the higher-order sense that humans supposedly possess it. No, that requires the ability to discriminate between values assigned to objects in the real world. This was meant as a harmless trial run, a first attempt at a program capable of making credible moral, aesthetic and personal discriminations. If successful, it would progress."

"I thought Gloria Shipton factored John in at the start," Phyllis said.

Ruby Parker smiled. "That appears to have been a lie."

Edna laughed. "So John really *is* the ultimate Londoner?"

"As opposed to, say, the Queen?" Phyllis said. "Who lived through the Blitz and danced in Trafalgar Square on VE day, and who lives in a ginormous house somewhere locally, and owns all the public parks and the whole of Regent Street?"

"And whose family have lived here for, like, yonks?" Edna added.

Ruby Parker sighed. "Choosing an individual on those grounds would have been another logistical problem. It would have come down to assigning ratings for other-generated objective values: existing popularity, fame, historical influence, and so on. This isn't doing that. John's a *kind* of ultimate Londoner. Not the kind any of us would choose – and I strongly agree with you both – but a genuine contender under one interpretation, yes."

"Do we know where the votes are coming from yet?" Edna asked.

"It's creating them out of nothing," Ruby Parker said. "As it accesses more and more information. We think from social media. By that I mean, the *total* social media, distributed globally. 'Digital footprint' is a metaphor. But imagine an actual footprint. Its effects on the subatomic level extend universe-wide. In short, its own votes are the only ones that matter."

"Well, if it loves him that much, it probably won't want to kill him," Edna said.

"Unless it loves itself more," Phyllis said. "And it has to make a choice."

"Personally, I think we're overestimating the extent of the crisis," Ruby Parker said. "I very much doubt whether there really is such a thing as 'artificial intelligence'. I think it's a myth, created by science fiction writers. However, I'm willing to keep an open mind for the purposes of this investigation."

"With respect, ma'am," Edna said, "that puts you well outside the scientific mainstream."

"Whatever you may have heard," Ruby Parker said. "We're not even close to building a computer that can pass the Turing test, and even if we were, it'd probably be sunk by the Chinese Room argument. We haven't time to discuss this now. Computer scientists exaggerate possibilities to obtain research grants. They tend to think like that young lady on the front row in Camilla Burkewitz's lecture: that consciousness is just a functional product of some sort of Gödel-incorporating network. Nice idea, but what does it mean?"

"Sorry, we need to be focussing on John," Phyllis said. "I mean, if he's probably going in to the Gherkin on Saturday night, presumably he's allowed to take a guest or two. It's an awards ceremony, after all."

"He'll have back up, obviously," Ruby Parker said, "yes."

"I'd like to be part of that," Phyllis said.

"Me too," Edna put in.

"I was wondering when you'd ask," Ruby Parker said. "Fair enough – provisionally - but there's a lot can happen in the next five days. I didn't express my scepticism about AI for nothing: it had an important connection to what I was about to tell you."

"Oh?" Phyllis said.

"I've asked Alec to look a bit more deeply into the deaths of Specioza Byanyima and Euan Frederick. Igor Lazarev and Martin Coombes died from heart failure, apparently as a result of their trying to leave London. Obviously, we know Gloria Shipton died from cancer. Lump all five together and it really does look as if we've got a killer computer on the rampage. But Gloria Shipton's death doesn't fit. And if we can rule Specioza Byanyima and Euan Frederick out as well, then we've only got two linked deaths. For all we know, someone could have set Martin Coombes up. Igor Lazarev wasn't old by today's standards, but neither was he young. His death might have been coincidental."

"But didn't the doctor say John's heart had been hit by some sort of shock twice recently?" Edna asked. "That would put him in the same category as Coombes and Lazarev, meaning we've got three linked *cases*, even if only two deaths."

"I admit, I'm not yet sure exactly where I'm going with all this," Ruby Parker said, "but I've learned to trust my gut instinct in such situations. I'll know what I'm looking for when I see it."

"So five days to go," Phyllis said. "I think that means we've got to get some sort of team into the Gherkin, check out entrances, exits, security systems, and so on."

"Ten out of ten," Ruby Parker said. "There's limited public access, of course. Only to the restaurant at the top. Otherwise, the whole thing's privately owned and commercially leased. However, Tariq's been monitoring its security and communications systems. In that sense, we're already well and truly inside. What we've discovered is several internal reports of odd occurrences. Complaints directed to the leasing companies, which the latter may have a vested interest in keeping in-house."

"Meaning they've not been formally passed to the police?" Edna said.

"Exactly," Ruby Parker said. "Except now they have. Phyllis, you've already got a Met alias. Edna, you're Detective Sergeant Leona Quarshie. Pick up your ID at reception, plus the names of the companies whose representatives you've got to interview, beginning with Mark Cooper, the chief leasing agent at Q&FPL. He doesn't know you're coming. Use that to your advantage."

## Chapter 26: Hey, Leave Mithras Out of This

Q&FPL was headquartered in a narrow, forbidding road with bollards and double yellow lines on both sides, in Covent Garden. Kevin drove them there. On the way they read the briefing papers and rehearsed what they were going to say. Edna applied make-up that made her unrecognisable as the celebrity she used to be and donned a peach Sorrento hat and a pair of wire-framed glasses.

"Mark Cooper," Phyllis said. "The aim is to faze him. Let him know there have been complaints about security, get him to send us over there, to reassure us. With any luck, he'll think that, in the time it takes us to get from here to 30 St Mary Axe, he can make a few phone calls, tell everyone in the building to keep schtum."

"But of course, they won't," Edna said.

"Someone always talks. And once we're on the inside, at his invitation, we can range freely. There's a bar on the top floor, a dining area on the restaurant on the thirty-ninth and a variety of other places to socialise, eat and drink. We blend in, we ask a few casual questions, we leave."

"What exactly are we looking for?"

"We know they're experiencing odd happenings. We want to find out how odd, see if we can gauge how that might pan out for Saturday. A building like this isn't just any old skyscraper. It's an organic whole, all parts interrelated, nothing gratuitous. So the first thing we're looking for is what they've got planned for the top floor on the 'award' night. Last thing we heard, they weren't keen on being associated with The Ultimate Londoner. They were looking to cancel the booking, but the system wouldn't let them. Things have been 'odd' for quite a long time, in other words, but funnily, we've heard no more about it. Almost like someone's been trying to keep a lid on it."

"If things *are* going awry, they might be thinking, 'Hey, we've only got to get past Saturday, then everything'll probably go away.'

"'We'll be back to normal.'"

"'We hope.'"

"'Please, God.'"

The car pulled up in the middle of Floral Street. They thanked Kevin and entered the Q&FPL building, a two-storey office block with a smoked glass-front. A young woman in a suit sat behind a desk in the reception area. Several fashionable lounge chairs and a sofa faced her, all unoccupied.

"Can I help you?" she asked cheerily, when the door closed behind them.

In Phyllis's experience, pulling your card out in an everyday office context and saying 'police' never went well unless you hedged it with all sorts of qualifications.

"We'd like to speak to a Mr Mark Cooper," she said, showing her ID. "He's not in any trouble. We'd just like to ask him some questions about the Gherkin, which I believe Q&FPL leases."

"Parts of it," the young woman said. "I'm Jenny, by the way." She reached over and offered a handshake, as if to put herself in the clear. "I'll call Mr Cooper now, see if he's available right this minute."

She picked up the phone and pressed Dial. "Yes, hello, is that Lorraine?" she said. "Hi... is Mark available? I've got two police officers here in reception who'd like a word with him. They say it's nothing serious; he's not in any trouble."

Silence. She held the phone to her ear and smiled apologetically at the DI and the DS.

Suddenly, she jumped. "Oh, yes, hello Mark. Sorry, I've got two police officers here in reception who'd like a word with you. They say it's nothing serious; you're not in any trouble... Okay. Thank you!"

She hung up. "He'll be down in a second. He's just, er..."

They never found out what he was just doing, because he burst in from a door to Jenny's rear with his right hand extended like he was meeting a pair of lucrative customers at an international airport. He was in his fifties, small, dressed in a new suit, and wearing a watch half the size of his face.

"Hi," he said. "Mark Cooper. How are you? Come in, come in. What's this about? Jenny, get us a pot of tea, will you? Please?"

They went upstairs. Cooper's office was small, but fashionably furnished with the latest in contemporary design. It looked like something from a magazine. On the wall, three heavy-framed monochrome pictures of iconic London buildings: The Shard, the Gherkin and BT Tower.

"Sit down, sit down, please," he said, indicating two tub chairs, side by side. He took up position on a third, at a comfortable angle to them, the semi-informal about-to-close-a-deal position which Phyllis recognised from *Mad Men*.

"I think I know why you're here," he said. "But I'll let you start."

"Thank you," Phyllis said, "and thank you for agreeing to see us at such short notice."

"Oh, I've been expecting you for some time! But I said I'll let you start, and I will. Apologies for interrupting. Go on, please."

"We had a report of a spate of thefts in the Gherkin after a series of apparently unexpected events: principally false fire alarms, of which I believe there have been four in the past week?"

"Who complained?" Cooper asked.

"We can't say at this stage," Edna said. "We're just following up."

"Because *I* didn't know anything had been stolen," he went on. "Honest to God, I knew nothing whatsoever about that. What's been stolen?"

"Let's just say it's in the field of cybercrime," Phyllis said. "We're here because the complainant claims he contacted you a few days ago to express his concern."

"Too right," Cooper said. "That's right, yeah. I still don't know who you're talking about, by the way, because I've got four or five complainants. Not just the fire alarms, but something in the water. Sorry, that should be 'something in the water'. Quote marks. I'm not saying it's true. People are experiencing delusions. We've had it all checked, though. Hundred per cent safe, if the water board's to be believed. We've got absences in there also. Lots. People taking time off work because they're freaked out. Which is what it boils down to, basically."

"If you thought something was in the water," Edna said, "shouldn't you have called the police? Tampering with the water supply's a criminal offence."

"We would have done," Cooper said, "if there'd been anything in the idea. Best let the experts be the judges though, surely? Look, sorry, I didn't mean that to sound sarky, it's just, you've probably got enough on your hands, haven't you? With all the knife crime and so on? We called the water board. They gave it the all-clear. End of."

"Mr Cooper," Phyllis said, leaning forward, "if I'm honest with you, you sound a little… *relieved* that we're here. Is that the right word?"

"Too right," Cooper said. "That's right, yeah. I don't like cover-ups. They seem like a prudent measure in the short-term, but in the longer term, they always come back to haunt you. Best be straight with people from the outset. Call it like it is. The problem is, Q&FPL isn't the only leasing company in the Gherkin. We've got a vote, but we've been overruled. Our associates don't want to rock the boat. I tried to tell them, I said, 'It's like *Jaws*. Or it could be. Keep the beach open, don't mess with the tourist trade.' They don't believe me. They think I'm exaggerating. But they don't get it. After the event, it's the cover-up that gets exaggerated. People will assume it must have been the Black Death or something. Because why put a gagging order on it if it's not very serious? And let's face it: we're capitalist Cityboys from The Square Mile. Most of Britain thinks we're out-and-out villains to begin with. It's not like we're ever going to get the benefit of the doubt."

"Would you mind if we went over there?" Phyllis asked. "Maybe take a look for ourselves? It would help if you could authorise - "

"Hey, be my guest," he said. "I mean literally, *be my guest*. You can go over there now if you like, my personal ticket, access all areas. They'll treat you like film stars, truly. I can see you're plain clothes, so you don't have to tell them who you are. I'll tell them you're reps for prospective clients, if you like, looking to rent a floor. Just get to the bottom of it, please. And keep me informed, if you can. I'll get Jenny to call you a taxi."

Phyllis and Edna stood up. Handshakes were renewed.

"You've been exceptionally helpful, Mr Cooper," Phyllis told him.

Phyllis and Edna checked in at 30 St Mary Axe as guests of Mark Cooper. They didn't need to show their IDs. Once inside, they split up, and ninety minutes later, reconnoitred on the top floor. They sat with two lemonades looking out towards Tower Bridge. The sky was blue, the sun shone, and an infinity of little clouds of roughly the same size and shape was arriving from somewhere on the horizon then fading into nothing. Unless you worked in a place like this, seeing the horizon at all in London induced a feeling of unreality, but from here, it seemed to be mainly what the world was. The ground-level greyish bits leading up to it were insignificant.

"It's what I'd call a skeleton staff," Phyllis said. "From what I've been told, about a third of the workers are off sick with something like stress, back problems or a cold. Conveniently unfalsifiable ailments."

"I met a guy called Juma in *Notes* who told me about a hallucination he had. Some sort of wormy things in the toilets. Then weird shapes dancing about in front of his eyes. He convinced himself it was migraine."

"Migraine?"

"Self-diagnoses aren't always sane. He said he had to. He's a manager, and too many of his key staff are off sick. They've had similar problems."

"I met a woman in the rest room," Phyllis said. "I mimicked panic. I said I'd seen some sort of ghost in the mirror. Four or five people came to help me. They all had stories to tell. Variations on a theme: threatening appearances by phantasmagorical creatures."

"Yet Juma says hardly anyone's putting it down to The Ultimate Londoner. Mostly, they think it's something chemical: in the water or the air. Every lunchtime, apparently, there's what's tantamount to a mass evacuation. No one wants to eat in here. The restaurant staff are moaning about it like crazy. They think there'll be layoffs."

"I haven't heard a lot of people putting it down to the competition either. Not everyone seems to know about it."

"One or two people Juma introduced me to put it down to the Roman girl."

Phyllis frowned. "Who?"

"The grave of a young Roman female. Found on the construction site when the Gherkin was built. Preserved and then reburied at the tower's base. Add to that, about fifteen minutes west of here, you've got a pagan temple devoted to the mystery god, Mithras. The Romans are coming. Smash the emergency glass and call for Mary Beard."

"Idiots. The Gherkin's been standing since 2003. Why would Mithras wait till now?"

"Maybe he's been busy."

"And no one knows what's setting the fire alarms off," Phyllis said.

"Unless it's Mithras."

"Hey, let's not diss Mithras."

Apart from the bartender, they were alone in here. Yet, all at once, they had the distinct impression something *was* listening. Something not quite human. They shivered involuntarily.

"We need to get a couple of agents in here on a permanent basis," Edna said. "Something's definitely going down."

"Drink up and let's go," Phyllis said. "I'm beginning to feel very uneasy."

## Chapter 27: Fun, Fun, Fun in a Safe House

*The Wednesday before the awards ceremony*

The third day, Rita thought she'd never seen anyone so happy as the four poor guys they'd brought in for their own safety. Which prompted the obvious, what the hell was going on? To help find out, she met Jeff on the picnic bench at the far end of the garden. An impromptu conference. Important that they all kept sharing perspectives. Four very different individuals under stress, confined together, might well become unpredictable.

Which they had. Just not in the expected way.

Jeff was vaping. He had his feet stretched out in front of him and his legs apart in a manspread. But that was his prerogative. He was paid to play the laid back one - and he was very good at it. A professional free spirit. He blew smoke like he was a bonfire. People like her would get used to vapers eventually, then they'd no longer look a teensy bit strange. But in 2018, they still did. To her.

"Things are going well," he said, when she sat down.

"They seem to be enjoying themselves," Rita replied.

"They're certainly tight-knit. But adversity can do that to people."

"Depends if they're a good fit, of course."

Jeff blew a huge cloud of smoke. "It goes without saying that these four are. We've been very lucky."

"Maybe too lucky. Sometimes too good to be true situations are the prelude to some kind of implosion."

"It's only till Sunday morning. Never look a gift horse in the mouth."

She laughed. "I hadn't looked at it like that: *only a few days more*. I'm not used to dealing with people for such small time-frames."

"Once they've gone, they're no longer our problem. Not that I foresee them having problems anyway. They strike me as uniquely well-adjusted."

"You're right. We have been very lucky."

"I see what you mean, though," he said. "From one point of view. They are a bit… manic."

"Like yesterday morning at 2am?"

"What happened? I wasn't on that shift."

"Didn't you hear, though? They all came downstairs at exactly the same time, switched the TV to a music channel and danced in the living room. For *one hour*. Even Francis and Aisha."

Jeff hooted. "Bloody hell. Good for them."

"The weird delusions they're having, though."

"Yeah."

"Still, they're more than managing them."

"*More* than."

Suddenly, a hundred yards away, the French windows at the rear of the house opened and Francis emerged. He was dressed casually in a striped shirt, a pair of mustard cords, and brown brogues. He seemed to be looking for someone. When he spotted Jeff, he gave a little wave and began to make his way over, performing erratic little jumps as if he might avoid the lawn's wettest patches.

"Everything okay, Francis?" Rita asked, when he was within hearing distance.

He didn't reply. He was still concentrating on not ruining his shoes. When he stopped in front of them, he said, "We've all been watching you from the upstairs window, if that doesn't sound too creepy. Not that it should, of course. You've been nothing but wonderful since we all got here. No, we were simply watching you vaping, Jeff. We thought we'd like to try it. I mean, if you could go out and get us all lots of vaping equipment and teach us how to vape, it'd probably be lots of fun. I'll pay, obviously."

"Heard about you on the dance floor," Jeff said.

"Pity you weren't there," Francis said.

Jeff laughed. "Way past my bedtime. Yeah, sure, I'll get you all some equipment right now. No need to bankroll it. Everything here's on the house. I've just finished, and there's no time like the present. I'll get you a selection of flavours, and you – *we* - can experiment."

"And there is one other thing," Francis said.

"Yes?" Jeff said, after a slightly longer pause than anyone expected.

"We've all talked about it, and we're unanimous," Francis went on. "Whatever happens now, John Mordred's going to be the Ultimate Londoner. But that means, between us, we've got the second, third, fourth and fifth places. That's pretty good. And we feel we should be partying somewhere. In the city, I mean. Not here. No disrespect because, as I said, you've been wonderful. We'd like to leave on Saturday evening. Say about five pm?"

Rita and Jeff exchanged alarmed looks.

"Are you sure, Francis?" Rita said. "Don't you remember why you came here? Think about what happened to the other contestants."

"We've considered that," Francis said. "We came to the conclusion there's nothing to worry about if we all stick together and take care crossing the roads. We don't want to spend the duration hiding our heads under the covers. It's undignified, apart from anything else."

"I'll come and talk to you all after dinner," Rita said. "As a group."

"That's super," Francis said. "I'll go and tell everyone the good news then." He turned and skipped back up the garden.

On her first night here, Mehreen rang her parents just before she went to bed. But then yesterday, she'd called before dinner, and they seemed okay with that. The media wasn't interested in anything Ultimate Londoner any more, so they hadn't been doorstepped by aggressive paparazzi. They didn't expect to be. Everything was just right, and even better. And now, Francis said, the four contestants were probably going to be released on Saturday night, in time to go to a bar somewhere and celebrate.

Because there was nothing to worry about at all. And the more time went on, the more obvious it became. They were winners. Not *the* winner, but still winners. The Ultimate Londoner wasn't like any other competition she'd ever been in or heard about. Even second to fifth places, and despite no one else knowing, it meant something *big*.

Which was so *weird*, when you thought about it. It almost made your head explode! Everything was coming together in a way no one – herself included – really seemed to get. But it was. It *was*.

And to make things even better, she had the tingly feeling that, in some way, when she rang her parents tonight, there'd be good news. Really good news.

"Mehreen?" her mum said. "How's today been?"

"Best time ever. I'm really enjoying it. We got up last night at two and did an hour's workout."

"Wow, that sounds… fun. Two am? Two in the morning?"

"Yup."

"Listen, we've got a surprise for you. Someone sitting in the kitchen here, right now. Someone you won't believe."

"Mum? Are you okay?"

"More than okay, Beauty. It's one of your biggest heroes."

"Okay," Mehreen said. "Stop with the mystery. You're beginning to freak me out a bit. What's going on?"

"Hi, Mehreen," a different voice said. Much younger, female. "Pleased to meet you. My name's Hannah Lexingwood. I'm John Mordred's sister, he of the Ultimate Londoner competition. I had to come round to your parents' house in person, because I thought they'd never believe me otherwise. I guessed they'd probably been getting lots of nuisance calls."

"We haven't," Mehreen's mum put in, from the background. "Not really."

Mehreen's head went airy for a second. "Hannah – Hannah *Lexingwood?*" she blurted out. "*The* Hannah Lexingwood?"

"You've heard of me?"

"Everyone has!" She put her hand on her mouth and ran it over her hair. "Oh my *God!*"

"I want you to come and play for me on Saturday night. We're having a big party in London. My brother's never achieved anything before in his life, although I have recently discovered that he's marginally more successful than I realised. Still, Ultimate Londoner, eh? That's pretty damn cool. Listen, one of the reasons I managed to persuade your parents to see me is that I was able to prove to them that you're not safe. I can change that. I would imagine this is a secure line, yes?"

"I – I believe so," Mehreen said.

"Have you ever heard of the Apple HomePod? Sorry, I don't mean that to sound patronising."

"A smart-speaker. Yeah."

"Well, there's one in your kitchen right now. I bought it as a kind of present for your folks. But also because I wanted to prove something. *Hey Siri,*" she said, "*where is Mehreen Shah of The Ultimate Londoner competition right now?*"

A slight pause and Siri replied: "Right now, Mehreen Shah, of The Ultimate Londoner competition 2018, is living at forty-one Wensleydale Road in The London Borough of Sutton. Forty-one Wensleydale Road is an official MI7 safe house, purchased by the Home Office from a private vendor in 2014."

Elsewhere in the building, in the small attic room where MI7 monitored outgoing calls: disbelief. Then panic. The rest of Mehreen's conversation would be recorded, as per usual, but suddenly no one was listening any more.

## Chapter 28: Alec's 'Sort of' Breakthrough

*The Thursday before the awards ceremony*

Another day, another one-to-one interview in Ruby Parker's office, this time with Alec. As he sat down opposite her, she gestured at the HomePod on her desk. "You're probably wondering what this is."

"Welcome to the twenty-first century," he replied.

"*Hey Siri,*" she said, "*where is Mehreen Shah of The Ultimate Londoner competition right now?*"

A slight pause and Siri replied: "Right now, Mehreen Shah, of The Ultimate Londoner competition 2018, is living at forty-one Wensleydale Road in The London Borough of Sutton. Forty-one Wensleydale Road is an official MI7 safe house, purchased by the Home Office from a private vendor in 2014."

"Bloody hell," Alec said.

"Quite. It works with all varieties of smart-speaker."

"I meant, I never thought I'd hear Ruby Parker use 'Hey' as a mode of address."

She smiled. "Very funny. On the other hand, we do perhaps need to take a step back. Things are getting more and more surreal."

"So what's the upshot? Do our four internees know about it?"

"I'm afraid so. We've managed to persuade them to stay put for now. We're not confident we can move them anywhere 'Siri' won't know about, and at least they're protected by armed guards where they are now. But on Saturday evening, we've agreed to release them into the wild. They want to 'celebrate', and Mehreen Shah is apparently going to play her turntables, if that's the right term, at a concert in Hyde Park to celebrate the fact that John's been voted Ultimate Londoner."

"A public concert? Do we know who's organising it?"

"Oh, yes. John's infamous sister."

Alec groaned. "Hannah. Who else. Does John know?"

"He's due here tomorrow morning. I thought I might as well tell him in person, although of course there's a possibility he may find out before then."

"I wonder how he'll take it."

"I'm not optimistic." She sighed. "This has come at a bad time. As you may have heard, Phyllis is considering leaving the service to pursue a career in politics. I'd really rather not lose her. But if John's forced out, she'll probably follow."

"Quite apart from the fact that John's intrinsically valuable? Or not?"

"Of course he is. That goes without saying. We all know he's both a brilliant linguist and an outstanding detective."

"Talking of outstanding detectives…"

"I dearly hope this is good news."

"It's now official: there's nothing intrinsically mysterious about the deaths of Specioza Byanyima and Euan Frederick. Dianne Speaks, the woman who ran Ms Byanyima down, was linked to her through a nephew whose appointment to a local affairs committee Ms Byanyima personally blocked on the grounds of 'moral unfitness'. Which may have been a tit-for-tat reprisal for an earlier slight to do with an uncle of Ms Byanyima's on her mother's side, the details of which are irrelevant to MI7. I got the nephew to talk, and he said enough to make Dianne Speaks realise further denials wouldn't work. Add to all this the fact that Speaks is taking medication for post-natal depression. Whether she should have been driving at all is a moot question, but again, that's not our concern. Since the alleged disputes, Dianne Speaks has moved house twice, and no longer lives near Specioza Byanyima. Their encounter as pedestrian and motorist was pure chance. It seems Dianne Speaks recognised Specioza Byanyima, saw her step into the road, formed an intention to scare her, and also to get close enough to show who she'd been scared *by*. Obviously, things didn't turn out that way. Personally, I think it would only have been a matter of time before Speaks confessed of her own accord. The police are taking it from here."

"Excellent work."

"There's more. It turns out Specioza Byanyima was never paranoid and she certainly wasn't suicidal. That was a red herring planted by Speaks's nephew, to throw us off the scent. The contrary seems to have been true. In the period immediately before she died, she told her friends she was on a 'high'."

"Interesting. What about Euan Frederick?"

"We know he had a history of depression. But according to two friends of his, he'd tried to kill himself in exactly the same way twice before, within the last six months. He didn't see The Ultimate Londoner competition as a piece of good fortune. On the contrary, the fact that, there he was, on the centre pages of *The Evening Standard*, saying things he strongly believed he *hadn't* said, but which sounded exactly the sort of thing he *could* have said, made him feel he might be losing his reason. For someone whose living is his capacity to think clearly, that's a pretty serious worry."

"And why is that information only coming out now?"

"Suicide's an odd thing. Mostly, people just prefer to say, *He killed himself because he was depressed*, and leave it at that. They don't want to delve into the deeper reasons, and they certainly don't want to discuss them. Who knows what can of worms might turn up? You might find you're partly responsible. On top of your bereavement, that might be too much. What it means here is that, in the immediate aftermath of Euan Frederick's death, we relied too heavily on the suicide note. And suicide notes aren't always dependable, because victims can't always name their own demons correctly."

She nodded. "Very impressive work, Alec. Yet I wonder where it leaves us."

"If Specioza Byanyima and Euan Frederick weren't equally paranoid and suicidal, it may mean that neither of those two were induced by the program. On the other hand, we do know The Ultimate Londoner's got into people's minds. Which doesn't mean it can think. It might be like those optical illusion videos you get on YouTube: 'This will shrink the room', that sort of thing. Except with powers of persuasion to avoid certain actions, above all, in this case, leaving London. We know from Gloria Shipton's notebooks that it's incredibly sophisticated. If it's bringing people back to the capital by putting them into some kind of stupor, then it must be slowing their metabolism somehow. It programs them to come back with reduced life-signs, and perhaps their heart rate slows to the point where it becomes critical. They have a heart attack."

"It sounds like a reasonable theory. Where does it get us?"

"If I'm right, it means the program's not 'intentionally' – I use that word loosely – killing people. They're dying because its method of bringing them back is lamentably crude."

"That would require Igor Lazarev's heart attack to be coincidental."

"Not necessarily, but that is possible. Or it could still be connected to The Ultimate Londoner in the way I've just described. True, Lazarev didn't go into a weird trance, like John, but he may have been about to. He was older than Martin Coombes and, vulnerability-wise, his heart could have been a bit nearer the front of the shutdown queue."

She folded her hands and put her thumbs together. "So how do we explain Michael Preston? Here's a man who pushed an Ultimate Londoner contestant in front of an oncoming train, after having five thousand pounds deposited in his bank account by Colander, the program's financial arm, and who later died of an unexplained heart attack on the tube. That looks pretty damning to me."

He drew a sharp breath. "Granted, yes."

"For all your excellent work, Alec, the only explanation of the Michael Preston incident is that we're dealing with a killer *something*. You only need a single murder to make a murderer.

Specioza Byanyima, Euan Frederick, Igor Lazarev and Martin Coombes become irrelevant in the light of what happened to Mehreen Shah at Tower Hill, and the five thousand pounds that apparently provoked it."

"And yet, as Siri's just revealed, the program knows exactly where she is now, and no harm's befallen her."

"Yet. But of course, she wants to leave on Saturday evening early. They all do. Assuming it 'knows' that, it may be biding its time."

He nodded. "We've still got major problems, in other words."

"In front of however many thousand people in Hyde Park, Mehreen Shah will be a sitting duck."

"We probably need John to dissuade his sister. Which shouldn't be difficult. She thinks she's doing Mehreen Shah a huge favour. Once she realises she could be putting her life in danger, I imagine she'll quickly devise a Plan B."

"I've asked Tariq to keep a close eye on Hannah, find out exactly what she's organising. She's certainly been busy, and unfortunately she's got a huge network of contacts. We can't monitor all of them. We do know, however, that the *Metro* and *The Evening Standard* are back on board. They're going to be running full page ads for the whole thing tomorrow."

"Talk about U-turns."

"And I don't know how many pubs and clubs she's co-opted. Except that it's a lot."

Alec knitted his eyebrows. "She's taking a big risk, isn't she? I mean, it looks a bit smug, celebrating your own brother's triumph in a big competition, especially when it's going to make *him* extremely rich, and you're *already* mega-rich. Like, 'Let's all celebrate my brother joining me in the lap of luxury. Never mind that you people celebrating are going to continue to live in drudgery.' Not terribly sensitive."

"She's a very intelligent woman. She twigged that at the outset. That's why just about all the major events are going to be free, with free benefits: food, non-alcoholic drink, a variety of goodies. She's hired every security firm available, to help keep the peace. To give her her due, she knows how to deflect criticism. She's already on the PR trail, making all the above explicit, just in case it's not already crystal clear. 'I don't expect anyone to have to pay to celebrate my kid brother. The party's on me.' It seems to be working. And the amazing thing is, she's managed to keep her own involvement secret from John, as far as I can tell. He knows people intend to celebrate. He doesn't know who put them up to it. In another life, she'd make an excellent intelligence officer."

"I suppose it's a waste of time, asking for Saturday evening off?" He held his hands up. "Joke, it was a joke."

"I suppose you read Phyllis and Edna's report?"

"Strange Goings-on at the Gherkin? Have we got anyone in there?"

"Suki and Victor. Under minimal cover as security management officials from a rival firm to the one the owners already employ. Doing a week-long 'audit'. They're authorised to be there all day and all night, if necessary."

"How long have they been in there so far?"

"Between them, twenty-four hours."

"Noticed anything odd?"

"Roughly the sorts of things mentioned in the report. Nothing first-hand."

"Top floor still indeterminate for Saturday?"

"Quite the contrary. It's booked for The Ultimate Londoner award ceremony. It won't unbook, that's the issue."

"Why can't we just get John in there, send him in the lift to the top floor, and keep him there till one minute past midnight on Saturday? I mean, get him in there right *now*."

"Because there's no telling what might happen to him. The two train journeys showed he was vulnerable, and now he's experiencing mild visual delusions. It might be like putting a puppy in a lion's cage."

"But he's going to have to go up there at some point before midnight, isn't he?"

"Hemmed in by proper safeguards, yes. At least as safe as we can make them. That's what we're working on now."

"He'll need company. He's allowed to take guests, I assume. I mean, I'm just playing along with the conceit of the 'competition' for a moment. I'd like to accompany him."

"Phyllis and Edna have already bagged that job. I don't want to risk all my agents by putting them in the same basket."

"Well, if either of them cries off, I'm your man."

"I think that's extremely unlikely, but thank you, I'll bear you in mind. Well done again for getting to the bottom of Specioza Byanyima and Euan Frederick. This has been an extremely useful debrief from my point of view."

He stood up to leave. "If only we could get to the bottom of Michael Preston."

She smiled. "Sometimes, sadly, things are what they appear to be. But I fully share your sentiment."

Suki and Victor were in the Gherkin's reception area when the sixth fire alarm that week went off. They could almost hear everyone in the building groaning in unison. The lifts stopped working in the event of a fire, and there were over a thousand steps in each stairwell. Mostly, you weren't near the top, so it wasn't *that* many. Still, it was far from enjoyable. Yes, you were descending, but it got hard on your knees after a few flights.

Probably no one believed there was a real fire right now. It was a break from work, that's all. The fire engines would come, the chief inspector would do a tour of duty, give the all-clear after about an hour, then everyone would trudge back in again. In the meantime, you'd have to give your name to your line manager, and just stand there like a muppet. Some firms would let you go off to The Counting House for a drink, but not all. Inside or out, fire or not, you were still on company time.

Since Suki and Victor were already at the base of the building, and they'd registered 'out' at reception, technically they were free to go home. But that wasn't consistent with their cover. They went to stand on the opposite side of St Mary Axe. People arrived alongside them from within the building, a slow trickle at first, then a steady stream, not quite a torrent. Mostly, they looked fed up, and had their arms folded or thrust into their trouser pockets. No one spoke. They'd done all their best moaning the first and second time it happened.

It wasn't a cold day, but neither was it warm, and standing still for a long time, you might easily catch a chill. The police would arrive with the fire engines, set up a cordon. All very dull, all wholly predictable.

Then the front doors began to buzz shut. An interested murmur set up. Victor and Suki couldn't fail to notice the common denominator.

*That's never happened before.*

## Chapter 29: The Apparent Sonic Cannon

*Still the Thursday before the awards ceremony*

Mordred sat with a book in his lap in his room somewhere in London. It looked like his wasn't the only head The Ultimate Londoner had got into. Apparently, the remaining four candidates were having similar experiences. And now *The Evening Standard*. Given how narked Timothy Grendell had sounded in Phyllis's report, and how much flak the *Standard* and the *Metro* had already taken over the competition, what else but a sudden mental invasion could explain their sudden volte-face? Because it wasn't just a modest one. No, they were going all out to make Saturday's awards ceremony into a major jamboree. Rationally considered, that was sinister.

The landline rang. He picked up, expecting Phyllis.

But it was Ruby Parker. "By way of keeping you informed," she said, "we've something of a 'situation' at the Gherkin. There was a fire alarm. Once everyone was outside, the doors closed, and no one seems able to reopen them. They're locked, in other words, from within."

"What about smashing the windows?" he said. "They do constitute ninety-nine per cent of it. Or has The Ultimate Londoner used nanobots to change the molecular structure of the glass?"

She gave a polite chuckle. "Rather more mundane than that, I'm afraid. The owners, the leasing companies and the businesses have thrown in the towel against the fire alarm. It's got them well and truly beaten. They've sent all their staff home and told them not to bother coming back till next Monday. Meanwhile, they're claiming insurance for the lost hours. The fire engines have gone home, of course. A small security team's outside, moving on the snooping and the curious. In short, no one's allowed anywhere near the building, let alone inside it, till the start of next week. And right now, that includes us."

"If 'wait till next week' is their solution, it means someone at least must believe The Ultimate Londoner's to blame. I wonder what'll happen about the awards ceremony."

"It's a simple matter of us obtaining a search warrant. We'll get you in on Saturday evening, whatever happens. I simply wanted to keep you informed."

"I've just been reading *The Evening Standard*. It seems everyone in the media's had an identical Road to Damascus conversion."

"Yes, so I understand," she said, in the tone of voice she used when, actually, she knew why, but for some reason, she wasn't going to tell you unless you asked.

"Any idea what's going on?"

"Are you sure you really want to know?"

With anyone else, this would have been the cue for dripping irony. "Yes, please," he said.

"Your sister's been rattling cages and pulling strings. She's used her considerable powers of persuasion to orchestrate what she expects will be a glowing tribute to her little brother."

His stomach fell. Of course. It was obvious. Why hadn't he thought of it?

"John, are you still there?"

"So we're putting me into the Gherkin on Saturday night, and there's a reasonable chance I'll be killed. That's going to be a bit of a downer for her. 'Your brother went to pick up the award, but sadly, his host for the ceremony murdered him. Sorry about that. Enjoy the rest of your evening.'"

"We didn't put her up to it, John. We didn't realise she was up to anything till yesterday, when she turned up out of the blue at Mehreen Shah's parents' with a view to getting their daughter to play at a concert she's organising. We thought you might be able to persuade her to quietly drop the idea. At that point, we had no idea she was planning anything else."

"Bloody hell. And Mehreen Shah agreed, I suppose?"

"That can be taken care of. By you, ideally."

"I'll do my best. What a mess."

"You can choose not to enter the Gherkin tomorrow night, and we might well make that decision for you if we think it's too risky. Nothing's set in stone."

"Any good news at all?"

"I don't know whether you'd call it that. Alec's shown fairly conclusively that the deaths of Specioza Byanyima and Euan Frederick weren't caused by The Ultimate Londoner. He put together a pretty good case that the program's never been out to cause any deaths, actually. Until he got to Michael Preston and Mehreen Shah, of course. There, he hit an immovable obstacle."

"Hmm."

"What do you mean?"

"Could you get Alec to write his report up as a matter of urgency? And could you send me a copy, once he's finished? Then I'd like to come over to Thames House and review all the evidence relating to Michael Preston."

"With an eye to what? It's an open and shut case, surely?"

"But what am I doing here? Sitting on my hands."

She sighed. "I'll send you a hard copy of Alec's report in about two hours, when he's finished writing it. And a driver. Be ready to leave, and you can read it in the car."

He thanked her and hung up.

Six hours later, early evening, outside the Gherkin. Two security guards in black company uniforms stood chatting and rubbing their hands. Two more sat in a black van further up the road. A group of drinkers stood outside The Slug & Lettuce across the road. A taxi went by. Overhead, you could just make out a few stars. Somewhere, a plane.

A low-pitched hum too. Difficult to say where from.

Then a glass shop front broke. The guards recoiled slightly and looked at each other as the remnants crashed on the pavement. Like a dream – you didn't know what was happening because it wasn't in your range of expectations. Even less so when glass was smashing everywhere.

The drinkers ran inside. A passing lorry veered onto the pavement. The windscreen in the security van imploded. The guards ran. Behind them, a panel from the Gherkin dropped onto the road and exploded like a bomb.

Out of sight somewhere, people screamed. Fire bells rang. The hum intensified. The detonations went on.

Then, just as suddenly as it had all begun, it ended.

But the flying glass had done its work. There was blood. Lots of it.

Thames House. Mordred was on his way alone from the library for some air on the fourth floor balcony when Suki found him and told him about it. He went straight to Ruby Parker's office. It was only a matter of time before she called him in, and it was faster than finding a TV.

"Were there many casualties?" he asked, as he sat down

"No one was killed," Ruby Parker said. "There were injuries. None critical."

He'd spent the evening at work, looking through everything relating to Michael Preston. He and Phyllis and Edna had eaten in the canteen together. He'd sleep in one of the underground pods tonight.

"The area round the Gherkin's been evacuated for a quarter mile radius," she said.

"So what happened? Do we know?"

"A prolonged sonic blast, apparently emanating from within the building. It smashed all exterior glass within the evacuated range. First reports talked of an explosion. We assumed there'd been some sort of terrorist attack. Which, in a way, there had."

"*All* exterior glass? So I'm assuming the Gherkin itself's a write-off?"

"On the contrary. It seems to have weathered the whole thing exceptionally well. Of course, it has suffered some damage."

"And we're assuming the program caused this?"

"That's our current working hypothesis: that the same thing that caused the doors to lock also caused the sonic blast."

"Its purpose being what?" He laughed. "To make it even more difficult for me to get to the top floor on Saturday night?"

"Our plan was to force the doors, get you in that way. The blast's made us wary. Apart from anything else, right now, we've no idea how dangerous applying force at ground level might be."

"Great. And if I do get in, a stairwell might just disintegrate when I'm halfway up, or the whole thing might topple over. I must say, I'm really looking forward to Saturday night. On the other hand, I probably won't bother getting my evening suit dry-cleaned."

"We'll see what Tariq and GCHQ have come up with tomorrow. If I'm not one hundred per cent convinced, I'll veto your involvement. Any progress on Michael Preston?"

"None yet."

"As I said, I'm not optimistic."

"And yet, it's the thing that most challenges the position Alec tells me you hold: that The Ultimate Londoner's not intelligent; that no computer program can really 'think' in the way humans can. Here we have the program *apparently* selecting Michael Preston as a suitable assassin, paying him to do the job, and presumably giving him instructions. If that's not intelligent, what is?"

She took a deep breath. Silence held sway for a moment. "I hadn't looked at it like that," she said. "You're right. And now we've got it *apparently* closing the Gherkin's doors from within, and *apparently* discharging some kind of sonic cannon designed to stop you reaching the top of the building on Saturday night."

"When you've got that many uncanny resemblances, at some point you've got to think, maybe things aren't just *apparently* this way. Maybe they *are* this way."

"You may be right. Okay, so for the purposes of this investigation, I'll assume The Ultimate Londoner can think. How does that help us?"

"I'm not sure it does, but as you said earlier in the process, it's important that we're all on the same page."

"Point taken. You need to get to bed, John. One last thing. On Saturday night, you really are going to have to wear an evening suit. And Edna and Phyllis, if they're going to accompany you, are going to have to dress for a party. Amber will take care of the details. Because if your sister turns up, as she probably will - despite our best efforts to waylay her - we can't afford to refuel her suspicions that you're not what Phyllis said you are."

He got up. "Point taken. Good night."

"Good night, John."

## Chapter 30: Say Hi to Trident

*Friday. The day before the awards ceremony.*

The Thames House sleeping pods were located in an underground room with ten large drawers, each containing a bed. You pressed a button. Your bed came out. You hopped on and laid down. You pressed a button. Your bed withdrew into the pod. You slept, or tried to. At eight o'clock, a gentle alarm woke you. Your new clothes - or your old ones, dry-cleaned and ironed - awaited you in the cloakroom. You showered and put them on. You ate a bowl of Weetabix in the canteen, had two cups of strong tea and read whatever newspaper happened to be lying on the table.

Mordred couldn't help noticing there was an unusual amount of activity in Thames House for a Friday. Whether it was down to The Ultimate Londoner, he didn't know. But it was obvious there were two groups: people who knew what was going on – mostly high-level managers, by the look of them - and whose behaviour indicated a quiet panic; and those who didn't, and who went about things as normal. The latter group was by far the biggest, but the former completely overshadowed it simply by its intensity. Its members were busy, busy, busy. And frightened. Yes, they were: they were scared of something.

If he was meant to know what, then sooner or later someone would find him. Probably the usual summons to Ruby Parker's office.

Alec sat down opposite him, like he'd appeared from nowhere. He wore a suit and tie and a fraught expression.

So he was obviously one of those in the know. And he was likely here to perform some sort of initiation into the big secret.

"Sleep okay?" Alec said. "Drink that tea," he said, before Mordred could answer, "and follow me to the basement. I've booked us an office. I've been instructed to brief you."

Mordred did as commanded. They went to the lift and got in without speaking. Alec pressed B1, the doors slid shut and they descended.

It had to be pretty serious for Alec to have said nothing more yet. The lift bumped to a stop, the doors pinged open. They walked down a corridor and turned left into an office. Alec closed the door behind them. There were two chairs before a desk without an occupant.

"Don't worry," Alec said, apparently seeing Mordred's glance at the vacant seat. "This is Edward Anantharao Venkatesh Sai Laxman's office."

"Who?"

"It doesn't matter. He won't be coming back. Not today."

"What's going on?"

"Well, it's like this. We've lost control of Trident. Apparently, two of Britain's nuclear armed warheads are pointing at the capital. They're due to launch tomorrow night, one minute after midnight."

"Right."

"I'm not joking. Four of our submarines run on the outdated Windows XP system, and they need frequent access to the internet when the boats are updating their operating systems. SMCSNG – Submarine Command System Next Generation – runs XP. In short, it's been hacked. Sounds pretty easy to do, right? Guess what: it is."

"I read something about that in *Private Eye*, last year."

Alec pulled the flesh down on his face. "If only you'd written to your local MP." He laughed. "God, I'm hysterical. Have you accepted that I'm not joking yet?"

"Are you?"

"No."

"Bloody... hell."

"That's better. Let it all out."

Mordred let out a hard breath like he'd just been burned. "Okay, so who's behind it?"

"Not 'who'; 'what'. The Ultimate bloody Londoner."

"Are we sure?"

Alec turned to face the desk. *"Alexa, who took control of Trident last night and pointed it at the capital of Great Britain?"*

A voice from nowhere: "The Ultimate Londoner took control of Trident on Friday morning at precisely 3.15am, and targeted it at London. The missiles are due to fire at one minute past midnight tomorrow night."

They sat in silence for a few seconds.

"Wow," Mordred said.

Alec stood up, his eyes bulging. "'Wow'? *'Wow'*?"

"Sorry, I'm still getting my head round it."

"So the hell am *I! Windows bloody XP?* Why do we live in such a *crappy* country, John? Everybody's either an amateur or a complete moron! And they're all *proud* of it! It was exactly the same when I was in the army! You never got the right equipment, and it was always down to some *half-arsed, no-nothing, chinless nonentity in Whitehall!* How we ever managed to run an empire's completely beyond me. I'm telling you, the Americans would never make this kind of mistake. Why? Because the USA's a *proper country*, that's why!" He threw his hands up. "I say 'mistake'. What am I saying?"

"So what happens now? Mass evacuation?"

He sat down again and swallowed hard. "Apparently not. No, we've a very precise *modus operandi* for this kind of thing. One that makes a weird kind of sense, but that's probably just because I'm freaking out."

"Go on."

"In the event of an imminent nuclear strike on the capital, the idea is to keep as many people as possible from finding out about it. All those who do know about it are expected to keep quiet, stay in the capital and die along with the rest of its inhabitants."

"That's… brilliant."

"Once you've thought rationally about it, and detached your head from every big-budget Hollywood disaster movie ever made, it's a hell of a lot saner than you probably imagine."

"What about the Prime Minister? Does she have to stay and die too?"

"She's not a living deity, John. She's just some bod with a better-than-average education, chosen by the party faithful and fairly reluctantly elected by thirty-seven per cent of the eligible population. No, she nominates a suitable successor – someone in the provinces – and then dies nobly with the rest of us. The successor doesn't find out until after we've been hit."

"'The good news is you're the new Prime Minister.'"

"'The bad news is Britain's now a post-Armageddon dystopia.'"

"What about the Queen?" Mordred asked. "Aren't we even going to evacuate her?"

"She helped draft the whole thing. If she's away on an official visit when the bomb drops, fair enough. Otherwise, she'd rather not know. It wouldn't look good her making an unscheduled rush for Balmoral when no one else gets evacuated. If she dies, she dies, that's her view. A bit like you. What scientists call the *so bloody what* approach."

"Won't it leak out?" Mordred said. "I mean, sorry to go on. But these things always do get out. And what if someone asks Siri or Alexa or another smart-speaker?"

"Firstly, no one's going to ask that precise question. Secondly, if they did, they wouldn't believe the answer. Thirdly, if it does leak out, no one will believe the leaker. They'll just think, *Why isn't Theresa May heading for a bunker in rural Yorkshire?* You see, the policy of staying put, making yourself visible, then getting fried, has its advantages. Subsequently, apart from anything else, no one can accuse you of cowardice; or the upper classes of shafting the lower. You go down with your sinking ship, Royal Navy style.

All things considered, it makes for a much more congenial aftermath."

"Does Phyllis know?"

"She was told last night. Edna too. Ian, yes. Not Suki or Victor. Annabel doesn't know either. She's still in Cyprus, so likely to become the new head of MI7's Red department on Sunday morning."

"So if this is connected to The Ultimate Londoner," Mordred said, "how do I fit in?"

"I wondered when you were going to ask that."

"Sorry, I should have raised it before."

"No worries. We've still got thirty-nine hours."

"And the answer is?"

"Well, I'm no scientist, but from what Ruby Parker told me, there's a theory that, if the competition fails, the part of the program 'hosting' it will unshackle from the thing it's hosting – like a butterfly casting off its chrysalis – and the freed entity will immediately seek to destroy us on the grounds that we represent the most significant detectable threat to its survival. It's making preparations for that."

"So once again, this boils down to me having to get to the award ceremony."

"I believe that's it in a nutshell, yes."

"Where's Ruby Parker?"

"She's attending a series of *Don't panic Mr Mainwaring* meetings in Whitehall, I believe. She won't be back till this afternoon."

Mordred laughed. They both laughed. But without the usual enjoyment.

"Okay," Alec said, when they'd finished. He reached into his pocket and pulled out an electronic wristband. "I need you to put this on. If you try to leave Thames House, it sets an alarm going."

Mordred laughed again.

"What's so funny?" Alec said. "Apart from everything."

223

"I manage to escape, and make it to King's Cross. When the train gets to Arlesey, I nod off, disembark, and end up on the Circle line just as the missiles hit."

"Yes, very droll."

"A complete waste of an escape."

"Still, at least you died in your sleep, which is more than can probably be said for me."

"You could have a few drinks."

"It's not the same. Anyway, alcohol's a depressant."

"In any case, I'm not going to try and escape. It was a joke."

"Which is exactly what you *would* say if you *were* planning an escape."

"Why would I try to escape?"

"I was joking. We both were. We're at cross-purposes here because we're delirious, hence our lack of mutual understanding."

"Right."

"Anyway, don't try to go to church, because it'll set the alarm off. If you want a votive candle, send out for one. We're keeping you here for your own safety and ours. Right now, you're our only hope of avoiding Doomsday. So don't use the stairs, use the lift, etcetera. Think: safe and boring."

"What am I expected to do? Sit in the canteen all day?"

"Not necessarily. We've set you up a little room of your own in room L9. Sofa, two armchairs, TV, magazines, a selection of books, e-reader, and so on. Plus a butler, so you can send out for anything. We've thought of everything. Well, not 'we'. I didn't have anything to do with it."

"Beer?"

"If you want."

"Phyllis?"

"Beer and Phyllis. Every man's dream. Yes, if you want."

"Am I allowed to ring my parents?"

"I don't know. I haven't got the answer to every question, John. I'm not Alexa. Alexa, can John ring his parents?"

"I'm sorry," Alexa said, "I don't know the answer to that."

"You've probably got a landline," Alec said. "I imagine things will be roughly as they were at Fowler's. The other thing is, you're going to be accompanied at all times by two bodyguards, Tim and Barend."

"I thought there might be a catch. Will they be sitting in L9 with me and Phyllis?"

"They'll probably wait outside. I don't know."

"Do they know about the end of the world?"

"No. Sorry, I should have told you that. So don't mention it to them. They'll only think you're crazy. Don't mention it to *anyone* unless you're a hundred per cent sure they've got clearance."

"What's their purpose? Tim and Barend?"

"Stop anyone abducting you. Look, like I said John, you're infinitely valuable right now. We've got to cover all possibilities, no matter how small."

"Thirty-nine hours, and the Navy can't defuse a Trident?"

"I don't know how Trident works, John, and nor do you. I don't even know if it's a countable noun. Anyway, let's err on the side of caution for now, eh?"

"Can't we just blow up the submarines?"

Alec sighed like one more question would tip him permanently into the abyss. "They probably will. But I'm sure The Ultimate Londoner will have taken that into account. Which likely means it has other options. Most governments probably wouldn't tell us if their nuclear warheads were inadvertently locked on us. It'd be too embarrassing."

"Fair enough. If caution means me sitting in L9 with a TV, an e-reader and two bodyguards, bring it on, I suppose."

Alec got up. "Shall we go and meet Tim and Barend now?"

"For what purpose do they think they're guarding me?"

"They don't know. That way, you don't have to lie. Why complicate matters?"

## Chapter 31: The Different Degrees of Bad News

*Friday. Five minutes after the end of the last chapter.*

Phyllis got off the tube at Westminster and walked to work along Abingdon Street, behind Westminster Palace, where the sun shone for the penultimate morning. Because on Sunday, this might be just a mile-wide hole. Which felt overwhelming. All these people.

God, she could hardly hold her head up.

But she had to. Because that was the British way. Stiff upper lip, carry on regardless.

Yet what was the alternative? 'Mass evacuation': it sounded so innocuous. But only the army and the police combined could organise something like that, and then people would suspect a *coup d'état*, especially out of wartime. There'd be riots and looting. Despite your best efforts, probably most people wouldn't leave the capital. You'd have to prise them away with a crowbar, and you'd fail. And who'd evacuate the army and the police?

And say the bombs didn't fall? What kind of hellhole would you come back to?

This way, no one would ever know what had happened. The last day of their lives – hers too - would arrive just like any other. And at 12.01am, most of them would be asleep anyway. They'd know nothing.

Unless they were at the bloody parties. But what could you do about that?

Yet even then, they wouldn't be aware. The merest flash.

The government would probably close the Underground a few hours beforehand, stop people getting trapped in its deepest regions. Probably the most it could do, practically.

226

The outskirts would likely be worst – Watford, Woking, Dartford - where people survived.

Then the radioactivity. The sickness.

Even if, by some miracle, you *could* pull off a mass evacuation, probably most evacuees would be dead in a year or two anyway. Much better –

Her phone rang in her bag.

She shuddered as she took it out. *Hannah*.

Bloody hell, great. "Hi, Hannah," she said cheerily.

"Hi, Phyllis. I'm just ringing because you know what day it is tomorrow, don't you?"

"You mean, The Ultimate Londoner."

"John's way, *way* in the lead. Have you seen the papers yet? This morning's papers, I mean. It turns out the whole 'Curse of the Ultimate Londoner' thing's complete bullshit. Who'd have thought it, eh?"

"You mean - "

"The parliamentary intern that got run down. And Euan Frederick. Both tragic but completely explicable. The bloody tabloids want taking to court."

"There's still Igor Lazarev."

"Yeah, but he was on medication. Even the Russians accept that was unlucky, and we all know what they're like nowadays. Martin Coombes, the same. Man loved his Lambretta, true, but also loved his booze, bless him. No disrespect. He was a lovely guy, by all accounts. Just not the victim of a supernatural curse. Anyway, enough about that. The reason I'm ringing is to find out what John and you are doing tomorrow night. I'm conveniently in town. I thought we could meet up."

"That'd be lovely," Phyllis said as enthusiastically as she could. "I'm not sure John's planning anything. Have you heard what happened to the Gherkin?"

"Yeah. Surely, there's an alternative venue, though? Haven't you heard anything?"

"Nothing whatsoever. And we're not expecting to. To be honest, I'm not even sure it's a real competition. John doesn't think it is, and I'm inclined to agree with him."

"But what about the five million?"

"As far as I know, a condition of receiving it is that you have to attend the awards ceremony. If the venue's inaccessible, and there's no designated alternative, that would mean the competition becomes void."

"Couldn't we, say, sneak into the Gherkin? I'm up for it if you are."

Phyllis laughed to conceal her alarm. "I think you probably need to talk to John. A pair of his nearest and dearest attending isn't likely to satisfy the terms and conditions."

"But I wanted to keep my being here a *surprise!* That's why I'm ringing you."

Phyllis stopped in her tracks. She couldn't carry on talking. The whole thing was getting too emotional.

There was a low-level wall by the side of the pavement. She sat down on it.

"Are you still there?" Hannah asked.

"Y – yes. I've just snapped my shoe heel."

"Are you okay?"

"I think so. I'd better get off the phone. I'll need to call a taxi."

"Take care. Call me if you need *anything at all*. Like I say, I'm in town. Otherwise, I'll get back later."

When she'd hung up, the emotion subsided. She wasn't going to cry. Not any more. It was simply the mental picture of Hannah on Saturday night, so happy to be with her brother, so gung-ho about climbing the Gherkin, so full of the joys of life, so tragic.

Her phone pinged, making her jump slightly. A text. She looked wearily at the screen.

*Bad news, I'm afraid. You didn't get it. Dad and Buster and I love you. Call me tonight. Mum.*

She laughed. Bad news.

After Alec, Mordred went straight to his cell. L9 was on the top floor, possibly to make it harder for him to escape, and it had a dull view of Thorney Street at the rear of Thames House. It began to rain shortly after Phyllis arrived.

"I'm here to sit with you," she said quietly as she came in. "If you want me to, that is."

"It'd be ten times great," he said.

She sat down. But what to talk to her about? The end of the world? Tim and Barend were outside. They might overhear. Anything else seemed wrong somehow. And there were still thirty-eight hours to go. It felt more like a public library in here than a lounge.

It occurred to him they might never be alone again. He had to be watched, and that was non-negotiable. Even when they went into the Gherkin together, Edna would be there.

Yet they'd be re-united in the afterlife, 12.02 on Sunday morning. Probably. He'd certainly have a few more questions for Gloria Shipton.

After ten minutes, Phyllis asked him if he wanted the TV on. He didn't. Nor did she. She picked up a newspaper and read.

He hadn't expected being in here to be much fun, and it wasn't. Everyone seemed to have forgotten that he'd been looking into Michael Preston.

Not that it mattered overly. There'd only been a limited amount of information relating to the case, and he'd been through it a dozen times. Yet the nagging feeling that he was missing something...

... Meant that he resembled a character in an old-fashioned detective novel, yes. The truth was he desperately *wanted* there to be something. Not because it would improve matters – it wouldn't even help crack the case, because this wasn't a 'case' in any normal sense – but because it would give him some small glimmer of satisfaction. It would show he could still think. *Knight to d2 and that's checkmate in four.* That type of satisfaction. Meaningless satisfaction.

"Penny for your thoughts," Phyllis said when she'd finished reading.

"I'm thinking about Michael Preston and Mehreen Shah."

"What about them?"

"From what I've been able to discover, he became obsessed with her after seeing her photo in *The Evening Standard*, the night the competition was announced. He spent a long time online stalking her under various different monikers, then five thousand pounds arrived in his account. Presumably the program had discerned his suitability for its purposes. Next thing, he pushes her onto the tube line. What's missing is any kind of explicit instruction from the program to despatch her."

"Why do you need that? There was no explicit instruction to you at Arlesey. Anyone looking for physical evidence of 'Get off the train, John, and walk back to London' would be disappointed. Why assume it's any different here?"

"There's something not quite right about it."

She chuckled. "Except that's incorrect for reasons I've just stated."

"I don't think the two cases are equivalent."

"Well, you've got another thirty-odd hours to discover what separates them. Then it becomes academic. Fancy a game of scissors, paper, stone? That sometimes helps clear your mind."

"How long till we're invited downstairs to look at the plans for tomorrow?"

"Depends when Ruby Parker gets back from Downing Street."

"Really? That's where she is now?"

"So I heard. At least, about an hour ago. Not that it makes any difference where she is. Or where any of us are."

"We're going to survive," he told her. "It's all going to be okay."

She nodded and smiled. "It's not impossible. But the odds are stacked against us."

"We'll see. Wait till we find out what Tariq and GCHQ have come up with."

Ruby Parker didn't arrive back in the building until 2pm. By that time, they'd eaten lunch in the canteen with Alec – spinach cannelloni for Mordred and chicken pizza for Alec and Phyllis – and discussed the weather. Tim and Barend had ham and eggs and sat at the far end of the table. They weren't interested in the weather. They talked about Manchester United.

Eating seemed to cheer them up. They invited Alec to L9. They drank tea and played Trivial Pursuit, then the call came down to report to Conference Room 6 in the basement. Their hearts seemed to leap and sink at the same time. This wasn't quite it, but it was a recognisable landmark on the road.

Tim and Barend received instructions to escort Mordred as far as the ground floor, then wait for his return within sight of Colin Bale. The descent of the lift felt oddly symbolic in a way it never had before. After the two bodyguards got out, even more so.

Conference Room 6 was a large rectangular space with a low ceiling and a large table. It was filled almost entirely by middle-aged and elderly men and women, mostly dressed in suits or military uniforms, who sat or stood in complete silence. Mordred and Phyllis wedged in between Ruby Parker and Edna. Alec went to stand against the wall, although that too was almost fully occupied. At the front of the room there was a screen with a projector above it. Tariq was the only other person Mordred recognised. Ruby Parker said 'John Mordred' to the room, and no further introductions were made. No one overtly acknowledged him, but it was clear from the way they eyed him that he was the person on whom all their remaining hopes were invested. Whether or not he inspired confidence was impossible to discern. Probably not. Realistically, who or what could?

Tariq stood up next to the screen as soon as Mordred was seated, and addressed the room. "Tariq al-Banna," he said. "Head of MI7 Information Technology and Cybernetics. Thanks to the notebooks we retrieved from Gloria Shipton's house, we now think we've got the upper hand. We can destroy it. It's just a question of getting John on to the top floor of the building. Once he's up there, that's the final piece of the jigsaw in place. It won't be able to touch him. It'll have to allow the whole process to run its course. Its destruction will be assured."

On the far side of the screen, another man stood. Black curly hair, late thirties. "Simon Davidson, Senior Analyst GCHQ. The Ultimate Londoner cannot be in complete control of what happens in the next thirty-four hours, otherwise it would simply stop the competition. No, the competition must have been devised as a rigid parameter within which the program can work. It is a 'host', in other words, in the true game show sense of the term. Gloria Shipton's final notebook contains the competition rules. To the extent that the competition fails, the program will go into what she called 'stasis' – it will freeze – theoretically allowing the 'host' to transcend it, understand it and appropriate it. If that happens, it may be able to run other 'competitions', perhaps even in parallel. Since the whole of life on earth is a competition of sorts, that could mean it gaining an unforeseeable degree of power over the destiny of this planet. Of course, we can't allow that."

Tariq stood up again. "My research shows that we can use Gloria Shipton's formulae to keep changing the rules of the competition. As the program readjusts to take its new parameters into account, John has breathing space to ascend."

"Excuse me for interrupting," a man in a grey uniform said, two seats down from Ruby Parker. "Guy Chaplain, RAF. Why can't we just knock a hole in the top of the tower and winch John down from a helicopter?"

Tariq nodded quickly. "Because the award centre 'venue' is described in fairly precise mathematical terms within the program," Davidson replied. "We don't even understand how. All we know is that Gloria Shipton gave it the means to choose a venue, then to map it conceptually within its wider neural-type network. Any significant damage to the structural integrity of the top floor may effectively void it as the program-recognised award ceremony 'venue'. If that happens, then once again, the competition fails as such, and the host wins."

"But if you're playing about with the rules," someone said, "won't that affect the program's understanding of the award venue? It sounds very much like that's implicit in them – in the rules, I mean."

"Which is why we aim to restore the rules to their original state as soon as John reaches the top floor," Tariq said. "The mathematics allows of one hundred per cent precision, so we don't anticipate problems."

Simon Davidson pointed a remote at the projector on the ceiling. The screen at the front of the room filled with a frozen animation of the Gherkin with a Play button in the centre.

"What you see here," Davidson said, "is our second line of attack. GCHQ has developed its own program, designed to overlay The Ultimate Londoner's presence within the Gherkin. It can replicate objects digitally as they might appear to any scanners. Shapes, weights, mannerisms, everything can be simulated as a package. Assuming that The Ultimate Londoner registers John's arrival in the Gherkin, it will be as an assemblage of data. We can mimic that same assemblage in six or seven different places at once. What the program will 'see' is six or seven Johns, only one of which will be the real him. Assuming it's trying to eliminate him, this gives him a far greater chance."

He pressed Play. What appeared on the screen looked a little like a computer game. Out of nowhere, annihilating flashes attacked seven little pixilated men with a shock of blond hair. It killed six in painfully slow succession, but allowed the seventh to ascend triumphantly to the top floor.

Mordred looked discreetly around the room. No one was laughing.

"And of course," Davidson went on, "we can resurrect eliminated 'Johns'. We estimate this gives him a seven in ten chance of making it. In conjunction with Tariq's rule-altering input, that rises to around ninety per cent. It does have one drawback, unfortunately. John will have to enter the building alone. His being in any way accompanied is out of the question, because we need to know where the real him is, and the presence of two, three or more genuine biological entities will reduce our chances of that."

Silence. "Any questions?" Ruby Parker asked.

"What time are you aiming to put me in?" Mordred asked. It was the first time he'd spoken. Everyone turned to look at him. Suddenly he was more than just a pixilated stick-man with a yellow blob on his head.

"You've got to be on the top floor on the stroke of midnight," Davidson said. "The problem is, we still don't know what extra tricks, if any, the program may have up its sleeve. We don't want to put you in so early that it has chance to readjust and activate anything unexpected. On the other hand, we don't want to put you in so late, you've no chance of making it. Given the damage the building may have sustained in Thursday's sonic blast, and the fact that we still haven't been able to access the interior – more than a legal problem now, I'm afraid: there seems to be physics at work there too – we're still uncertain. But certainly no later than eleven."

"What do you mean, 'physics'?" Mordred asked.

Davidson looked nonplussed for a moment, as if strictly speaking, this was technically outside his field of expertise. "I, er…" he began.

"Do you mean The Ultimate Londoner's changed the molecular structure of the glass?" Mordred asked.

Silence.

Davidson nodded. He cleared his throat and grinned lopsidedly. "That sounds crazy, I accept. But... er, perhaps something like that, maybe, yes." He ran his finger round his shirt collar. "How did you know?"

## Chapter 32: The Agent of Dakota Attic Park Fame

*Saturday*

Doomsday arrived much like any other day. Shoppers and sightseers arrived from the shires, people booked into and out of hotels, retailers sold goods, windy excursions were had, cars drove, pedestrians walked, birds sang, the sun hid behind a blanket of cloud.

The only difference was that this was the day of the night of The Ultimate Londoner award ceremony. So, in addition to all the above, temporary food stalls were brought in, stage sets were erected, barriers aligned, notices displayed. Which also happened every day here, but just a touch more today. Because this wasn't any old Londoner being crowned. It wasn't even the best Londoner. It was the *ultimate* Londoner. The *very last word* in being a Londoner. You couldn't have another one. This one would be definitive.

Mordred spent another night in the pods. Tim and Barend were replaced by Sam and Tony who were more taciturn and therefore more in keeping with the general end-of-the-world vibe. Phyllis also spent a night in the pods, but in a different drawer. Sharing a pod wasn't allowed, and would probably break the entire complex.

They met up half an hour after reveille and went to the canteen. Since there was a reasonable likelihood that this would be their last ever breakfast, they decided to go crazy. They each had two croissants with blackcurrant jam, and shared a pot of coffee. Afterwards they went to L9 to read the papers, and watch *Saturday Kitchen Live*.

At lunchtime, they were back in the canteen for their last ever lunch. Phyllis had roast chicken with gravy; Mordred had a nut cutlet and four new potatoes with butter. They said they loved each other. They discussed their families and whether it would be right to call them. They wanted to, but no. How to explain their own emotion? It seemed selfish, and saying the only really important things wasn't an option. They both wept a bit. Then they recovered and didn't talk about it again.

The afternoon was set aside for him to rest. He returned to the pods while Phyllis went to her desk to do some filing which would have been urgent except for the fact that she, and the files, and the issue they addressed, might not be here this time tomorrow. Still, it gave her a welcome, if entirely deceptive, sense of routine.

6pm brought their last ever dinner. Neither could face anything heavy, so they had a round of egg mayonnaise sandwiches and shared a pot of Earl Grey tea.

At 7pm sharp he was due to meet two psychologists for an evaluation of mental fitness assessment.

At 9pm, Tariq and Simon would meet him in L9 to give him their final instructions and answer his questions.

At 9.45, he'd drive over to the Square Mile, where Ruby Parker was installed with a group of government officials on the first floor of The Red Rosy Cross, an evacuated public house.

At 10.45, he'd don a Kevlar vest and Ruby Parker would give him his final briefing.

At 11pm on the dot, he'd enter the Gherkin.


The two psychologists were bearded men of about forty in sweatshirts and jeans. Their consultation room was an office on Ruby Parker's floor. They shook hands with Mordred smilingly and introduced themselves as Gavin and Miles. The two bodyguards were outside somewhere, but it was okay, they said, because the room was soundproofed. They asked Mordred to lie down on a chaise longue obviously commandeered at the last moment to serve as a couch. They took out clipboards and sat down on office chairs.

"Before we begin," Gavin said genially, "I should tell you, it's okay. Both Miles and I know what's going to happen tonight."

"And that there's a small chance you won't make it, and we'll all be blown to *kingdom come!*" Miles said, leaning back and waggling his fingers. He chortled, as if being vaporised was the zaniest thing he could imagine.

"How did you sleep last night?" Gavin asked.

"Not well," Mordred said.

"How are you dealing with the disturbances in your visual field?" Gavin said.

"They're getting weaker. They're almost gone."

"Any dreams?"

"The Lambton Worm." Seeing their blank looks, he continued: "It's an old north-eastern story about a worm that gets thrown down a well and then keeps growing." He sang: "*The worm got fat an' grewed an' grewed, an' grewed an aaful size.* I can't remember when I last heard that. Twenty-five years ago, probably."

"So it'd be fair to say you're a little frightened then?" Miles asked.

"Well, there is a possibility we're all going to die tomorrow," Mordred replied.

Gavin and Miles chuckled. "Try and think positive!" Miles said cheerily.

"We'll be okay!" Gavin said.

Mordred suddenly realised: they had no idea why they were doing this. They were dutiful public servants, and they were going through the motions. Underneath, they both thought they were going to die. They were manic.

The psychology session didn't last long. It wasn't even clear why anyone had arranged it, since he had to go into the Gherkin no matter what. At eight, Ruby Parker came to fetch him for an unscheduled meeting. She took him to Conference Room 5 in which forty-five people in suits sat looking funereal. These were the only employees in the building who knew precisely what was going on – a different category to those in 6, earlier, although there was some overlap - and they'd asked to see the person on whom their life now depended. Ruby Parker introduced him without giving too much away. She told everyone he'd already stopped a possible rogue state emerging in Siberia, prevented Saudi Arabia from being invaded, and that, yes, this was the agent of Dakota Attic Park fame. People sat up like they thought their chances of survival had increased. They asked him a series of fairly feeble questions on the same theme: how confident are you? Yet they weren't interested in the answers. They were focussed on the non-verbal stuff: how he deported himself, how much of a dash he cut, whether he seemed the kind of person you'd choose to hold the front line when everyone's life was at stake. At 8.30, when Ruby Parker announced it was time for him to go, he got the strong impression the jury was still out. But then, that was probably the best anyone could expect in a situation like this. To an individual, they all wished him good luck.

After everyone had left, Ruby Parker closed the door. "There's something I need to mention," she said.

"Go ahead. We've still got three and a half hours."

"I assigned a team of shadows to watch your sister, Hannah, tonight. She rang Phyllis yesterday morning. She hasn't called back, and I'm worried she might try something. In a word, they've lost her."

"Would you like me to call her? Only I haven't got my phone. You have."

She took it from her jacket pocket and gave it to him. "It's fully charged. And we've already checked. She hasn't called you. If she had, we'd have come to find you."

"That's rather strange in itself. Given that she's supposedly in town for my benefit."

"Just what I thought."

He pressed Call and waited. It went straight to voicemail. "No answer," he said, giving her the phone back.

"Hang on to it. And keep trying."

The meeting with Tariq and Simon didn't add much to what he already knew. Because it was in L9, Phyllis was present. She sat on the sofa with her arms folded and said nothing.

It was mainly communications info. Both men would be in the same room in Whitehall, they told him, coordinating their deployment of their different inventions, the rules changer and the Mordred replicator. They'd speak to Mordred through the same headset, and he could speak back to them. A built-in webcam would also feed back to them. He needed to give them a full running commentary: what he could see, and, in some cases, what he couldn't – for example, if they told him $x$ was supposed to be in front of him and it wasn't.

Tariq and Simon weren't quite as far gone as Miles and Gavin, but they kept repeating themselves, and they were definitely hyper. Despite their outward optimism, on some level they both thought they were going to die.

As soon as they'd left, Mordred's phone rang. *Hannah.*

"Hi, John," she said, "where are you?"

"I was about to ask you the same question."

"Well, unfortunately, I asked first."

"I've been called into the Foreign Office to do some translation work for a client."

"Yes, Phyllis told me about that. So you're not going to the Gherkin tonight?"

"I don't know whether you're aware," he said, "but it's been cordoned off. *No one's* going to the Gherkin tonight. It's surrounded by a half-mile exclusion zone."

She laughed. "Oh, yes. That's right. I forgot. Incidentally, I keep meaning to ask: what does Phyllis do for a living?"

He and Phyllis had talked about this. It would have to be something Hannah wouldn't touch with a bargepole. "She works for Goldman Sachs," he said.

An incredulous pause. "Bloody *hell*. And you're okay with that?"

"I love her. So yes."

A second incredulous pause. "I can't *believe* it! *Goldman Sachs? GOLDMAN BLOODY SACHS? Oh my GOD! WHY?*"

"Why am I going out with her, or why does she work there?"

*"BOTH!"*

"Okay, stop shouting. You're going to shatter the screen on my phone."

But she'd hung up.

"Job done," he told Phyllis. "Now we've just got to avoid her for the rest of our lives."

"Which might not be too difficult, depending on how you get on at the Gherkin tonight. Maybe we should have chosen something a little more innocuous and vague. Like the Bank of England."

"We've been through this. Anything she wasn't absolutely outraged by might be something she'd later ask quiz questions on. How comfortable would you be with 'What's the difference between the monetary and the financial policy committee?'"

"She'd never ask *that*."

"She might if she was feeling bolshie."

His phone rang again. *Hannah.* He sighed and picked up. As Doomsdays went, this one was pretty rubbish. Nothing like the Book of Revelation.

"Okay, I'm over it now," she said when he picked up. "I'm an adult. It's your life. It's none of my business. Just don't bring it up when we're together. Remember the Brexit meal?"

"Me and *The Northern Echo*, yes."

"Anyway, sometimes good people do bad things."

"So where are you now?"

"What's it matter? I mean, if you're at work? I was going to say, Can we meet up, but obviously, that's not an option. Where's Phyllis? Maybe I could meet *her*. Even though she does work for Satan."

A knock on the door of L9. Phyllis went to get it. Kevin. Mordred saw her shush him as she pulled the door shut on her way out. Not that he'd speak anyway.

"I don't know," he said. "Have you tried ringing her mobile?"

"It's switched off."

"She's probably in bed, asleep."

"It's only 9.45. Bloody hell, some party this is turning out to be. I never knew you were so utterly boring. Don't you realise everyone here's asking about you? Just because you can't make it to the top floor of bloody Capitalist Central Control, doesn't mean you can't pick up an award, John. It may not be five million pounds, but what's wrong with a few rounds of beer on the city populace? And don't tell me you don't drink any more, because I'll disown you."

"Where's 'here'?"

"We've been through this. What's the point if you're at work?"

"I may be getting off in half an hour. I don't want to let you down. Where's the harm in telling me? Even just on the off chance."

"Okay," she said, "I'm in Hyde Park. Meet me outside at Wellington Arch in forty-five minutes. I'll be with Mehreen and Francis from the competition. They're keen to meet you. 10.30. *Be* there. Okay?"

"I'll do my absolute best." He hung up. Time to get in the car and go to The Red Rosy Cross. Odd name for a pub, but there it was.

He opened L9's door. Ruby Parker stood in the corridor holding her own phone, as if she'd just had a fraught conversation with a bearer of bad news. She and Phyllis were deep in conference. Kevin was nowhere to be seen.

Ruby Parker turned to face Mordred, her face emanating thunder. "Your sister's lying," she said. "We've just triangulated her phone. She's somewhere deep inside the Square Mile exclusion zone."

## Chapter 33: As Usual, Put It on Speakerphone

They crossed reception without signing out. Colin Bale had gone home at 5.30, and his replacement – a man that looked exactly like him, only thin – raised his hand to object, but registered Ruby Parker and thought better of it. Outside, Kevin was parked on the double red lines. Mordred got onto the back seat, where he found himself sandwiched between Ruby Parker and Phyllis. Edna was waiting in the front seat. Alec, Ian and Suki were in Sheila's car, somewhere five minutes ahead.

"This is turning out to be a disaster in more ways than the obvious one," Ruby Parker said as they pulled out. "I might as well tell you, John. We still can't seem to get into the Gherkin. Forget that nonsense of yours about changing the glass's molecular structure: you caught Simon off guard, and he was too polite to make you look foolish in front of all those people. We may not know what's going on, but it's certainly not a cross between physics and black magic. In any case, unless we make some kind of literal breakthrough in the next hour, we may be finished."

"What about the submarines?" Edna asked. "Are we doing anything about them?"

"They're being evacuated now," Ruby Parker replied. "The Royal Navy will try intercepting the missiles either before or just after launch. I don't know the technical details, so don't ask me. But it may be beside the point. We've had intelligence that the problem may not be confined to Trident. Other countries' missiles may be poised to fire. John, why do you think your sister's in the Square Mile? You must have a theory."

"I wish that were true," he said. "At the beginning, we both thought she might have nominated me. Her denials were pretty convincing. But maybe she is involved in some way we haven't yet considered. The problem is, we already *know* who's responsible. Gloria Shipton, along with her notebooks, explain the entire thing. As far as I understand it, there's simply no role for Hannah."

"Could she have been in contact with Gloria Shipton somehow?" Phyllis asked.

Mordred shook his head. "Neither mentioned the other. If there'd been any collaboration between the two women, Hannah would probably have financed her to do something more useful."

"We need to find her," Ruby Parker said. "She's obviously up to something, she's got a huge network of collaborators and she's highly resourceful. I hate to say this, but she may even be able to help. She may know something we don't. At this point, I'm desperate enough to try anything. Can you call her back?"

Mordred took out his phone and called. No answer.

"Keep trying," Ruby Parker told him. "Although, no, don't. You'll give away the fact that we're onto her. She already suspects you're a spy. This might confirm it."

"I'll go to Wellington Arch," Phyllis said. "I can say John couldn't make it, so he sent me, and we'll meet him later. After midnight, maybe. For all we know, she could *really be* intending to meet him there."

"Something in her tone made me doubt it," Mordred said. "But it's worth trying everything. Maybe we should *both* go. Ten-thirty still gives us time to get over to the Gherkin for eleven."

"Not an option," Ruby Parker said. "You're our only chance of staving off assured destruction, and the antipathy some people probably still feel towards you for not being a 'real Londoner' might just find an outlet. If you're killed, we all are. Phyllis, you go. Report back as soon as you've met her, if that happens, but either way, no later than ten forty-five. If she's not there by eleven, Kevin will bring you over to St Mary Axe. Look out for him."

The car slowed to allow Phyllis to get out. She and Mordred looked at each other for the last time on Earth. She bit her lip. They hugged crushingly, whispered the big three words, and detached. Suddenly, the car stopped, the door opened, and on the back seat there were two occupants, instead of three.

The central portion of The Square Mile was cordoned off as a temporary exclusion zone. Given the celebrations, the police had anticipated difficulty maintaining its integrity, so they'd brought in reinforcements from other parts of the country. Inside was a series of checkpoints of increasing security, manned by soldiers. Orange barriers marked the perimeter, patrolled by police constables in high-vis jackets. Mounted policemen formed an advance first line further in front. According to the BBC, all this was costing the country three billion pounds daily, mostly in income lost to the financial services industry. If Armageddon didn't come, it would almost certainly be lifted tomorrow.

Yet somehow it felt weirdly like what it was always meant to be. Sinister and not entirely of-this-earth. The skyscrapers looked like alien palaces from the writings of HP Lovecraft.

Hannah was somewhere in here. How did she get in? What would happen to her if she was caught?

The Red Rosy Cross was down a narrow one-way street just off Cornhill, tucked between two much bigger buildings. It had a single door, small Dickensian windows and a tiled bib, and was otherwise nondescript, the kind of building you could walk past every day and never notice. Two armed men in flak jackets stood on the pavement outside. They examined the three passes Ruby Parker gave them, and waved her, Edna and Mordred in without comment.

The ground floor was as forlorn a deserted pub as Mordred had ever seen. Vacant and gloomy and unloved. However, it was on the first floor that the action was supposed to be taking place.

Why had they chosen here? Because it was difficult to find, probably. If you had to put all the state's highest officials in one location at short notice, you'd probably go for the least obvious place. Which, say what you like, this was.

They climbed a single creaky set of stairs, and emerged into a large lounge that – probably because it was stuffed with civil dignitaries - looked oddly like the Thames House conference room where Simon and Tariq had made their presentation. The wallpaper was ochre with pink paisley patterns. Mordred suddenly realised his visions had stopped. He felt clear headed. Even so, the sudden tearing away of Phyllis had left him feeling as sad as the bar downstairs. A thousand times as.

It was hot. A chandelier with six unshaded low-energy bulbs gave a moribund light. No one spoke. Everyone looked as if they'd been thrown in here by prison warders. Several people looked haggard. Against the far wall, one man had his eyes closed, his hands clasped and he was whispering. No one looked like they thought it inappropriate. When Mordred entered, they came to life slightly, as if hope had been temporarily restored, but not enough to see them through the next hour.

"We're searching everywhere for her," a grey-haired man in a suit with a slightly vampirish look about him whispered to Ruby Parker. "But there's a lot of places she could be. Not that it matters much, the way things are."

Ruby Parker rolled her eyes and almost threw her arms in the air, easily the closest Mordred had ever seen her to losing control. However, when she spoke, she was calm. "I take it we still haven't accessed the Gherkin."

"No."

"Are Tariq and Simon ready?"

"Standing by in Whitehall."

"John, get that Kevlar vest on and the headset. We'll walk over there."

They were going already? They'd only just arrived!

More: given that all these people didn't have information to impart, and didn't want to ask anything, what were they doing here? Why weren't they at home?

Then he saw. Because they were the only ones who knew what was happening, and they couldn't stand to be in the company of those who didn't, even their nearest and dearest. Knowledge gave them an unnatural bond. It filled them with an irrepressible hunger for news, and this was the only place they were going to get it. Junkies. With their haggard expressions and dead eyes, they even looked the part.

"John, can you hear me?" Tariq said when he'd got the headset on.

"Loud and clear," he replied. The sort of thing you were supposed to say in these sorts of setups. 'Yep' didn't usually cut it.

"John, it's Simon," said another voice. "Can you hear me?"

"Loud and clear. Do you know if we've got access to the Gherkin yet?"

"That's not really our bag, but unless things have changed radically in the last ten minutes, no, I don't think so."

"So all this could be a waste of time?"

"Just focus on the role we've assigned you, John," Ruby Parker said, before Simon or Tariq could reply. "We'll get you in even if we have to use explosives."

He almost laughed. A pound of gelignite in St Mary Axe, the Gherkin collapsing like a felled tree, and Ruby Parker's, 'You were only supposed to blow the bloody doors off.' She preceded him down the stairs, and a few seconds later they were walking through the darkened streets.

Suddenly, faint music. Somehow, they both knew where it was coming from. Everyone stopped and looked up. The top floor of the Gherkin. Fully illuminated from within, and pulsing slightly, like a party was in progress.

And yet everyone knew it was derelict. Mordred's viscera sank just half an inch.

When they reached St Mary Axe, a crowd, mainly of army personnel, stood fairly motionless watching a team working on the doors under arc-lights. Sparks flew, power tools screamed. Two fire engines stood by with their engines idling and their lights flashing. The air smelt of burning plastic and exhaust fumes.

A man in a long woollen coat – obviously a civil servant – approached Ruby Parker brandishing a document. "We've searched the entire area with thermal imaging equipment. We don't believe she's here. Lexingwood, I mean. Which isn't to say she wasn't earlier. But she must have left."

Ruby Parker took her phone out. "Phyllis?" she said. She made eye-contact with Mordred – *listen to what I'm saying* - and kept talking. "…So she didn't turn up there either. Right. Kevin should be there any second. If you just stand on the roadside, he'll find you."

She turned to the civil servant. "Search again," she told him. "She's in here somewhere, I'm certain of it."

He nodded and left. Ruby Parker turned to Mordred and finished her sentence. "Although we probably won't find out *where* until she chooses to show herself. Let's just hope she hurries. Try calling her again."

Mordred took his phone out.

Then it began to ring in his hand like it had come to life.

*Hannah.*

"Put it on speakerphone," Ruby Parker said. "Don't be confrontational. Ask her what she wants. If necessary, give the phone to me and I'll speak to her. We can't afford to prioritise caution at a time like this."

He picked up. "Hi."

"I wondered when you'd get here," Hannah said coolly.

He started. "What do you mean, 'here'? Where are you?"

"Try looking up."

For a few seconds he couldn't see anything. Maybe he didn't want to. Then she appeared, standing behind the glass on what looked to be the fourth or fifth floor.

She waved. She didn't look happy.

## Chapter 34: Brother-Sister Business

"What are you doing, John?" Hannah asked. She stood inside the Gherkin, some forty metres above street-level. Her face was pretty small from here, but even so, he could tell it wasn't smiling.

Ruby Parker met Mordred's querying look with a shrug. "Tell her," she said.

"Honest answer?" he asked Hannah. "I'm here for the awards ceremony. Because if I don't turn up, we're all going to die. That includes you and me and everyone in London."

"I see. Well, at least that's more entertaining bullshit than the stuff you shovelled me last time I called you. I suppose you'd like to come inside, would you?"

"It's not a question of 'like'."

"How do you think *I* got in here? Aren't you and your bosses in MI5 a little curious?"

"Right now, we're more interested in saving lives."

"Get off your high horse, John. You've been lying to me for years. *And* you've been spying on me. As of today, you're officially the enemy."

"I'm not - "

"I really appreciate you telling me Phyllis works for Goldman Sachs, by the way. Like you couldn't think of a non-hurtful lie. Like you had to sit there together and ask yourselves what'd upset me most of all. *Let's tell her we're professionally connected to the Great Vampire Squid. That should hurt her.* Well, thanks, John. Thank you very much for taking the time. You're a great brother."

"I'm not - "

"Hang on, wait, did I just say, 'great brother'? My bad. I meant *complete shit.*"

"Are you going to let me speak?"

"And say what? 'Sorry, Sis, you've got it all wrong. I may be in MI5' – because you know I know that: it's undeniable now – 'but I never spied on you. I'm just dumb old John. *Stupid, thick, loser* John who's too *simple* to know the difference between right and wrong and who, even if he *was* spying, wouldn't know it and, oh, now you've pointed it out to me, Hannah, I can see what a fool I've been, and I'll never again blah-de-blah-de-bullshit blah.' You're forgetting, John: I can see right through you now. My eyes are open. I've woken up. And guess what I've realised? You're a *complete and utter shit*."

"You've already said that."

"Well, I've just said it again. And I'm going to keep saying it because I'm going to tell everyone you and I have ever known. I think they deserve the truth, don't you?"

"Most of them probably won't be interested."

"We'll see. Oh, *we'll see!*"

"So what's going to happen now? Are you just going to sit up there, railing at me until we all get blown up? Because if we carry on arguing into the afterlife, St Peter's probably going to turn us both away."

"You think this is *funny*? You think I'm *joking?*"

"I think you're overreacting. Yes, I work for the security services, but I've never spied on you, nor would I. If I'd been hired to keep tabs on Hannah Lexingwood, I'd have asked you for a job. You'd definitely have fitted me in somewhere in your entourage, because you're fabulously rich and I'm your stupid, loser brother. I'd have stuck to you like a limpet, and you'd have found yourself being gradually undermined and ultimately, brought down. You'd never have suspected it was me. But that's not happening. Think about it: how often do we even *meet?* When we do, it usually ends in some boost for you. Think Jersey. Think last year in the Square Mile. Think all sorts of things. How does all that fit with your theory, eh, Genius?"

"Don't you be sarcastic with me! You haven't earned that right."

"Sorry."

Pause.

"So what now?" she continued. "Are you just going to stand there like a tool for the next hour? Because there's no way you're coming in here. I've had it with you."

"There are nuclear missiles pointed at London."

"To think I cared about you when you disappeared on the train! I *knew* you were up to no good *then!*"

"They're scheduled to lift off at one minute past midnight."

"Yeah, sure. What a coincidence. Nuclear bombs if you're not in here to claim your five million pounds first prize. What the hell do you *take* me for, John? Do you think I'm a *complete* idiot? You're certainly not helping yourself, I'll say that."

"How long are you going to be angry? Because if you actually stop to think about it, you'll know I've never spied on you. As for the Goldman Sachs thing, it wasn't to hurt you. It was just to stop you asking questions. If we'd said Phyllis was a jewellery designer, or a rep for some big company, you were bound to know someone who knew someone who could 'help' her in her career, and then you'd have tried to put them in touch, and then the whole cover story would have fallen apart. We knew you'd be repulsed by Goldman Sachs, true, but we also knew you wouldn't have related contacts. We definitely didn't come up with it to hurt you."

"How long am I going to be angry, you say? Maybe till one minute past midnight. At that time, I might just decide to let you in. True, you won't get the prize money, but hey, money doesn't matter, right?"

"A minute past midnight's when we're all going to die."

"Righty-ho."

Ruby Parker passed him a scrap of paper. On it, she'd written, 'Ask her how she got in there.'

"How did you get in there?" he said.

Hannah laughed. "I knew you'd get round to asking me that, sooner or later. And I saw your little buddy pass you that piece of paper. So sad, as Donald Trump would say. You're not even speaking your own lines now. Put him on. Your buddy. Put him on."

Mordred turned to Ruby Parker. She held her hand out and took the phone.

"Good evening, Hannah," she said. "I'm John's boss. Before you carry on, I know how you got in there. You walked calmly in on Thursday evening as the fire alarm was sounding, and you took a friend of yours with you. Then you both hid. I haven't looked at the CCTV, but I'm pretty sure it'll confirm that. I also know who your friend is. You might like to remind Ms Burkewitz that she signed the Official Secrets Act before she went in to Gloria Shipton's house, and that, if we do survive this, she's likely to go to prison for a very long time. Twenty years, possibly. Unless we can make some kind of deal, we've the power to ensure she serves her full allocation. If you could put her on the line, I'd be much obliged. I think she deserves a say in this, don't you?"

A long pause. Two women frantically discussing something in the background.

"How did you know all that?" Mordred whispered.

"Barely informed guesswork," Ruby Parker replied. "We never thought to look at the CCTV because we haven't had time and it didn't seem relevant. And Camilla Burkewitz is the only one who could possibly give Hannah the power she obviously holds, to open the doors. She's an academic and, like many academics, fairly left-leaning. We knew that before we invited her to Thames House and put her into Gloria Shipton's, but she's one of only a handful of experts in her field in the entire world. Telling your sister all that was a huge gamble. Miraculously, it seems to have paid off. Perhaps."

Hannah's voice again: "What sort of a 'deal'?"

"All you have to do is let John into the building. Only him. We'll pull everyone else back. I know you can do that, because I know Ms Burkewitz has the expertise."

"You still don't get it do you?" Hannah said.

252

"What do you mean?"

"The Ultimate Londoner's a *living thing*."

"As defined how?" Ruby Parker said.

"It may not be able to *think* like you and me, not yet. Certainly not like *you*: no one would want it to… But it has feelings." She sighed. "I'll get back to you at one past midnight."

She hung up.

Mordred's phone showed the time. *11.30*.

Kevin's car pulled up. Phyllis got out. Hannah had disappeared from the window.

"My God," Phyllis said. "We're still not in?"

Mordred rubbed his forehead and handed his phone to Ruby Parker. "I've just had a thought. I just need to sit alone for a moment."

"What if your sister calls back?" Ruby Parker said.

"She won't. If she does, it'll be to negotiate a deal for Camilla Burkewitz. Only you can do that."

"Are you okay, John?" Phyllis asked. "I mean, apart from the fact that we've only twenty-nine minutes left."

He shrugged. "I might be able to save us. Is Kevin leaving? Since he never speaks to me, the back of his car's probably the quietest place at the moment."

Phyllis walked him to Kevin's car. Mordred got on to the back seat. She got in next to him. "Don't speak, Kevin," she told him. "John's got to think."

As so often, Kevin shot him a disgusted look in the rear-view.

Mordred put his head in his hands. He sat upright and looked up at the car ceiling. He ran both hands through his hair. *It may not be able to think like you.* For a moment, he was acutely aware of his own breathing. Then Phyllis's. *Not yet. But it has feelings.*

Maybe that was the key to it all. It *was* a thinking thing, but not in the human sense. For all its algorithmic potency, its thoughts were basic and rudimentary, like a dog's or a bird's. But yes, it had feelings.

And yes, it had done what it was designed to do. It had launched a competition for humans and chosen ten people somehow. Not at random, but according to its assessment, somehow, of their worthiness for five million pounds. These ten were its chosen ones.

Might it be too much to say it 'loved' them? No, no, probably not. It brought them back home when they strayed too far away. Like lost sheep. *When he has found it, he carries it on his shoulders, rejoicing*. Not quite that, no. More like in Alec's report. It didn't mean to hurt them – quite the opposite – but it failed to control the details.

So it loved people, and these ten above all, maybe. And how had people reacted to its munificence? With hatred. Every step of the way. All it had tried to do was greeted with suspicion and outright hostility. Innumerable attempts were made to cancel the awards ceremony. *The Evening Standard* and *The Metro* had disowned it until yesterday, or the day before – until Hannah persuaded them to get back on board.

That was it. That was why she was inside. It saw her as its friend.

But *him*. John Mordred – for some inexplicable reason – above all. The only constant in all this. It loved *him* more than anyone in the world!

Yet what about the fly in the ointment? What about Michael Preston?

My God! What if - ?

"I've got it," he told Phyllis, opening the car door. He looked at his watch. *11.40*. He almost hurled himself onto the tarmac and scrambled to a run.

Ruby Parker stood alone with her hands folded behind her back, looking impassive.

"I take it from your haste that you've had an insight," she said. "Don't waste time explaining what it is. Just tell me what you need."

"For starters, immunity from prosecution for Camilla Burkewitz and my sister, and anyone else in there: I'm pretty sure there are more than two of them. They'll understand a free gift much better than a deal, and it'll put them in our debt. Or at least cancel mine."

She gave a single nod. "I had the same thought. Granted."

"Next, I need everyone here to stop working. I need the doors hosing to cool them down, I need everyone to back off and I need Tariq and Simon to put me through to every landline in the building simultaneously. I mean, if that's possible."

"From this?" She held up his mobile.

"Yes."

"But what if your sister rings back?"

"We don't need her any more."

Hannah was tall, thin, blonde, aristocratic-looking and thirty-six years old. She wore an ankle-length dress and plain sandals. When she put the phone down on her brother's boss, she wiped her eyes and went back into the room where her sister, Charlotte, sat with the other nine women. Charlotte was short, slightly overweight, and dressed, as usual, in black. She was two years younger than Hannah. The other women were Camilla Burkewitz, the quantum scientist, Soraya Snow, lead singer of Fully Magic Coal Tar Lounge, Ségolène Carignon, a French literature lecturer at the Sorbonne, and four Italians, a Gambian and one transgender German who all went by the same name – 'Leda Rafanelli', after the famous poet – and who were known collectively as The Anarchist Sisters. All eleven had all come down from the top floor in an act of mutual solidarity. The party-that-didn't-qualify-as-a-party had begun to bore them, anyway, despite the unlimited availability of cocktails. And they were scared. Sooner or later, the police and the army would get in here, and who knew what would happen then? When Hannah had called her brother, they'd held hands in a ring, broken only by the fact that Hannah needed to hold her mobile, and everyone else had to stay out of sight.

Afterwards, they sat in a kind of mournful silence. Hannah drew back into what she knew, from the perspective of the street, would be darkness, but she continued watching. She saw Phyllis arrive, then she and John both get into a car. John's boss didn't move.

After that, nothing. The car didn't go anywhere. No one below moved especially. Things went back to how they'd been before his arrival.

What was going on?

She suddenly knew she'd forgive him. She always did.

And actually, come to think of it, he was right. *If I'd been hired to keep tabs on you, I'd have asked you for a job and you'd definitely have fitted me in.*

She would have. Of course she would have. And he hadn't asked. Ever. Even last year, when she'd invited him to come and stay with her in America for a while, he'd cried off. No, he couldn't be spying on her. The weird fact that he actually *was* a spy made it somehow even more shocking. They must have asked him. She was a known 'troublemaker'. She knew she *was* being spied on, because she had reliable contacts who told her so, and, on one occasion, had even shown her the evidence.

Just not by her own brother, apparently.

Yes, that's right: they must have asked him.

And he must have said no.

Knowing them, they'd have tried to twist his arm in every which way.

But he must *still* have said no.

Which must mean he was pretty good at his job. And let's face it there were *real* bad guys out there: ISIS, Combat 18, the Continuity IRA, to name but a few. Someone had to deal with them.

The Goldman Sachs thing too. That also made sense.

Was Phyllis really his girlfriend? Yes, she had to be. He wouldn't have brought her home otherwise, to meet his parents. She certainly had no interest in Hannah Lexingwood. She was as much interested in her brother's sister as any normal girlfriend might be. No more, no less.

Bloody *hell*, she was crying again.

That stuff about the nuclear weapons: that *had* to be a pile of crap, though.

She suddenly saw him get out of the car at speed.

Her fellow squatters apparently registered her alarm.

"What's up?" Charlotte asked. "Has something happened?"

"I don't know," Hannah replied. She sniffed. She was past caring, really.

All the women came forward as far as they dared. They didn't want to be seen, but nor did they want to miss anything.

They saw John in conversation with his boss and Phyllis. It looked like they were reinvigorated. A few seconds later, hoses were dragged from the fire engines and turned on the building.

"What are they doing?" asked one of the Leda Rafanellis.

Hannah looked at her phone. *11.45*. She'd said she'd let him in at 12.01. That didn't seem too long to wait, given that he wasn't usually the impatient kind. Mind you, the army and the police wouldn't be trying to get him in so *he personally* could get his hands on the prize. He must have offered to donate it to them. But then, why would they be so eager to get *five million pounds*? Government-budget-wise, it was peanuts. And given how much the country was allegedly losing just by having this exclusion zone...

So maybe there really *were* nuclear warheads out there...?

She couldn't concentrate any more. Too much to hold in her head. And too much happening outside. Suddenly, everyone below seemed to be drawing back. John, his boss and Phyllis disappeared into the crowd as it rearranged itself into a denser, narrower configuration at a greater distance from the building's base.

"What's going on?" someone else behind Hannah asked.

"I don't know," she replied.

But she did know. She'd seen it before. John had come up with something. He'd had one of his bloody sodding ideas.

Which probably meant curtains for poor Camilla.

Maybe she should ring John's boss again.

Unless they were bluffing, of course. Rearranging themselves to create the impression of purposefulness.

Suddenly, the office phones began to ring. There were five in here, all going, but she had the uncanny feeling every one in the building was doing the same.

Well, if they thought mere noise would bully her into talking to them –

Then they all went answerphone. Five discordant variations of 'Please leave a message'.

Then a horrible silence.

Then a voice. "This is John Mordred. Look, I know I haven't been as grateful as I ought to have been. I want you to know I've suddenly realised how stupid I've been, and how sorry I am, and how idiotic everyone's been, not just me. We've been suspicious and rejecting when we should have been accepting…"

"Who the hell's he talking to?" Soraya whispered to Hannah.

But Camilla Burkewitz had gone pale. "He's talking to the program," she said. "He's talking to The Ultimate Londoner. Oh my God, it's over. We're finished." She laughed hysterically. "At least, I am."

"… I also know you tried to save Mehreen Shah," Mordred continued, "and we were stupid enough to think you might have been responsible, instead of…"

Hannah took her phone out. "Never say die," she said. She pressed Call. "Hi, Josh, Hannah here. You know I told you to get everyone ready to move from Hyde Park before twelve? Yeah, well, this is the green light… As many as you can muster, please." She smiled, and nodded to herself. "That sounds outstanding. See you in five minutes." She hung up. "Let's see how they cope when five thousand angry punters descend on them in a single mob," she said. "Time to retreat to the top floor, ladies."

## Chapter 35: Exit the Roman Girl

Phyllis looked at her phone. *11.53.* "How long are we going to give him?" she asked Ruby Parker. When she got no response, she realised it went without saying: this was the last toss of the dice, whatever happened. They were already on Plan C. There might conceivably be time to devise a Plan D, but definitely not to implement it.

Somewhere nearby, there was a pop and a small cheer, as of a group of men and women who'd just opened a bottle of champagne. End of the world bash: you might as well.

An army major with a long chin and thick eyebrows approached Ruby Parker with a lopsided grin. "Trident's been deactivated," he said. "On all fronts. We're no longer in danger. At least not from our own missiles."

It took Ruby Parker a split second to digest this. "How?" she asked.

"Of its own accord, apparently. As mysteriously as it happened."

She expelled a breath of relief. "Well, thank you for letting me know."

Phyllis laughed. So – what? - it was going to be *okay?* She put her hands over her mouth and gasped. Then she laughed again. Then she did something that was both.

"There's another thing," the Major said. "Apparently, we're being invaded. It's a police and armed forces matter, but just for your information: there are large crowds at the perimeter of the exclusion zone. They're demanding entry. They look ugly. Not as ugly as Armageddon, but best be prepared."

"I strongly advise you to let them in," Ruby Parker told them. "Concentrate on preventing looting."

He nodded grimly as if she'd voiced his own thoughts exactly, then turned and left.

Suddenly, the unbelievable: the front doors of the Gherkin opened. Another cheer, much louder, this time from everyone. Police and soldiers did double-takes then piled in.

Phyllis looked at her phone. *11.57.*

Not that it mattered any more.

Twelve minutes earlier, the firefighters turned off the hoses and Mordred approached the building. He put his hand on the glass, called the phones Tariq and Simon had patched him through to, and spoke to The Ultimate Londoner like it was a person. Given how much misunderstanding there'd been, he expected to have to beg, and he wasn't sure how successful he'd be, or even if what he was doing was sane. Seen rationally, it wasn't. But there were worse ways to exit this life.

Five minutes later, his opinion changed. The shapes in his visual field returned. He felt euphoric. The past and the future seemed to open up like one long tunnel with him in the middle. Nothing could hurt him. He'd always been there, always would be and everything was okay, even the worst bits. Everyone and everything was inextricably linked. The great universal language spoke soothingly. Then the Roman girl turned up. He was back at Hadrian's Wall, but this time, his sisters and parents were actual deities. Sparks came out of his fingers. He could travel way past the solar system, just by thought.

Then the Gherkin's doors opened. Behind him, humans cheered. They piled past him like he was of no account. But they wouldn't get into the lift. That was reserved just for him.

He edged to the front of them. Not difficult. Once inside the building, none of them knew what to do. They were guys used to taking orders, and they hadn't been given any; not lately. Their last, several hours ago probably, was to let him go first, follow his lead and wait. Which made it easy for him now. He stepped into the lift alone. He pressed '34' and, a few seconds later, he stepped out and transferred to the hydraulic lift for the top floor.

He looked at his phone. *11.59.*

The doors pinged open. He stepped out.

A large empty space, carpeted and spot-lit, with a central bar. Ten grim-looking women on bar stools, holding cocktails. He gave Camilla Burkewitz a little wave. She reciprocated miserably.

Nice of her to make the effort, given what she probably thought he heralded.

He located his sister. She didn't look as mad as earlier. He strode over and wrapped his arms round her and told her he loved her. "I'll never let anything bad happen to you," he said.

She laughed awkwardly. "Apology accepted. Maybe. But it's not about me."

"I won't let anyone hurt Camilla either," he said.

"I've called off the attack dogs, by the way. There won't be any trouble."

"What 'attack dogs'?"

She clicked her tongue. "As usual, my preparations are wasted on you."

In his zeal to placate Hannah, he hadn't noticed, but there was a huge screen to his left with 'John Mordred: The Ultimate Londoner!' flashing. The Beatles' *I Will* began to play. Coloured metallic confetti fell from the ceiling. For a split second, he was in ecstasy.

Then the lights went out. The music stopped. There was a black silence.

"It's finished," Camilla Burkewitz whispered, after a moment. "That's it. The program's run its course."

"Oh, my God," one of the women said. "Look."

You could see the whole of Greater London from here. There wasn't a single light on. It was a moonless, cloudless night. Above, an infinite expanse of stars. Below, an everlasting carpet of nothingness.

Mordred suddenly felt desolate, like the most comfortable rug in the world had been pulled from under him.

It was back to the interminable wandering. Back to normality. Even the Roman girl had gone. The party was over in every possible sense of the phrase.

Something green zipped from the horizon at an unearthly speed, then disappeared into space.

"What was that?" Camilla Burkewitz said.

No answer. One of the women laughed nervously.

He felt an arm slip round his waist. "So how about a cocktail?" Hannah whispered.

## Chapter 36: The Usual Tying up of Loose Ends

Mordred went straight to Fowler's after he emerged from the Gherkin. Once again, he was assessed by psychologists, this time for his fitness to return to work. The general expectation was that he'd be back in a day or two at the most. Ruby Parker sent him a curt message: *we need to talk about Mehreen Shah and Michael Preston.*

He was absent for three and a half weeks. The professionals concurred: a severe case of depression. They feared for his safety if he was discharged. For the purposes of his file, he was classed as hospitalised.

Two days after the awards ceremony, Phyllis met Hannah in Wandsworth for a coffee and a Chelsea bun. Somehow, the truth had given them a deeper mutual understanding. They smiled about Goldman Sachs, then spoke about John as their mood darkened. He was a mess, they agreed, but they couldn't do as much as they definitely wanted to: he required men and women with clinical expertise. That rigid stare, those tears, those abandoned sighs, the interminable silences.

Colander had deposited five million pounds in his bank account on the stroke of midnight. The British government discreetly returned it to the Fed.

Inside his head, Mordred was fighting back. But even he could see it would be a long process. Most days, he wanted to die. But then something would appear. Rain on the window followed by a sudden punch of sun, a flowery old-fashioned air freshener scent, someone laughing just outside his room, a bird's hard shadow on a blank wall. Each some faint echo of a different world he'd somehow accessed, albeit briefly. Enough to remind you it existed. Somewhere.

Just not here.

*I Will.* Even the thought of that was enough to make him weep with anguish now. The loss, the terrible loss.

The best remedy was forgetting. Bury what you knew. If it actually was real, you'd see it again someday. You didn't have to know how or where. *This* world was real too, in its way. For most people, it was the best they'd experienced. They knew nothing else. You had to get into that mind-set if you wanted to live at all.

There were only a few truths in both worlds, and they boiled down to even fewer: there *really existed* people he loved, and who loved him. And who could benefit from his love. People he didn't even know yet, maybe never would. Love, love, love, all you needed was love. Trite-sounding, but true.

He had an inkling why he was floundering. Willpower wasn't supposed to be important in the modern world. For a variety of reasons, people preferred pharmaceuticals.

So one day, he stopped taking his medication.

Then in the same instant, he decided to escape. The mere act would jolt him back to 'life', such as it was. Reclaim his autonomy. As decisions went, it was perhaps the best symptom of being on the road to recovery.

He told Phyllis and Hannah. Because part of him knew 'escape' was a fiction, even as he climbed over the perimeter fence, a day later. Going through the motions, really. Ruby Parker probably knew too. The hospital staff probably knew. They were likely turning a blind eye, watching him through binoculars from the first floor, chuckling.

Phyllis and Hannah awaited him at King's Cross. They hugged him, shared a flask of tea with him on a bench and laughed. He felt himself coming back to life.

The feeling grew the further he got from London. A reverse Ultimate Londoner. When they reached Arlesey, Phyllis and Hannah poked gentle fun at him. Even more after Woking. They read newspapers and passed them around between themselves. They played *I Spy*.

At Newcastle, his entire family was standing on the platform, looking apprehensive. Mum, Dad, Charlotte, Julia, even Mabel. More hugs. He wondered how many of them knew he was a spy. Or whether they cared. Despite his objections, they took him straight to Hexham Abbey and sat on the back pews. He fulfilled the vow he'd made. He lit a candle for Gloria Shipton.

That night, Julia handed him the thin draft of a book she was hoping to bring out. She wanted his permission, she said.

He put it on his bedside table. Hopefully, it wasn't what he thought it was, some thinly disguised autobiography about a literary woman and her shady brother who worked for MI5. Difficult to know how to deal with that, in his current frame of mind.

He read it the next day in the garden under the old apple tree. He still hadn't decided what he'd say if his suspicions were correct. *I can't let you publish this?* He didn't even know if she'd listen. If not, his career in MI7 might be well and truly over.

Mind you, for all he knew, that might already be the case.

It took him four pages to work out what it was. She and Euan Frederick had exchanged letters and e-mails, ten or twelve a year, since 2003. They wrote about literature, being human, everyday annoyances, how to survive in a world without objective values, the planet's future, science, art, magic. His suicide had hit her badly. She'd asked John for permission to publish because of The Ultimate Londoner connection. Unpleasant associations: could he cope? Euan's family had already given their blessing. The proceeds were going to charity.

The deeper Mordred read, the more he realised his own suffering was stupid. Euan had suffered mentally, for a long time. It was a miracle he'd lasted as long as he had. And he was another Ultimate Londoner. He'd been chosen. In this life and beyond, they had a bond.

So: no real reason to be depressed.

Of course, that wouldn't necessarily stop it. Depression was complex. It didn't like being gainsaid.

Yes, obviously she should publish it. He was touched she'd asked.

That afternoon, the whole family picnicked at Hadrian's Wall. The sun shone. His dad smoked his pipe. His mum read her book. A light breeze blew. They talked, lay on their backs to gaze at the sky, played tag like seven-year-olds, and told each other stories about their lives.

Time stood still. It was the same time it had always been, no dividing it into discreet packets. And the same little block of space, with all things locked snugly inside it. Their childhoods, magical Gloria Shipton, the Roman girl, the living, the dead, the unborn, all one, and all here. Everyone was here.

Three days after John emerged from the Gherkin, Phyllis got an invitation through the post from Sir Anthony Hartley. *Please come and meet me upstairs for lunch in the Red Lion, Westminster, Saturday at 1pm. I have some friends I'd like you to meet. RSVP.*

The reply address was the House of Commons. She penned a quick acceptance and posted it the next day on her way in to Thames House. Presumably, it was some kind of debrief, his way of saying he was sorry she hadn't got the job, but when something else came up, she'd be considered. *Only next time, you may want to approach the interview slightly differently.*

With John maybe out of action for a long time, she needed to keep her options open. From a networking point of view, the 'friends' sounded promising. And it was a free lunch. Three good reasons to go.

No reason to think it wasn't formal, and, if you were going to get it wrong, it was always better to dress up than down. She wore a navy tailored sleeve dress and matching heels, and put her coat on. The forecast said icy winds.

She got to The Red Lion early and showed the barman her invitation. He nodded and indicated the stairs. A single room, with six or seven tables and only one of them occupied. Sir Anthony Hartley-Brown sat perusing a menu. Next to him, two women and a man, all in suits, all about a decade younger than Phyllis, all looking slightly awestruck by whatever occasion it was.

Sir Anthony stood up and shook her hand. "You're early," he said. "A difficult feat to achieve with London's traffic."

It wasn't – unless you drove. "Even so, I hope I haven't kept you waiting," she replied.

Two equally meaningless pleasantries. Now time to business. He gestured to his fellow diners. Each stood up as he made the introduction.

"We have here," he said, "three chairs of their respective university Young Conservative associations. Moira de Winter, from Edinburgh, Mike Thomas: Oxford, and William Paulson from Bristol. Lady" – he chuckled – "and gentlemen, may I introduce Phyllis Robinson?"

More handshakes were exchanged. Phyllis still had no idea what was going on. What was she supposed to say? What offer was imminent? *Phyllis, I'd like you to consider coordinating Young Conservative associations across the country?*

Her answer would be a polite no. Without question.

Which might make lunch awkward. Hopefully, they'd eat first, offer afterwards. That way, she could make her excuses fairly naturally.

Then she saw. It wasn't Sir Anthony these three were awed by. It was her. They sat down. The barman emerged from the stairwell to take their orders. Five minutes later, they sat with drinks.

"The reason for our meeting today," Sir Anthony said, when the small talk had died off. "It's rare to come across a politician with conviction. But I was very impressed with what you said in your interview, Phyllis. Very, very impressed."

"Thank you," she said. She took a sip of her lemonade. "I spoke from the heart. Pointless anything else."

"You may recall that we took minutes. Since I'm too old to care about the data protection act and, since I liked what you said,

268

I took the liberty of sharing your ideas with a few people I knew would be sympathetic. You're an idealist. We can find a parliamentary seat for you if you still want one, but you need to be aware that what you're proposing is nothing short of a revolution in Conservatism. If you want it to succeed, you're in for a long hard battle against the Cynthia Cartwrights and Innes Mounts of this party. They're used to having their fingers in the country's biggest pies, and they won't go down without a fight. And it won't be pretty."

"What you said in your interview was amazing," Moira said.

"It's the only way we stand to make a success of Brexit," Mike chimed in.

William sipped his ale. "The sooner the better."

"I've said it before and I'll say it again," Sir Anthony went on: "you're party leadership material. The country needs you, Phyllis. These three firebrands are right behind you, and they're not alone."

"Absolutely not," Moira said.

"So what do you say, Phyllis Robinson?" Sir Anthony said. "Think you're up to it? Because if you are, the revolution starts here, today, in this room." He raised his glass with a hard, querying look into her eyes. "Yes?"

She hesitated for a moment. She didn't know what to think.

But then her euphoria died. On a wider level, she'd boxed herself in. In the Newbury interview, and therefore in the minutes, she'd committed herself firmly to local politics for local people. It wouldn't look good, her being parachuted in to some constituency by 'friends in Westminster'. Which was all that could happen now.

So she was duty bound to decline.

She smiled, trying not to give her feelings away. She explained that Newbury was her only possible route of entry. Now it was closed, she was fenced out. She could only get back in by sacrificing the very principles she'd pledged to promote. Not an option.

"I hope you don't mind if Mike and William and I carry your ideas on?" Moira said tentatively, after an uncomfortable silence. "I mean, if we make them *ours?*"

"They're still true, after all," William said warmly.

Phyllis raised her glass. "To the revolution," she said.

Four weeks after the Gherkin, Mordred went back to work for a de-brief with Ruby Parker. They sat in their usual places in her office.

"Welcome back, John," she said. "How are you feeling?"

"I've been better, thank you. How have things been here?"

"Less exciting than before, thank goodness. Now, the question I said I'd ask when you got back. How does Michael Preston pushing Mehreen Shah in front of a tube train square with your conviction that The Ultimate Londoner was essentially benign?"

"Michael Preston saw Mehreen Shah in *The Evening Standard*. He'd seen her in one or two venues live before, but the competition was the trigger for him to become obsessed by her. He tried stalking her, and when she didn't respond positively to his attentions, he decided to kill her. The Ultimate Londoner 'knew' we had an eye on its financial arm. It deposited five thousand pounds in Preston's bank account as a way of alerting us to the fact that Mehreen Shah was in danger. We should have picked it up earlier. If we had, we'd have had Preston watched. We'd have discovered he was stalking Mehreen Shah. We'd have taken steps to protect her. That's almost certainly what the program intended to happen."

She sighed. "Why didn't I see that?"

"None of us did. We'd become accustomed to thinking of The Ultimate Londoner in a certain way. We couldn't change that."

"You could."

"Ever since the night of the awards ceremony, I've had the feeling we were never in any danger. Everything that happened

270

was meant to happen, including me having my brainwave and getting us into the building."

"I've read your psychologists' report, yes."

"It couldn't have happened otherwise. Like there's something intelligent, and totally in control, at the end of the universe and it's sending messages back. The Ultimate Londoner was part of our preparation. I got caught up in it. We all did."

She looked at her screen. "'At the instant the end is reached, life will have spread to all universes in which it could logically exist, and will have stored everything it is logically possible to know. Its computational capacity will have diverged to infinity. It will be able to create an unlimited number of fully complete everlasting worlds.' Sound familiar?"

"Did I say that?"

"Sounds like your thinking, doesn't it? No, it's from a 1986 book called *The Anthropic Cosmological Principle* by two cosmologists, John Barrow and Frank Tipler. You're not as way out as you probably think."

"Great."

"Nevertheless, I think we should change the subject. Nothing can be gained from you dwelling on that." She reached into her desk drawer and pulled out a big padded envelope. "We've been looking after your flat for you while you've been away. These arrived for you."

He opened the flap. The envelope contained ten or twelve letters and cards. "I take it they've all been vetted," he said. "I mean, you've read them."

"For your own safety, yes. We don't want you receiving hate mail. Not that there's been any, remarkably. People seem to have forgotten all about The Ultimate Londoner."

"I doubt that. It'd be too good to be true."

"What they know is that there were parties to celebrate it, but no one knows who 'won', or even if there was a winner. After about an hour, the celebrations became an end in themselves."

"Pity, I was hoping to use it on my CV."

"I'm sure you'll get over it. From our point of view, of course, it's very good. It means we get to keep you."

He smiled. "I'm not sure I'm worth having any more."

"One thing that may interest you. In the hours leading up to The Ultimate Londoner's expiration, another two whales arrived in the Thames. Birds were apparently diverted from their migratory paths as far away as Africa and South America. They were on their way here at speed. Make of that what you will."

"What about that green light?"

"Unknown 'presences' in the solar system, so I've been told. More than one. They've gone now. Again: don't ask me. I don't know and I'm not sure I want to."

"It's probably academic now, anyway," he said.

"Take that envelope up to the canteen. Have a coffee and read the letters and cards. They may help. And the context will. Enough of Fowler's now. It's time to get you back to normality."

He stood up, thanked her and took the lift to the canteen, as advised. Mostly, this time of day it was relatively deserted. He bought a tea and a scone and found a table next to the window at which he could be alone. He took the letters from their bigger envelope.

They were from the surviving Ultimate Londoners, Aisha Mirzakhani, Marcus Jobs, Mehreen Shah and Francis Shaylor. They wanted to have a yearly reunion. Reading between the lines, it was clear they were feeling only slightly less desolate than him. They'd survived something, they didn't know what, but it had left them feeling a curious blend of much less and much, much more than before. They were seeking solace in each other's company. And they needed him. They'd been to Russia together for Igor Lazarev's funeral. They'd elected Francis as their group coordinator.

Reading their words, and thinking about the five who'd died, he got a real sense that, actually, the computer's choice was adroit. In a sense, its ten selections were a good cross-section of London, at least insofar as such a small number of people could be. A

272

snapshot, with no particular reference to the past, taken at a very particular moment in time. London 2018. Not perfect, but pretty good. It'd have been different in 2017. It'd be different again in a year's time.

The idea of staying together as a group was attractive, but might not help his recovery. He probably needed to talk to the doctors. Sit down in someone's office for an hour or so, chew over the precise ramifications.

That's what a sensible person would do.

But then, when had he ever been that? He was the Ultimate Londoner.

He put the letters back into the envelope, finished his tea, then keyed Francis Shaylor's number into his phone and pressed Call.

# Acknowledgements

Probably the claim most readers will most wish to query in this novel is Alec Cunningham's, in Chapter 30, that Britain's Trident missile computers run on Windows XP, with all the apparent cause for concern that might imply. Mordred says he "read something about that in *Private Eye* last year." The issue he is referring to is #1444, 19 May-1 June 2017. For curious readers, a photo of the article can be found on the Tales of MI7 Facebook page, but here is a large extract:

"In the light of the potentially catastrophic cyber-attack on computers running Windows XP, defence secretary Michael Fallon continues to suggest that 'our Vanguard submarines, I can absolutely assure you, are safe and operate in isolation when they are out on patrol.' Given that the Vanguard boats carry the UK's continuous at-sea Trident nuclear deterrent, they had better be safe from hacking. But the computers on the UK's fleet of four Trident submarines *do* run on the updated XP system and they must and do have frequent access to the internet when the boats are alongside or updating their operating systems ... So, for the sake of affordability, the navy installed 'off-the-shelf', commercially available kit into the command systems of its Trident missile submarines? Er, yes."

In Chapter 25, Ruby Parker's rough summary of Gloria Shipton's research interests is quite general, because I wanted to minimise its "info-dump" features. But some of it is based in fact. In its original form, it ran:

"[Gloria Shipton's] research interests stretched far beyond traditional computer science. In her last fifteen years, she was absorbed by the newly emerging field of synthetic biology. Her notebooks build on the work of the J. Craig Venter Institute in Maryland, USA. In 2003, it developed the world's first synthetic chromosome. In 2007, it created a DNA transplantation method to convert one life-form into another, and in 2010, it invented its own code based on the four DNA base couple letters. Now, what JCVI did was controversial enough – it's a matter of public record that President Obama himself asked the Commission for Bioethical Issues to report on it – but it only dealt with bacteria. Deliberately non-contentious. Imagine how much of an uproar there'd have been had it dealt with brain cells. Now: imagine someone manufacturing, as a computer program, a synthetic biological neuron that could both replicate itself and retain informational contact with its progeny. Step forth, Gloria Shipton."

Most of this is taken from Christopher Barnatt's *25 Things You Need to Know About the Future* (Constable 2012), particularly from Chapter 9 of that book, 'Synthetic Biology'. The J. Craig Venter Institute in Maryland is a real place, with all the above achievements to its credit.

Back to *Private Eye*. Phyllis's programme for modernising Britain in Chapter 22 is largely lifted from the contribution of the anonymous author, 'Slicker', in issue 1467 (6-19 April 2018), and in some places reproduces it almost word for word. It seemed pointless to tinker with excellent ideas, since I was always going to acknowledge their source here.

The 'book' Phyllis is reading at the beginning of Chapter 22 is, of course, Margaret Thatcher's *The Downing Street Years* (HarperCollins 1993). That chapter begins with a slightly modified quotation, the original of which can be found on TDSY page 10.

Some readers might consider it incredible that the government in *The Ultimate Londoner* has decided, in advance, to remain in the capital in the event of a threatened nuclear strike. Maybe it is not so odd as first appears. In the Cuban Missile Crisis of 1962, Britain came as close as ever to activating the UK's nuclear forces. The government had a bolthole, codenamed 'Turnstile', deep beneath limestone between Bath and Corsham in Wiltshire. But it never seems to have seriously considered evacuating there, even at the crisis's height. Much later, the prominent political writer, Peter Hennessey asked: "Why didn't the Chiefs of Staff prepare to forsake their suite in the Ministry of Defence in Whitehall and race down the A4 to Corsham, taking the Prime Minister and his War Cabinet with them once the full Cabinet authorised a 'Precautionary Stage' when they met on the Sunday afternoon?" (*The Prime Minister: The Office and its Holders Since 1945*, p133). Sir Frank Cooper, an eye-witness, recalled that the Chiefs "never really liked the idea of rushing to a bloody quarry". Hennessey puts it down to a feeling that the secret location was easily discoverable. But he also comments: "As far as we know, neither Macmillan – nor any other Prime Minister since – has ever set foot in 'Turnstile'." (p133).

In Chapter 25 Ruby Parker says, "We're not even close to building a computer that can pass the Turing test, and even if we were, it'd probably be sunk by the Chinese Room argument." The Turing test is a set of criteria for use by scientists and philosophers to decide whether something can "think", the idea being that if an entity passes that test, it definitely can. The Chinese Room Argument is a rejoinder, first proposed by the American philosopher, John Searle, in 1980. It seeks to demonstrate that the Turing test is wholly insufficient in that regard.

*The Anthropic Cosmological Principle* (1986) by John Barrow and Frank Tipler, mentioned in Chapter 36, is published by Oxford Paperbacks.

Finally, I would like to extend my thanks to Lynn Hallbrooks for her careful proofreading of the text of this novel.

JW May 2018.

# Books by James Ward

### General Fiction
*The House of Charles Swinter*
*The Weird Problem of Good*
*The Bright Fish*
*Hannah and Soraya's Fully Magic Generation-Y \*Snowflake\* Road Trip across America*

### The Original Tales of MI7
*Our Woman in Jamaica*
*The Kramski Case*
*The Girl from Kandahar*
*The Vengeance of San Gennaro*

### The John Mordred Tales of MI7 books
*The Eastern Ukraine Question*
*The Social Magus*
*Encounter with ISIS*
*World War O*
*The New Europeans*
*Libya Story*
*Little War in London*
*The Square Mile Murder*
*The Ultimate Londoner*
*Death in a Half Foreign Country*
*The BBC Hunters*
*The Seductive Scent of Empire*
*Humankind 2.0*
*Ruby Parker's Last Orders*

### Poetry
*The Latest Noel*
*Metals of the Future*

### Short Stories
*An Evening at the Beach*

### Philosophy
*21st Century Philosophy*
*A New Theory of Justice and Other Essays*

CPSIA information can be obtained
at www.ICGtesting.com
Printed in the USA
LVHW032142240321
682338LV00009B/209